18 WHEELER

JF RIDGLEY

Printed in the United States of America

ISBN: 978-1-951269-00-5 ebook

ISBN: 978-1-951269-01-2 Print

R Pride Publishing www.rpridepublishing.com

JFRidgley www.jfridgley.com

Cover art: Cathy Helms www.AvalonGraphics.org

Formatting: by Book2Bestseller.com

To my hero…Joe
&
Thank You, Spike

Truck Talk

= 10-4 – Yep/ okay/copy/ y'all be safe and careful. I'm out.

= 10-20 – your location

= Big-Road – interstates

= Big-truck or rig – an 18-wheeler

= Bobtail – truck cab without a trailer

= Bone-box – ambulance

= Box – basic dry trailer

= Brake-Check – slow traffic

= Broker – an agent who arranges the loads for pickup and delivery

= Bull-Hauler – trucks loaded with livestock

= Canteen or Thermos-bottle – tanker truck full of liquid, but not fuel

= Chicken-Coop – weigh station

= Copy – I understand, got it

= Covered-wagon – flatbed trailer covered with a canvas

= Crotch-rocket – sport motorcycle (i.e., Ninja)

= Dead-head – drive empty, without a load

= Dragon-wagon – tow truck

= Flip-flop – return trip

= Four-wheeler – Car or anything with four tires

= Gator – retread rubber blown off a tire and left on the highway

= Granny-Lane – slow right lane

= Greasy – Icy or slippery roads

= Hammer-down – speed up

= Hand – driver

= Happy-Happy – Happy New Year

= Lie-book/comic book/swindle sheet/funny-pages – all truckers must keep a record of their days on the road; here they log in everything from stops, fueling, sleep/rest time.

= Loop – interstate highway around cities

= Lot-Lizards – prostitutes at a truck stop

= Lumpers – casual labor that loads or unloads a trailer, often requiring cash from the company or driver

= Owner-operator – a driver who owns his own truck

= Parking-lot – traffic jam on the highway

= Pete – Peterbilt

= Pig-Pen – truck hauling hogs

= Pig-tail – electrical connection between truck and trailer

= Reefer – refrigeration unit on a trailer

= Rig – a semi-trailer truck

= Rubberneckers – people who slow to gawk at an accident, creating traffic jam

= Run – a delivery trip

= Saltshaker – snowplow

= Seat-cover – female passenger

= Skateboard – flatbed trailer

= Schneider-eggs – orange construction cones

= Squawk-box – CB radio

= Squirt-gun – fire truck

= Stop-and-rob – convenience stores

= Sunny-side up/greasy- side down – right side up

= TAT- (www.truckersagainsttrafficking.org) Drivers who sign
up to watch for and report sex trafficking to the authorities.
= The-Seventy – Interstate 70
= Ticket – speeding ticket
= Yardstick – mile markers

Law enforcement

= Smokey-Bears – law enforcement
= Diesel-bear – a highway patrol that focuses on trucking.
= Disco-lights/gumball machine – flashing lights on a patrol car
= Driving-award/bear bite – speeding ticket

Cities

= Air-Capital – Wichita, KS
= Alamo – San Antonio, TX
=Beantown– Boston, MA
= Big-D – Dallas, TX
= Bright-Lights – Kansas City, MO
= Cactus-Patch – Phoenix, AZ
= Circle-City – Indianapolis, IN
= Dago - San Diego, CA
= Frisco - San Francisco, CA
= Gateway-City – St. Louis
= Guitar-Town – Nashville, TN
= Lost-Wages – Las Vegas, NV
= Mardi-Gras – New Orleans, LA
= Oil-City – Tulsa, OK
= Sack-of-Tomatoes – Sacramento, CA
= Salty-City – Salt Lake City, UT

= Shaky-City – Los Angeles, CA

= Shaky-Town – San Francisco, CA

= Steel-Town – Pittsburg, PA

= The-Alamo – San Antonio, TX

= The-Apple – New York City, NY

= The-Dirty – Cleveland, OH

= The-Flag – Flagstaff, AZ

Kudos to Many

Spike and Barb for helping this story get a life. My hubby who believed in me. Friends who encouraged me. Cathy who put up with me and still made the cover right. Editors Cindy and Deb who helped get this story right. Lisa of Book2bestseller who got this out there. Yvonne and Patrick, Thomas Vlad, Kennedy who handles everything Internet. And you dear readers for your patience. And God for everything. Love you all

CHAPTER 1

A LONELY SNOWFLAKE FLUTTERED down onto the blue hood of her car. Carrie Marshall punched 9-1-1 on her cell phone again and prayed that it wasn't entirely dead as her car seemed to be.

Wasn't there emergency power on the cell phone for things like this? After another failed try, she tossed the damn thing into the passenger seat.

The sky was darkening with heavy winter clouds. And no one had passed on the interstate for at least half an hour, and she had only two granola bars and two bottles of water left in the car.

Her only hope was to reach the highway patrol and, if they didn't come, she was going to freeze to death inside her car.

Frank's unwanted voice rose from his grave, *"Carrie, you know you had no business taking off like you did. You should have flown to Sacramento. But like always, you won't listen. You—"*

"Shut up, Frank. I don't need another one of your lectures," she snapped at his ghost.

A layer of snow began covering her windshield. Great. Just great. Instead of seeing her grandsons open their Christmas presents, it was very likely that she would be joining Frank because of her impulsive desire to go on a road trip over Christmas holiday. Now what was she going to do?

A deep-throated rumble shot Carrie's attention to the rearview mirror. The black semi-trailer truck, which she had passed many times, growled to a halt behind her car. And then the chrome-plated monster released a loud hiss as if a warning.

Worse than any threatening snowstorm, a new fear consumed her. She was alone. On Utah's Salt Flats. With no help. No phone. With a dead car. And a strange truck stopping just inches from her rear bumper.

The instant the driver's door opened, and khaki pant-legs climbed down the silver steps of the black truck, every crime episode that Frank had told her about screamed through her brain.

"Shut up, Frank. I don't need this now."

When the trucker stopped to zip up his leather jacket, Carrie yanked the keys from the ignition, clutching them as a weapon. Somewhere she had heard about doing this to protect herself. The metal bit into her palm as the trucker appeared at her car window.

"Ma'am are you okay?" he asked. His sky-blue eyes and weathered face reflected concern more than malicious intent.

That's what Jeffrey Dahmer's victims thought, too.

"Frank, I'm warning you," she seethed. Faking poise, she bolted out a lie, "Yes, I'm fine. I'm fine." What else could she say? "The…the highway patrol. They're coming. I called them."

His sandy-colored hair danced in the punishing wind as his mouth tilted in a sympathetic grin. "Ma'am, the *smokeys* can't. There's a major accident on 80 West past Wendover. It's a damn *parking-lot* and every *bear* is there."

Gripping her keys tighter, Carrie glared at this guy. *Smokeys. Parking lot. Bears.* She wasn't a fool. Nodding as if to thank him for that information, she stated, "Then, I'll just wait until they get that taken care of."

The trucker shoveled his hands deeper in his coat pockets. "Ma'am, a major snowstorm's coming in fast." To prove his point, he glanced at the snow piling on her car's hood, and the scenery around them was barely visible.

Oh, God. If he was right, they might never find me until spring. "No. No. I'm fine. I…I'll wait."

He shrugged. "Okay. Start the engine to keep warm, but don't run it constantly, or you'll run out of fuel." He stood, waiting for her to start the car.

She turned the ignition, and nothing happened—of course.

He leaned down, concerned. "Try again."

The engine didn't even turn over or make a sound other thank *click*. "Can…can you give me a jump?"

He sagged slightly as if an invisible weight had just dropped on his back. "Sure. Pop the hood." He walked to the front of her car as a wind nearly swept him onto the empty highway.

Carrie peered through the space between the dash and the raised hood. Frank's voice sounded in her brain again. *'Watch him. He could cut a hose.'*

"I don't need that right now, Frank," she said through her teeth.

The trucker frowned when he cleaned the oil stick and checked it again. He glanced toward his truck, deciding on something. No answer apparently came, so he walked to her window and presented her oil stick like a sword. "No oil."

She could see he wasn't lying. There was no oil showing on that stick. "It was fine when I checked it in Salt Lake."

"It isn't now." He nodded toward his truck. "Best you wait in my *rig* 'til the *smokeys*, I mean the highway patrol, can get here. So, you won't freeze."

John rubbed the sleeves of his leather jacket for any amount of warmth. She was scared and he could see that. Rightly so. But he couldn't let her stay in her car, not with this storm coming in. Hell, it was colder out there than the frozen beef inside his trailer.

He could see she was clutching her car keys like a weapon. Couldn't blame her for that. He wouldn't want Janis getting into a rig with a strange man. Neither would he want this *seat-cover* to freeze to death, which would happen if he left her stranded here with no hope of rescue.

"Look, ma'am, you can call for help in my *rig*. I have better reception, I think. While you do that, I'll see if I can get your car started. I think I have a quart of oil that you can have."

"Uh, sure. Do you mind if I charge my phone?"

"Sure. No problem."

The locks popped after a moment of hesitation and, praise the Lord in Heaven, she was getting out. And then she stopped to read his name, "*John Graham-owner-operator* that was written next to a decal of TAT surrounded by '*Truckers Against Trafficking*,' and the identification numbers on the side of the cab door.

John knew she was committing it to memory, and he wanted to say, 'yep that's me and this is my *rig*,' but didn't. He just wanted them both inside before he froze to death. He opened the passenger door to the blessing of warmth pouring out of the cab like an avalanche.

As if already frozen, she didn't move. Flashbacks of his first climb into a *rig*—a million years ago—raced through John's mind. He almost laughed. "Don't worry. I won't let you fall."

She turned stiffly toward him. "You're sure…about the weather? And…and the wreck?"

John nodded. "I'll show you the weather report once we are inside." He motioned to the lowest step. "Step here and hold here. Put your other foot there." He pointed to the next step. "And grab here."

She stuffed the keys in her coat pocket and grabbed the first handle and hoisted herself up the first step like a trooper. But, the toe of her boot caught on the next step, and she swayed out like a drunk.

To stop this *seat-cover* from falling, John had no choice but to place both hands under her butt and shove her inside, sending her belly first onto the tan leather seat with a screech. Bolting upright on the seat, she glared down on him, hand diving into the coat pocket.

"Phone plug is there." He pointed to the dash before her. "And I'll go see if there is anything I can do for your car. Wait here," he said and shut the cab door.

⌘

The moment John climbed into the cab of his *rig* and slammed his door closed, warmth seeped deliciously over him like a blessing. Now, he had to be the bearer of bad news. He turned to his new *seat-cover* suddenly plastering herself against her door, ready to escape.

"Something cracked your oil pan, because your engine block is locked up tighter than…well, tight. Your only option is to have your car towed."

A jolt of electricity couldn't have struck her any harder. "Towed? A-Are you sure?"

John nodded. "Must've run over a *gator* or something?"

Confusion flooded her face. "An alligator? Up here? In this? Seriously," she said cynically.

"Sorry, I meant a piece of retread tire. Truckers call them *gators*."

She nodded. "Yeah, I couldn't dodge the damn thing when it flew off the back of the pickup full of junk."

He remembered that rusted out *four-wheeler* full of shit passing him. "It's likely that's what did in your car."

"Retreads can do that?" she asked.

"I've seen them smash in a windshield."

"Oh, God." She pulled away from the door handle to stare at her snow-covered car. "How long, do you think, before the highway patrol can come by?"

"No telling. As I said, they are dealing with a *parking-lot*…I mean a major accident just past Wendover. Where were you headed anyway?"

"Sacramento for Christmas with the grandkids." Her voice seeped with disappointment.

"Well, I am going through Wendover and can drop you off at the airport. You could catch a flight out from there. If the storm lets up, it'll only take a little more than an hour to get there. You want me to get your things out of your car?"

"I don't have much of a choice, do I?" she said, nearly crying.

"Not unless you prefer turning into an ice cube." He nodded to her, knowing what she was thinking. "Look. You're safe here. I won't do anything, I mean…,"

She tried to smile. "I'll help get my things."

"No. Stay here. I'll get it." He hesitated before leaving the truck. "By the way, I'm John Graham, *owner-operator* of this *rig*, I mean truck."

She smiled, "Carrie Marshall. *Owner-operator* of a dead car."

CHAPTER 2

THE FALLING SNOW had turned into a full-blown blizzard while Carrie waited, watching John's every move. Maybe she was safe like he promised. Every pore in her body wanted that to be true. Nothing about this guy gave her the impression otherwise. Still, she had to watch him.

When John climbed back into the truck, he looked like the abominable snowman. "Here's your luggage," he said, while hoisting both suitcases behind the seats.

He handed her a manila envelope from inside his coat. "Stuff from your glove compartment." He pulled her two bottles of water and granola bars from his pockets and placed them on the dash. "Your kids' gifts are in the outside storage compartments. Things get crowded in here fast, but I'll get them if you want them up here."

"No, that's fine." She wouldn't need them if…. Carrie blocked her mind to that thought and sank back in the seat.

John rubbed his hands for warmth and asked, "Anything else you need?"

"No. I don't think so." Carrie inspected the contents of the envelope. Everything was there. She forced a grateful smile. "Thank you…John."

"Glad I came along when I did. This storm is not going to get any better." John started out of his door again. "I'll be right back."

Fear clutched her insides again. "Why? I-I mean, don't you have everything?"

He hung for a moment in the open doorframe, letting every ounce of heat escape. "I just have to check the trailer before we can pull out in this…stuff."

"Oh." She felt ridiculous bringing this up, but she had to pee. "Can I ask you something…personal?"

He stopped from closing his door. "Sure. What?"

"Where can I go to the bathroom?"

John climbed back inside, slid between seats to go to the back of the cab, and pulled out a Porta-Potty from beneath the double bed. "Use this, while I check the trailer."

He unsnapped the folded curtains behind the seats, letting them drop, and then escaped back out into the blinding snow.

Once in the back, Carrie noticed a microwave, mini refrigerator, small shelves, and cabinets…neater and nicer than most homes.

While relief poured through her, horrid thoughts bombarded like stones. Had she not been listening to the audiobook, she would have heard about the approaching storm, and stayed in Salt Lake City. Instead, she was now at the mercy of this man who could be either a saint or a rapist or a murderer.

How could she explain any of this to the kids, especially Frankie Junior? Heaven help her, her son would never believe that a simple piece of rubber tire could crack her oil pan. She found that hard to believe herself.

And she could hear Frankie's lectures lining up right alongside his father's. Carrie shut her mind off to it. This was the situation, and she had to deal with it. She settled, again, in what she guessed was her assigned seating.

∽

John swung up through his door, flopped onto his seat, and reached for a notebook from a small bin over the windshield. He checked his wristwatch, wrote his time on a page, and noticed her watching his every move.

"I have to log this stop, or it will be added to my driving time." He finished filling out the entry, returned the notebook to its bin, and glanced at both mirrors outside the doors. "Ready?" he asked, pointing at the ignition button, ready to push it.

"I think so." She snapped the seatbelt over her and started twisting her wedding band, remembering that he had said that they'd be in Wendover in two hours. Just two hours.

The hungry sound of the engine vibrated through the entire cab like a lion. This was real. No doubt about that. She was leaving her life behind in that dead car. This could be the nightmare that Frank was threatening from his grave--or a new adventure.

Once again, her world shifted in a new direction without asking for permission. A small prayer was said as she bit one side of her lip.

The snow-covered cab vibrated beneath Carrie and growled, eager to move. The truck began inching forward onto the snow-covered interstate. It jerked forward and then pulled out onto the road, grappling with the weight behind it.

"How long have you been driving?" Carrie asked, while trying to breathe.

"Thirty-five years." Once they picked up speed, John relaxed back in his seat. "Where in Missouri are you from?"

Carrie watched her car disappear from her rear-view mirror. "How'd you know that?"

"License plates."

"Kansas City."

"Ah, *Bright-lights*. That's what we call KC," he explained and glanced at her side mirror. "I can't believe your husband let you head to *Sack-of-Tomatoes* alone this time of year?"

"Sack of what?"

He chuckled. "We call Sacramento *Sack-of-Tomatoes*. I can't explain it."

"Frank would never let me go on any kind of road trip by myself…any time of year. However, he died six months ago. Heart attack."

"I'm sorry." The sparkle in John's eyes evaporated. "I understand. I lost my wife Janis to breast cancer five years ago."

Carrie nodded, grateful for the chance of talking about that miserable episode in her life. "Then, two months ago, I was granted early retirement. It was either that or be laid off with nothing." She never realized that the memory of being forced into retirement hurt worse than Frank's death.

She stopped the emotions that came with that fact and continued, "I never knew walls could creep in on you; but they can. I had to get out or go stark raving mad. So, I decided I wanted to see the grandkids on Christmas morning and just took off. I realize, now, how stupid that was. I should have flown."

Snow was blowing more viciously outside the windshield. The engine downshifted as it slowed. "I know what you mean. After Janis died, I couldn't take sitting around our house either. I sold everything except my Harley and bought this *rig*. Road's a lot better than four walls. That's for sure." Pain lingered in his voice.

"How long were you married?" Carrie asked, figuring that if it was a long time it was good—short, maybe not so good.

"Woulda been 35-years in two months. You and…Frank?"

"We would have been married thirty-three years this fall." Hers—not so good. But there was sadness when John spoke of his wife. Hopefully, that was a good sign.

He nodded and then asked, "Would you be willing to get me a soda out of the fridge?"

"Sure." Carrie left her seat and went to the black mini fridge behind her seat and opened it. A quart of milk, old fruit, and leftovers in a Styrofoam container greeted her, along with a stack of frozen dinners filling the freezer compartment. Like the truck, the fridge held more than she ever expected.

She reached for one of the cans of soda lining the inside of the door. She popped one open and handed it over John's shoulder. He took it, and she slipped back into her seat.

"Thanks." He toasted her with the can and returned to driving. "Most marriages don't seem to last anymore."

"No, they don't." Sheer determination and stubbornness had kept hers and Frank's intact. It wasn't love. "Did you and Janis have any kids?"

"Two boys. Little Johnny and Billy. Both boys are married and live in Florida now. Three grandkids. Little Johnny's boy, Eli, is ten and Barbie is eight. Billy has a girl Sarah, who is seven, and there's another one due in July."

He checked the mirrors and turned the windshield wipers on high to stir the thickening snow. "You?"

"Three. Frankie has two boys. Sam's five and Roy is eight. They live in Sacramento. Oldest daughter Carrianne has two girls, Mary who's eight and Annie, four. They live in Kansas

City, like our youngest daughter Emily, who graduates with her master's in marketing from the university this May."

He smiled as he drove. "Grandkids are awesome, aren't they?"

Carrie huffed. "Enough to make you do stupid things like take a road trip in the dead of winter."

John chuckled. She liked the sound of it. Carrie allowed her eyelids to close just for a second.

"Shit!"

She jerked out of the delicious beginnings of slumber. "What?" Fear crippled her insides as the truck eased to the shoulder and slowed to a stop. "What's wrong?"

He didn't answer and reached for the CB mic. "*Diesel Bear.* You out there? Big John here. Taking a forced vacation."

"Copy Big John. What's your *twenty*?"

"Not far from *yardstick 43* is my guess. Can't see 'cuz of the snow."

"Well, get your suntan lotion and enjoy your two-day vacation Big John. Will come as soon as we can."

"Copy. Lookin' forward to your visit."

Forced vacation, twenty, yardstick suntan lotion? "Why are we stopping?"

John nodded toward the windshield. "Can you see the road out there?"

"No…but—"

"Me either. Can't drive in this. I just told the *smokey bears,* I mean the highway patrol, we're out here. You heard. They'll come when they can."

When John turned off the ignition, the engine settled to the hum of a generator battery. He checked his cell phone. "Yep. *Diesel Bear* is right. Forecast says this one could last for a few days. We'll have to wait till this blow over." He showed her the phone screen. A huge, blue cloud on the radar screen proved that it was just beginning to move over them.

"A few days! We can't survive in this out here. No way!" They were dead. It was over.

John settled back with a smile. "Carrie, we're fine. There's plenty of fuel, enough until the *saltshaker*, I mean the snow-plows, can get through. I'm sorry. It's trucker talk. My life."

He nodded toward the rear. "Plus, I have plenty of food back there for us to last three days or more. Trust me, the generator will keep things plenty warm."

CHAPTER 3

"*S*ON OF A bitch! Oh, sorry. I didn't mean to say that." John placed the laptop on the dashboard and slumped back in his seat, pissed. "I hate computers. Thing's been arguing with me for the last few months. No clue why."

Carrie's green eyes sparkled with curiosity. "Mind if I take a look?"

"Knock yourself out." John waved his hand at the piece of shit that he hated worse than anything the technological world had cursed on him.

He grinned as Carrie claimed the laptop like a pet and went to work on the damn thing. He leaned against his door while her fingers shot all over the keyboard, popping up screens he never knew existed. Bars were streaking across small boxes. Bells were dinging.

He enjoyed watching her until she frowned. "For heaven's sakes, John, didn't anyone ever tell you to scan or update your computer?"

"Since when do I need to do that?"

Carrie gave him a cute, but scathing, glance and continued working. Just like Janis would have.

Every day, every mile of the last five years without Janis, had kept him driving. God, he missed her, missed coming home to the smell of stew, missed the aroma of good coffee in the mornings, and missed sitting out in the backyard together. Life was good back then.

Now, the road offered him a different kind of solitude. One he knew well. Being needed. Back then, he had a reason to drive the long dark miles—family. Now everything felt like an empty bucket with a large hole in the bottom.

"There. Got it. No wonder your computer ran so slow."

His trance broke, and John sat up to look at a new screen. "Got what?"

Carrie's eyes lit her impish face. "A big bad bug."

"Big bad bug?"

"Actually quite a few big bad bugs. But they are all gone now." She lifted the laptop back to the dash.

"Where did you learn all that?" he asked.

Carrie relaxed back in her seat like a satisfied kitten. "You have to learn a lot of things about computers when you're the only secretary in the office." Pride blazed on her face.

He shrugged. "I guess that would have some benefits."

Carrie wilted slightly. "Some, but I miss having a reason to get up to go to work, like being needed."

John nodded. "That's why I went back to hauling."

He needed to take a leak and, as much as he wanted to use the pot, he didn't think it appropriate with Carrie in the cab. "Be right back. Hey, if you are hungry, help yourself."

Claiming his coat from the back of his seat, he climbed out of the *rig* and into an ankle-deep drift of snow. Bitter cold cut through his body as if a bucket of ice had been dumped on him.

When John climbed back into the warmth of his cab, he was greeted with the fragrance of cashew chicken. Nostalgia slammed him like a fist from days when Janis would do that. He shook off the feeling and settled in his driver's seat. "Smells good."

"I can work a microwave, you know," Carrie said. She opened a second frozen dinner. The microwave dinged, she switched the plastic plates and handed him the finished one. "Here. It's hot."

"That's yours. I'll take the next one."

"No. Go ahead. Eat."

If married life had taught him anything, there was no point in arguing with the cook. He took the dinner and dug out the plastic forks from a drawer. Everything felt good and rotten at the same time. So, he shut up and ate the food.

❧

"*Mom? Where the hell are you?*" Carrie's son's voice roared from her cell phone like a public announcement system. "In…" She dare not tell Frankie that she was trapped in a truck, with a strange man because of the snowstorm raging outside. "Salt Lake City."

John grinned while she continued, "I'll be there soon—when the highways are open, of course. A few more days. I'll call. Okay?"

"Just get a flight. I'll pay for it."

John's grin just kept enlarging. She glared at him.

"I…I can't. The flights are full. And, Frankie, I don't want to leave my car…here."

John knocked her bottle of water over on the floorboard. "Shit."

"Well, whatever…Who was that?" Frankie demanded.

"No one, nothing. I…I'm at Denny's, and a trucker just knocked over his…coffee. That's all."

"Stay away from those barnyard perverts, Mom. Remember what Dad told us about truckers. Nothing good."

John looked at her with questions blazing in his gaze.

"Oh, Frankie, you are breaking up. Gotta go." She shut down her phone, wishing it had not charged, and then slid it into her purse.

"If you want to leave this Denny's, you know where the door is," John said with a smirk.

"I can't tell Frankie the truth. After watching all those true crime shows on television with his father who never had anything good to say about truckers. I don't even want to think about what Frankie would do if he knew I was here."

John tossed the wet paper towel in the small wastebasket on the floorboard. "I take it 'Frankie' is Frank Junior?"

"Just like his dad. And once I get to his house, I'll hear all about why I shouldn't be out here driving alone and hear about every other mistake I've ever made."

John nodded and smiled. "I'd say the only thing you did wrong was not check the weather forecasts, or you would be in the *Salty City* instead of being here."

"You mean, Salt Lake City?"

He grimaced. "Sorry. Trucker talk."

Carrie stared at the snow piling up the massive windshield, while feeling all warm and cozy in the passenger seat next to this trucker, who was showing absolutely no signs of being a pervert.

John was just an ordinary man dealing with life and doing an everyday job. And Frankie would never listen to a word she told him about John even if he were a saint. And that was the reason she had put off calling Frankie, knowing that he would rant like his father, and she couldn't bear it. That was part of the reason she had chosen to drive.

"Well, I didn't have a survival kit like I should have, like blankets, food, and water," Carrie muttered.

"You'd be surprised at how many people don't and make the trip just fine. It is better to have one though." John started to get up. "Want something to drink?"

Having someone make her feel halfway intelligent felt nice for a change. "Sure."

A pop and fizz sounded behind her and then a can of Coke appeared, followed by pings of a microwave and the sound of popcorn popping like firecrackers. When the cab filled with the fragrance of a movie theater, she had to giggle.

John resumed his place behind the massive steering wheel with a bag of hot popcorn in his hand. "What?"

"All we need is a movie."

He handed her the popcorn bag, reached into the pocket behind his seat, and retrieved a handful of DVDs. "What would you like to see? *Gladiator, Band of Brothers, Alamo*, or *Secretariat*. Here, you pick."

"Never in a million years would I ever believe this possible. Never," she muttered and shuffled through movie choices. "This one. *Gladiator*."

John opened his laptop and then slipped in the disc. In a few minutes, the previews began. He did all this with a well-practiced flair, something he must do every night that he spent in the truck. Maybe he did. She didn't know.

"All I can say is this truck is a home on wheels."

"*Rig*. You call it a *rig*," John said with a grin. "Your car is a *four-wheeler* for obvious reasons. And the highway patrol and police are *bears* of some sort: smokey bear, Care-bear, diesel-bear." He shrugged the rest.

Carrie smiled, feeling as if she were being inducted into a special class of people. "And a big highway wreck is a *parking lot.*"

"You're a quick learner." The movie started.

CHAPTER 4

BY THE TIME Commodus faced Maximus, Carrie knew her car would be buried by now, and she would have been frozen stiff. Instead, she was warm and toasty inside John's *rig* watching gladiators kill each other. When the movie credits started, John took the empty soda cans and the empty popcorn bags and stuffed it in a trashcan by the small sink.

Carrie picked up a kernel from the floorboard and added it to the pile. "How did you meet Janis?"

He returned to his driver's seat. "High school sweethearts," John said. "Went together since we were freshmen. When we graduated, she wanted to date around."

His hands caressed the steering wheel while his gaze became lost in the snow-covered windshield. "I didn't agree, but what choice did I have? So, I joined the rodeo and toyed with bulls as a clown until one gored me in the thigh." He rubbed his left leg as if the wound remained.

"I had to go home to recoup and started walking around Walmart for exercise. Didn't have fitness centers back then." He shrugged with a knowing grin and then continued. "One day I spotted Janis looking at winter coats.

We got to talking, went out for dinner, and woke up in bed together the next morning."

A satisfied smile appeared on John's face. Must have been a copy of the one he had worn the next morning when he woke up with Janis, Carrie thought.

"I'll never forget the look on Janis's face about a month later when she called to tell me that she was pregnant and was scared shitless. I couldn't have been happier.

We got married in *Lost Wages*, or Las Vegas, and I started trucking for a company. Janis loved riding with me until Little Johnny put an end to that. We bought a nice place in Fort Lauderdale. She set up house, and I kept on trucking." He drew his attention back inside. "So, how'd you meet Frank?"

The question broke the romantic reverie. Carrie readjusted in what had been a comfortable seat and studied the glove box before her. "Frank and I met in an accounting class after I cancelled my wedding because I caught my fiancé in bed with my best friend. While I was trying to put my heart back together, Frank managed to get me through that accounting class.

"Frank always said marriage was a team effort like a team of horses or something like that. It sounded romantic at first. Safe. However, after we were married for a while, I discovered it was more like slogging through mud. To him, flowers, jewelry, cards, candy were wasted expenses. He'd rather use that money to pay off a bill of some kind."

"Sounds like an accountant."

She grimaced. "Frank loved doing taxes, of all things. Frankie took after him. Exactly like his father, even down to the lectures." Wanting to change the topic of conversation, she looked at John. "Your sons didn't go into trucking like you?"

John shook his head. "Never developed the love of the road. The kids hated not having a father at their little league games, birthdays, holidays, and things like that. But Janis made sure they understood that the road paid for everything."

He yawned and rubbed his face with his hands, which brought up a sudden reality. Sleeping.

Carrie glanced back at the double mattress stretching like a lonely acre across the back of the cab. Her heart made a slow climb up her throat.

"Gotta go check on the trailer. Be right back. Pick out another movie if you want to watch another one. Don't know if I can stay awake though."

"Maybe. No. I…uh…don't think so."

John opened his door to a swirling mass of snow and disappeared in the darkness. After going to the bathroom again, Carrie searched for a way to put the back of her seat down.

John swung back up into the cab. "What are you looking for?"

"Does this lay back?"

He shook his head. "You take the bed." He stepped toward the back and grabbed a blanket.

"No. No." She tried to claim it from his grasp. "I'll sleep in my seat."

He shook his head. "Take the bed, Carrie. I'll sleep here." He tossed the blanket on her seat and sat down before she could move.

"No. I mean…" Why was he taking her seat? "Why there… I mean—"

"That's one thing I don't do…sleep where I drive."

❧

John didn't care how warm his cab felt. Every chill from beyond the door had seeped into his spine. Oh, he'd slept in worse places before, but he was a hell of a lot younger then.

He glanced at the mattress where Carrie slept, snoring softly, and grinned. Janis had instructed him that women snuffle and men snore. Just thinking of Janis could still swell his heart to bursting. He loved her with every mile he had ever driven.

However, Carrie talked about her husband as if she hadn't been all that happily married. Nevertheless, he had to hand it to her for staying. Few did anymore.

He well knew the fear of another man in his wife's bed and how it ate at nearly every driver's guts with each mile closer to their front door. Then others had come home to the shock of divorce papers instead of their wives' arms.

Janis always welcomed him with warm arms and an even warmer bed. He remembered the time he had returned home for Christmas and presents hemmed the tree that he had never bought. Half the time the kids knew more about what was under the tree than he did. He had been one lucky trucker and he knew it. Janis's last words whispered in his memory. "I love you, John. Be happy. That's all I ask."

His heart melted to tears. He shifted, trying to avoid them.

"I can scoot over." Carrie said from the back. "There's room."

"No. I'm fine."

"No, you're not."

John glanced over the back of the seat to see Carrie sitting up, fully dressed, shielding herself with a blanket.

"You sure?"

She nodded. "You're miserable."

Truth never sounded so right. He struggled to his feet, feeling sweat cover his flesh as if he'd become a dumbass teenager again. He'd never slept with another woman since that night he found Janis in Walmart. But this wasn't sleeping with anyone. Anyone! He was just sleeping.

CHAPTER 5

CARRIE'S EYES POPPED open the instant an arm slid around her waist, drawing her like a fluffy pillow. She had forgotten how nice it was waking up to a man's body so nearby, so warm and assuring. Smelling of Old Spice.

She loved Old Spice. It reminded her of her father. No. No. Not her father. And this wasn't Frank. It was John. A very tired man whose bed she had claimed. Nothing more.

Well, it was more in a way. Frank hated snuggling. He had his side of the bed and she had hers. There were times she even questioned how they ever had three kids.

John jolted to his feet. "Oh god, Carrie. I'm sorry. I'm sorry." His hands dove through his sandy brown hair while he turned in a circle in the meager space.

Carrie sat up, instantly missing his presence. "John! John! It's okay. It's okay."

He stopped. "I'm sorry. I didn't mean to—"

"John, nothing happened. You slept. I slept. That's all." Slept better than she had in years.

"I, uh, I've got to go check on the trailer."

Carrie glanced out the side window and saw snow still falling like an avalanche. He had no business out there. "John, use the Porta-Potty."

She got up, released the dividing curtains, and slid into her seat. "I had a husband and a son. I don't think things have changed much."

§

She studied the white wilderness still enveloping the truck, until John pushed back the curtains and snapped them in place. He held the portable bucket in one hand, slid across his seat, and opened his door. He climbed down far enough to toss the contents behind the cab.

"Want some coffee?" he asked after shutting his door to the frigid air and snow.

"I'd love some."

He began working like a kitchen maid behind her. While the coffee brewed, filling the cab with its fragrance, he tidied up. "Never could stand a messy truck. I know some truckers who don't give a damn. They just want a place to sleep and can drive. I can't live like that. Janis never…Cream or sugar."

"Both."

Soon the coffee with cream and sugar warmed her hands. Carrie adjusted deeper in her seat while John settled back into his with his steaming black Peterbilt mug of black coffee.

"Gotta be three and a half feet out there. Maybe four," he said lazily.

"At least," she said. "Wonder what the weather is like back home."

John pulled his cell phone out of his pocket and tapped at an app. "*Bright-lights,* dead brown, no snow, 34 degrees the high today."

She sipped coffee. "I love falling snow and enjoying my coffee in the breakfast room." In truth, she preferred being here in his truck rather than at home.

"Janis and I enjoyed coffee out back. We had a swing where we'd sit and listen to the birds." His face softened with the memory and then he grinned. "We didn't watch snow fall. Rain, yes. But no snow."

Carrie chuckled. "Not much snow in Fort Lauderdale, huh?"

"Not much." His blue eyes sparkled.

"To snow then." She toasted him.

"To snow." He toasted back and then drank.

Silence filled the cab while a brisk wind made elegant white drifts outside. A warm purr vibrated beneath her feet. How long would the storm last? A week might be too short.

"I have cereal and milk if you are hungry. Or, there are your granola bars." He motioned to her contribution to the groceries still on the dashboard.

"I'm not hungry." Lies. She was starving. However, she was not eating John out of house and home or *cab, rig,* whatever.

After he handed her a granola bar from the dash, she toasted him again. "Here," he said, "Goes good with coffee. Not exactly coffee cake, but pretty close."

He ventured back by the bed. The microwave dinged and the smell of fresh coffee once again flooded the air. "More?" he asked.

"Sure."

The morning passed with a few rounds of card games and laughter. The afternoon passed with *The Alamo* and *Band of Brothers.* John answered her questions about all the buttons and gauges spreading across the dashboard that would challenge an airline pilot.

He explained the business of being an *owner-operator*, a driver who worked for himself instead of a company, and what a *Pete* was. A Peterbilt truck, which John assured her, was the best truck on the road, and then listed off the rest of the nicknames for the other trucks.

Carrie had to laugh realizing that a truck could even have 18 wheels, period.

She listened when John got on his CB, which he called a *squawk box,* and reported to the *smokeys* they were doing well. They assured him the *saltshaker* would be by as soon as possible…maybe tomorrow morning. She should have been happy to hear that but wasn't.

A tingle of long-forgotten happiness wiggled beneath her skin. This had been better than any romance novel. John had become her hero, not a villain. And she was an unlikely heroine.

She even considered calling her son and confessing to her lies. However, she didn't want to endure her son's forthcoming arguments over the issue. She'd deal with it when that time came.

John handed her a chilled bottle of water and then settled back into his seat with the next movie in hand. *"Secretariat?"*

"How many times have you watched that one?"

"A few, but never enough." He set things in motion in his laptop and rested back to watch the movie.

She could never get Frank to watch anything other than suspense thrillers and murder documentaries, and never twice.

What had she done with all the time married to such a man? Not much, other than go to work, which she loved and missed horribly, and made crafts for the house, their kids' houses, and now grandkids. She enjoyed cooking and holidays, which Frank enjoyed. Yet, he hated vacations. Cost too much.

All her life now seemed to have been a comfortable existence of watching television and talking about work or what the kids had done. Until Frank ripped their lives apart like a piece of cloth with his affair. After that, they rarely spoke to each other.

"You ready to eat again? I am." John's voice jolted her back from the Preakness playing out on the screen.

"Yes, I'll fix it. Do you mind?"

"Knock yourself out."

Just doing something other than remembering felt good. She placed another frozen dinner in the microwave. "What happens tomorrow?" Carrie asked.

John turned sideways in the seat. "I'm headed to *Sack-of-Tomatoes*, I mean Sacramento, to drop off meat. Then *dead-head,* I mean drive empty, to pick up a load of furniture in *Shaky-Town*…Los Angeles. At least, I hope the load is still there." He sighed.

"What do you mean you hope?" Carrie handed him a cold bottle of water.

"Thanks to this snowstorm, I'll be late getting there, so they could give my next haul to another driver. Carl will have to find me another load somewhere."

"Carl?"

"He's my broker." John read the confusion in her face. "A broker finds the loads, makes schedules of where to go, drop, and pickup. I just make the delivery."

"How do you stay in touch?"

"Computer usually. By phone. If it's an emergency, he'll call on my cell." He frowned again. "Now that you mention it, I should have heard from him by now." He reached for his phone and checked his recent call list. The frown deepened.

"What's wrong?"

"Nothing here from him, and that's not like Carl." John punched in a number. They both waited for the call to pick up. Someone answered. A woman's voice.

Carrie overheard the words 'hospital' and 'bypass' and then looked at the blanket of snow over the windshield. She remembered that call at her office and then seeing Frank laying in his coffin. The distraught looks on everyone's faces, especially their children's, cut through her. Something she couldn't wish on anyone.

"Keep in touch, Diane." John slumped back in his seat, beaten. "Carl is in surgery for a triple bypass."

Carrie rested a hand on his forearm. "At least they caught it in time."

He smiled bravely. "Diane said Phil is going to cover for Carl until he gets over this." He plopped his cell phone on the dashboard and then walked to the space behind her—she guessed they could call it the kitchen area.

His hand slid over his hair to rest on his neck. "Can't stand that prick…I mean, oh never mind." He sat down on the bed, staring at the floor. "I'll spend more on *fuel* than I'll get on a load, not to speak of enough miles to pay the bills."

"I'm sorry, John. Is there anything I can do to help?"

He smirked at her. "Become my broker?"

✍

John had been restless all night, as much as she had been. Carrie shifted the pillows that had separated them during the night and sat up on one arm.

She was worried about John and his broker. But it was more than that—she really didn't want to go to Frankie's now. Or ever. Actually, she wanted to stay right where she was.

Don't be ridiculous, Carrie Marshall. After she got on that plane in Wendover, she would never see John again.

An element of sadness crept into her heart. She knew she would be searching for him in every black *18-wheeler* she saw on the road now.

Just then, a white blur sped past, throwing up an avalanche of snow over the truck. "Big John, you breathin'?"

John bolted to the CB and grabbed the mic. "Yeah. Where'd you come from, *Salty*?"

"Outta the blue. Catch my tail and I'll get you to Wendover."

The plow drove through the deep snow like a boat in a lake, leaving a long black wake of highway behind him.

John slipped into his seat like a hand in a glove and pushed the ignition, waking the truck. The engine growled to life like a sleeping bear. Then, getting back outside, he cleared the windshield of every flake of snow.

From the side mirrors, she watched him check over the trailer until he disappeared behind the cab. Something rattled against the cab's back wall, startling her. He reappeared, settled in his seat, and checked the mirrors for nonexistent traffic.

Carrie felt a serious motion struggle beneath her, then a huge, strong shift gripped tread. The image of draft horses bearing down in their collars came to mind. Then John eased onto the black asphalt revealed by the snowplow.

A change had come over John. Before, he had been easygoing and chatty, quick with a smile or chuckle. Now he had turned into something totally different…something sharper. A truck driver.

CHAPTER 6

T HE BLUSTERY WIND blew thin white waves back over the black path where the snowplow had cut through the deep, dry snow.

John settled back into the lifelong rhythm of being a trucker, watching the road, watching his load, and seeing far beyond it all…. Into the past, present, and future.

Surprisingly, he did appreciate Carrie's company. In fact, he appreciated it more than he should. His arm, which had found her waist each morning, still tingled. Since Janis died, he had managed to forget how delicious a soft feminine form nearby could be. One that filled his senses with the fragrances of beaches and warm sun.

Even with the many offers from the *lot lizards* prowling the truck stops, he still had never slept with one, or any other woman. Nor wanted to.

He glanced over at Carrie, lost in the same netherworld. Her cell phone twittered. For a second, she stared at the screen and then answered. "Mom, what the hell is going on? Haven't you been getting my calls?"

Carrie held the phone from her ear, avoiding her son yelling through it. "No, Frankie. I haven't. Phone must have been on mute."

It wasn't. John grinned. Carrie had turned off her cell phone after his last call.

"Mom, there were plenty of flights available out of Salt Lake. Where are you? I—"

"Frankie, I'll explain when I get there. Okay?"

"I called all the hotels around Salt Lake, for God's sake."

Carrie rolled her eyes. "Frankie, I'm on my way. I'm—"

"How? How are you on your way? When will you get here? Just tell me…"

She waved the phone in the air until she could talk. "Oh dear, breaking up again. I'll call you back." She hit the end button hard enough to break the screen and sagged back in her seat.

This Frankie had not impressed John in the least. If the little creep was anything like Carrie's husband, why did she put up with either of them? Well, many women did.

The green highway signs began appearing for Wendover. "I need to stop for fuel. You can catch a taxi to the airport and fly out from there if you want. Or I could drop you off in Sack of…Sacramento if you want."

He could imagine her son's face when he saw his mother climbing out of the *rig*.

Carrie stared out the windshield. "Best I get this over with." She wiped something from her eyes and then looked at him. "Thank you, John. You saved my life, and I have enjoyed every moment of being here. I owe you dinner in Kansas City if you come through some time. I know where there's great barbecue."

"I'll take you up on that, but you don't owe me anything. I enjoyed your company. Would have been lonesome waiting out this snowstorm."

"I hope Carl recovers and can get back to finding you good loads."

"Yeah, me too."

❧

Carrie came out of the convenience store, carrying bags of frozen dinners, a large pack of water bottles, instant coffee, and fresh pastries. She walked toward the first fueling station and stared at John's rig coated with winter slush.

Even so, it seemed more like a tame dragon than the monster bearing down on her bumper, ready to swallow it whole. A yellow taxi pulled up next to John's truck and began taking her luggage from John. The growing smile faded from her face.

She didn't want to leave. She didn't want to deal with Frankie. She wanted to go on with John. Escape everything lying in front of her. However, she couldn't. Once again, life snowballed her down this miserable hill, and she couldn't stop it.

John hurried toward her, taking the grocery bags from her grasp. "Did you buy out the store or something?"

"For you and for all you've done for me, John. The fresh bear claws are still warm."

He hefted the meager load onto his seat and turned to her. "Carrie, you didn't have to buy all this."

"I know. Oh, and a new movie CD. I think you will like it. 300."

John pointed to a strange piece of luggage among her other two in the taxi's trunk. "I put your Christmas gifts in my suitcase for the flight. Hope that was all right."

Again, he had taken care of her. "But, John, what about you? I mean—"

His adorable smile made her insides ripple with joy. "I'll stop by for it when I come through *Bright-lights* next time. How's that?"

That thrilled her. "I expect you to do just that."

"Ready to go, ma'am?" The taxi driver's voice cut through her.

No. She fought every tendril taunting her to climb right back into that black *rig*. She was being stupid. John needed to make his deliveries. The grandkids were waiting. These last two days had been a gift from heaven. However, they were over. Put on your big girl pants and deal with it. She had no choice but to be…ready.

"I guess."

The driver opened the rear door and waited. Carrie rested her hand on John's arm. "Remember, you promised."

"Will do, Carrie. I promise."

She pulled a piece of paper from her purse, scribbled her phone number, and handed the paper to him. Not even as a teenager had she ever given out her phone number.

She stepped back, resisting the urge to kiss his cheek or even hug him to claim one more whiff of his Old Spice after-shave. "Don't lose it."

He slid the note into his jacket. "I won't. I'm already looking forward to some good ribs."

Chapter 7

CARRIE WALKED FROM the secure area of the airport to see her grandsons racing toward her. She knelt and hugged them like life itself. Their million questions all at once allowed her to laugh. Then Frankie and Diane approached. Her daughter-in-law's glance warned her about Frankie, obviously livid.

"Glad you found a flight, Mom," spit from her son's lips.

"Me, too." Before Frankie could retort, Carrie turned to Diane. "How are you?"

Diane brightened. "Great, Mom."

Little hands tugged on her coat. "Grandma, where's your luggage?" Roy asked.

Carrie pointed to the signs to baggage claim. "I believe this way."

They waited in cold silence for the parade of suitcases to pass. Carrie squatted down to Sam. "Is Santa going to bring you lots of toys?"

"Uh-huh. But you are the best toy, Grandma." The little five-year-old strangled her with another hug. She drowned in it until she saw John's piece of luggage.

"That one has all your presents. Roy, can you get it?"

Frankie snatched John's suitcase from the luggage belt before his son could and saw the luggage tag. John Graham. Fort Lauderdale Fl. His gaze skewered her. "Mom, this isn't yours."

"It is, and I'll explain later." Carrie jerked her attention back to the luggage belt. "Oh, there're my other two pieces."

Frankie all but tore the handles off each piece as he blustered his way to the auto park. Diane claimed both boys' hands to get them through the airport traffic while trying to keep up with her husband. The atmosphere in the car loomed colder than the snowstorm as Frankie drove as if under assault from the other drivers

Roy and Sam chattered in their car seats about what they wanted to do over Christmas vacation and what they wanted from Santa. Pinned between the boys' car seats, Carrie listened while trying not to think of John.

The moment of truth she had dreaded over the last few days had arrived. Yet she could not remember enjoying someone's company as she had John's. The sound of his laugh and the way he listened, really listened, had settled over her like sweet perfume.

She missed John, wanting him to protect her from her son's forthcoming wrath. Why did she need such protection? Frankie was her son. A child she had raised and dealt with all her life. Why let him intimidate her?

Frankie pulled up to a white two-story with red window shutters. A Christmas tree twinkled in the picture window near the front porch decorated with icicle lights. The only oddities were the puttering of lawnmowers drifting in the air and green lawns bristling with overgrown grass.

Carrie had never seen where Frankie and Diane lived until now. As expected, Frank would have found some flaw.

It would be too nice, too middle class, over landscaped. He would have found something.

Frankie slammed the car into park near the side door of the house, popped the trunk, and jerked around to Roy. "Show your grandmother where her room is. I'll get everything."

Roy scrambled from his car seat. "Come with me, Grandma. I'll show you."

"No. I will," Sam yelled after Carrie helped him from his car seat.

"Daddy said I had to."

"I want to."

"Both of you show her," Frankie growled from the rear of the car as he snatched each piece of luggage from the trunk.

Both boys clutched her hands and pulled her toward the door. "Okay. Okay. Wait a minute," Carrie said, laughing.

Diane opened the door to the house, releasing the smells of holiday cookies and pies. Every doorway had garlands of ribbon or greenery. Angels and Santas rested on every shelf and along each step to the second floor.

"You're up here with us," Sam announced.

Roy pushed Sam aside. "Idiot, Mom and Dad are up here, too."

"I know that, stupid."

"Which are your rooms?" Carrie asked to redirect the boys.

"Mine's here," Roy said, tugging her toward his doorway.

Sam pulled her across to the other doorway. "Mine is over here."

Toys from *Toy Story* filled Roy's room. *Marvel* characters filled Sam's. Being near the boys' bedrooms sent the first thrill for the holidays surging through her.

"In here, Grandma. This is your room." Roy pointed into a room across from Frankie and Diane's bedroom.

White lace curtains covered the two windows. Between the bedroom door and the windows stretched a queen-sized bed covered with a blue bedspread. The white afghan she had made for Frankie and Diane's eighth anniversary stretched across the foot of it.

Frankie bumbled up the stairs, carrying the three pieces of luggage, and then dropped everything at the foot of the bed. "Boys, go help your mother with dinner."

When the boys scurried off, the room became a vacuum. "Mom, where the hell were you? Why didn't you answer my calls? You had us all worried sick."

She slumped down in the blue chair by the farthest window. "Frankie, sit down."

He remained in place, as stiff as the bedposts.

She inhaled a brave breath to begin. "I left Salt Lake City, not knowing about a snowstorm. Somewhere along the way I ran over a *gator*, I mean a piece of retread, that cracked the oil pan."

"A piece of retread did that? Come on, Mom."

"Yes, and the car died, froze up the engine or something.

"Where is it now?"

"John—"

"I knew it. That filthy perverted trucker." He waved a hand at John's luggage. "You trusted him after all that Dad told you about them?"

Carrie stood up from the chair. "John saved my life! I would have frozen to death if I had stayed in that car."

Frankie stared out the window. "If you had flown, none of this would have happened. Nevertheless, you just had to drive, didn't you?"

"Yes, Frankie, I wanted to, and I'm glad I did even with everything that happened."

"With a trucker, for God's sake." Fury burned in his gaze. "And you lied to me, Mom. Why?"

Her gaze locked with Frankie's even though guilt cut through her guts. "To avoid this. You sound like your father."

"At least Dad would have known to pay attention to weather and avoid running over a retread, which you obviously did not. For God's sake, Mom, you had no business out there alone."

"Boys, stop that! Frankie, would you come down to help me?" Diane's call came like a saving grace.

"I'll be down." His glare tried to pierce through her. "We're not through talking about this." He motioned to John's luggage and then left, closing the door behind him.

⁓

If it weren't for the boys dancing through the paper-littered living room wearing her afghans like capes, Christmas morning would have been more like a funeral. Diane loved the white evening shawl. Frankie studiously examined his afghan, running a hand over the green and black squares, still his favorite colors. The feeling of success floated over her.

Carrie opened a gift card to a Kansas City yarn shop. *"Your life has changed so much in the last year. I hope this helps remake wonderful."* It was Diane's handwriting.

"We didn't really know what to get you, Mom," Diane muttered as she stroked the shawl.

Carrie teared up from all that had changed in her life. Frank's death. Forced retirement. Boredom. John. She dreaded the fact that she couldn't just live for her kids and grandkids;

crocheting blankets barely filled the hours. She wanted—no needed—something to do. There had to be more to live for.

Roy handed her a handmade card, his gaze begging her to adore his handiwork. She gushed over it and opened his gift card to get her nails done at a Walmart. "It's beautiful, Roy. I love it."

"Open mine! Open mine!" Sam yelled as she hugged Roy. His handmade card came with squiggles that resembled hearts or Christmas trees. It held another gift card for her favorite dress shop.

"Oh, Sam, I can't wait to go shopping for a new top. Will you go with me?"

His towhead nodded, his eyes sparkling. "We can go now."

"Sam, the stores are closed," Frankie informed. "It's Christmas."

"They can open for us," Sam argued. The little fella stood stalwart like a tiny warrior while Roy and Diane seemed to freeze in fear.

"No, they won't." Frankie handed Sam his afghan. "Now take this to your room."

"I don't want to."

"I said take this to your room."

"Sam, why don't you show me where you want to put it," Carrie whispered.

The boy brightened like a star. "I know the perfect place, Grandma. Come on. I'll show you."

✧

Carrie dried Diane's china plate while Frankie took the boys out to pick up a movie. The argument she'd had with Frank before their wedding rang in her ears. "Who uses china anymore, for God's sake, Carrie?" he had barked.

"It's on Diane's registry, Frank. She obviously will."

"Did you see how much it costs? Fifteen hundred dollars, for God's sake. If you invested that now, their kids would have their college tuition paid for. What's more important? Their future or eating macaroni and cheese off a damn piece of china?"

"Both, Frank. Both," had been her answer.

Carrie placed the dried saucer on the stack. Suddenly, Diane sank her hands in the white, fluffy dish soap and burst into tears. "I can't take it anymore, Mom. I can't," she said to the suds.

Carrie left the damp towel on the cabinet and enfolded Diane in her arms. "What? What is it?"

"Frankie. It's Frankie." Diane swiped a wet hand across her face, leaving traces of suds on her cheeks. "He controls everything. He won't even listen to us, or it's an argument. Never. He never listens. You don't understand."

"Yes, I do understand, Diane. I know." Oh, how well she knew.

Diane braced herself at the kitchen sink and looked out the window. "If we want to do something like…like go to Disneyland, it's when he wants to go, how he wants to go, and we do what he wants us to do when we get there." She grabbed the wet towel and slammed it on the counter. "Because he's paying for it."

Carrie had to get her hands busy. She started running fresh water to finish the dishes. "I do understand, Diane. Frankie is just like his father."

Diane sagged against the kitchen counter. "How did you do it?"

"Do what?" One saucer done and rinsed.

"Put up with it."

Another piece done. Carrie had to be careful, or she'd break something. "I chose to. For the kids."

Diane picked up a towel and started drying. "I don't think it is good for the boys. Besides, I want to go back to work. The hospitals are begging for nurses. I can't just stay here anymore."

Carrie swallowed the frustration, remembering that she went to work for that same reason. She wanted her own money to spend on the kids and on herself, without the lectures. Still the lectures came. Yet the question loomed in the air; why had she stayed?

Kids and the fact she didn't want "divorce" attached to her name had been why. She had been raised that you didn't just get a divorce. You worked it out. You dealt with it. Regret niggled deeper. What would her life have been like? Better? Worse? No answer.

Carrie rinsed the last plate and handed it to Diane. "Diane, that's a great idea for you to go back to work. It would be good for you."

"He won't let me." Diane set down the plate with the others. "He wants me home with the kids."

Carrie ripped off the apron and plopped the fabric on the wet countertop. "I heard the same nonsense." It was that same exact argument echoing in her brain.

Diane carefully put the stack of plates in the cabinet and turned. "Mom, just so you know, I've looked into a lawyer. I want a divorce. Once I get back to work, I can take care of the boys well enough."

"Divorce? The boys?" Carrie leaned back against the sink. "Seriously, Diane."

The girl begged for understanding. "Mom, I don't want this. I don't. I love Frankie, but I can't stand his control anymore."

"Have you considered counseling?"

Diane threw her hands to the ceiling. "A thousand times. What a waste of money. What do they know? Do you know how much they cost…per hour? That's all I hear each and every time I mention it." She walked toward Carrie. "Mom, please understand. I won't take the boys from you. Ever. We just can't live here. We can't."

Carrie studied the plea radiating from her daughter-in-law's tears and rested a damp hand on Diane's forearm. "You know you will always be my daughter. That I love you. But please, try to work it out first."

Tears ran through mascara, leaving black streaks down Diane's cheeks.

"I love you, too, Mom. I do." Diane enfolded Carrie in a tight hug.

The front door shut sharply. Diane swiped at the streaks covering her cheeks and rushed out of sight. The boys ran in the kitchen. "They didn't have *Cars* or Nemo, Mom."

Carrie intercepted their charge, squatting in front of Roy and stopping Sam in his tracks. "What did you get?" she asked.

"A dumb horse movie that Daddy picked," Sam said, fuming.

"Something about a horse being a secretary," Roy mumbled. "Dad said it was good." The tiny shoulders shrugged with nonchalance.

"Secretariat isn't a secretary. He was a racehorse," she told the boys. "Did you know that he really is a real horse?"

"Really?" the boys asked.

"Oh, yes. I saw that horse win that race. Well, on television."

"It really happened?" Sam asked, suddenly enthralled.

Carrie stood, took both their hands in hers, and led them out to the living room, past Frankie standing in the doorway, scowling at Diane as she joined them.

"I'll take that." Carrie plucked the small case from his hand and continued her oration on the horse. "Secretariat won the Triple Crown."

"He got a crown for winning a race?" Sam asked.

"Three of them."

"Horses don't wear crowns. They get trophies," Roy corrected and started settling on the couch. "Here, Grandma, let me. I know how to do that."

CHAPTER 8

S AM FELL ASLEEP before Secretariat won the Kentucky Derby. Roy gave up on the movie and went to bed after the Preakness.

Carrie helped tuck them in and then faced the idea of going down to watch Secretariat win the Belmont again, which always thrilled her. However, it died with the idea of being alone with Frankie. Going there would be like walking into a death trap.

Instead, she went to her bedroom. When she walked past John's luggage under the window of the room, a deep melancholy seeped over her like warm oil. Had he made his deliveries? Was he in Sacramento now, or on his way to Los Angeles?

How was Carl—his agent…no, broker? Every ounce of her wanted to be back on the truck with John, doing anything but standing in front of the window, wondering.

We're not through talking about this echoed in her brain. Well, maybe if Frankie wanted to continue his rant, fine with her.

But she was glad she had left Kansas City and had driven out on the Salt Flats where a knight, in a shining, black, chromed *rig* with more amenities than some small apartments, had saved her. Her melancholy changed to a feeling of homesickness.

"Mom? I don't like the fact that you lied to me about being with that pervert."

Carrie turned to see her son standing in the doorway like a shadow.

"He's not a pervert, Frankie. I should have been more prepared and—"

He sat on the foot of the bed. "Like I said, you should have listened to the weather forecast or, better yet, have flown."

Like father like son. "I didn't want to fly. I love driving and seeing the—"

"It's too dangerous for a woman alone. I would never let Diane do this."

Carrie stepped closer to the bed. "What would you do to stop her, Frankie? Lock her in her room?"

A glare lit in his gaze. "I would have talked sense into her." He braced both hands on his thighs. "Like Dad did you."

Oh, did he? Did Frankie really believe that? She glared down at her son. "And what if she still wanted to drive to Kansas City?"

Her son combed a hand through his hair and adjusted himself on the coverlet to face her better. "I'd make her stay here until I could go with her."

"Oh. Make her stay, Frankie? She's a grown woman."

His voice lowered. "And the mother of my children."

She stepped closer to drive her words in deeper, hoping they'd made some sort of sense. "They are her children, too, Frankie. And Diane is fully capable of making an intelligent decision on her own."

The snarling smirk on his face seemed all too familiar. "And likely would have the same experience you did." Bitterness laced his words. "You could have died out there, Mom. I bet you never considered calling the highway patrol, did you?"

Carrie inhaled and let it out slowly. "I did. They were busy with a *parking-lot*…I mean a pile-up. I told you on the phone that John stopped, because they couldn't come."

"John?" Saying his name brought her son to his feet.

Her feet rooted into the plush rug. "Yes. You saw his nametag? John Graham."

Her son's chin jutted out with indignation. "Dad would be turning over in his grave if he knew you were with another man again."

That slapped her back a step. "What do you mean … again?" Had he lost his mind?

"This isn't the first time you did as you pleased with someone else. Is it, Mother?" Glaring at her, Frankie spewed his words like a hissing snake.

Confusion twisted around in her brain. He was accusing her of having the affair? Her hands curled at her sides. She had never slapped her children. She wouldn't start now.

Frankie's arms flung open like wings. "Dad told me and Carrianne the real reason why you moved into your own bedroom. And it wasn't because of his snoring." He slowly nodded with a sick smirk. "Like you wanted us to believe. And he said this wasn't the first time."

"That's a lie."

A cold, deeper than any snowstorm, swept through her. "I was *never* unfaithful to your father." Carrie started toward him. "Not once. Not once." Her fingernails bit into her palms. "I cannot believe he told he you this."

"You think I would make that up about my father?"

She had to sit down. She had never once said a word to the kids beyond the idea of snoring. Obviously, Frank had-- and lied to not only Frankie, but also Carrianne to protect his ass. The last respect for her dead husband just died.

"I. Never. Had. Any. Affair," she spat. "Your father did that. Not me. Is that clear?"

"Really, Mom? Dad would never do such a thing. He said he could never please you no matter how hard he tried."

"Get out. Get out of my room. And so, you know, I'll be leaving in the morning."

How could she stay and even look at her son after this? She lifted her chin in defiance. "Since I don't have a car, I'll be flying home."

Frankie melted slightly. "Mom. Come on. The kids. It's Christmas."

"Get out, Frankie."

CHAPTER 9

FRANKIE RACED TO beat her to the front door. "Seriously, Mom. The boys. What do I tell them?"

The taxi honked from the drive. Carrie clutched her luggage and John's suitcase and started for the front door. "I'm sure you'll figure that out like your father did."

"Look, Mom, I'm sorry. About last night. I shouldn't have said anything about all that shit. Dad let it go. I should have too." Frankie looked desperate.

She stopped to face him. "I'm glad you did, Frankie. Nevertheless, I can't believe you would believe him."

"Mom, Father would never—"

Carrie glanced at Diane wrapped in her housecoat. "Be happy, Diane. You and the boys deserve it." Her gaze locked directly on her son, and then she stepped closer to the door.

Frankie put his hand on it to stop her. "I can't let you do this, Mom."

The taxi honked again. Carrie looked directly at Frankie. "Yes, you will. I'm your mother. Now move."

⸻

Tears leaked the entire way to the Sacramento airport, through security, and on the plane ride back to Kansas City. People avoided her. A lady on the plane offered her a tissue and obviously wanted to listen. Words refused to come.

Every mile that the taxi got closer to her house, the thinner the air became, to the point that she might have passed out. Then she saw the shadowed silhouette of the Tudor-styled house hidden in the late wintry dusk. The driver stopped and got out to open her door. "This the right address, ma'am?"

"Yes."

She couldn't tear her gaze off the house that had consumed her life with a liar. She never dreamed Frank would stoop low enough to lie to the children. But why not? He'd destroyed hers with such lies.

"You want me to help you to the door?" the driver asked.

"No."

Carrie shifted her attention to the restless man. No part of her could face all those memories that awaited in there. She couldn't do it.

Taking in a deep breath, she forced her mind to shift out of the past to face the uncertain future. "No. I…Not here. I need to go…to a hotel. Do you know of any close?"

The taxi driver smirked. "The Plaza? I could take you to the Sheridan Suites."

She shook her head. Still too close to home. "Uh, no, uh, Embassy something?"

"Embassy Suites. Yes, I know one. You want to go there?"

Yes."

⌘

The farther the taxi got from her house, the more the vice around her chest loosened. She managed to hold together until she stood in front of her room. Her key card shook so, she barely got it in the door slot.

A flood of tears intensified behind her eyes until the green light blipped, and she shoved her way into the room. She yanked the luggage inside seconds before sobs crumpled her into the nearest chair.

"Damn you, Frank! You are lying son of a bitch!"

She had given her entire life to her family, to Frank, to her kids, only to find out they assumed she was a whore, while their father remained a saint.

She didn't have anyone now. No job. No family. Nothing but a house she couldn't even walk into. Nothing but memories that had turned into lies. How could she face any part of that?

Swiping desperately at her cheeks, Carrie looked around at the area of the unlit room. Light from the parking lot beamed through the distant bedroom.

Just what should she to do now? Her luggage lay about the floor like pieces of her life. John's piece remained upright, stalwart like a warrior. If she could be any place right now, it would be in his truck. However, she likely never would be again.

"Breathe, Carrie. Get a grip."

Her cell phone buzzed and she instinctively pulled it from her purse. Voicemails from Frankie, Carrianne, and Emily filled her screen.

"Mom, where are you? Frankie said you should be home by now. We're worried. Mom? Is this you? Mom, call the moment you get in."

Carrianne.

Then the next voice mail came from Emily. "Mom, really? A trucker? Totally awesome. I want all the details. So cool."

Carrie almost smiled. It died with the next click.

"Mom, what the hell did you tell Diane? She just up and left, right after you did. She's taking the boys. Thanks for a great Christmas. Have a happy New Year. I won…."

She simply listened, with no interest whatsoever in calling any one of her children back, and then poked the end button to end the sound of his voice. She needed a shower. A long hot shower.

❧

"When do you think you'll have it ready?" John asked the service manager.

"Coupla days at the most, Big John." The slight young man pushed the order slip toward him to sign.

"See ya in a coupla days then." John signed the papers.

The door to the KC service center dinked as someone walked in. "Hey, Big John, comin' with me, or do you wanna walk to the car rental?" one of the drivers asked.

John heard the man's *rig* running outside. "On my way, Bill." He hated leaving his truck anywhere, even here where he had purchased it. "Take good care of it."

The service manager chuckled. "We'll see it's diapered each night before we put it to bed. Will that do, John?"

"Likes to eat around midnight."

"No problem."

John walked past the fancy coffee makers that made single brews of special coffees. Bet Carrie would enjoy one of those played through his mind. She said she really liked French Vanilla. Guilt itched.

He shouldn't be thinking of Carrie or caring what kind of coffee she liked. That was over. Past. Forget it. However, for the last three days, John couldn't stop wondering how things were going between Carrie and her son.

The answers the road had given him weren't good. Even though he knew Carrie would still be in California with her grandsons, his mouth hadn't stopped from watering for bar-beque. That had pushed him to get to the *Bright-lights*.

Bill pulled out of the parking lot. "Heard about Carl?"

"Yeah. Unfortunately, he's going to be laid up for a while. Can't wait until he's back on his feet. Phil is really screwing me with the miles, givin' the best loads to his trucks."

"Yeah, I heard," Bill grumbled and checked his mirrors. "Phil is like that, or so I hear."

"Guess I'll have to deal with Phil until Carl is back, since I don't have a family like you. By the way, how are they?"

"Wife's bitching about me never being home, you know. Kids and all."

"Yeah, Janis went through that." A comfortable lie because Janis understood he'd be home every chance he could. However, it was the general bitch of all trucking families, especially through the Christmas holidays. Kids' birthdays were the worst.

Bill glanced at him with a smirk in his eyes. "Heard on the *squawk box* that you had a new *seat-cover*."

"Who the hell told you about that?"

"Overheard the *smokeys* sayin' how you helped one out when they had that *parking-lot* on 80. Then Charlie saw you putting her in a taxi over by Wendover. Couldn't believe it. Had to ask." Bill turned into the rental car parking.

"She's not my *seat-cover* by any means. But lucky for her, I stopped, or she'da been an ice cube after that storm." John started out of the cab. Frigid cold instantly slapped him.

"Glad I was in Kentucky for that one. See ya on the *turn-around*."

"*Ten-four.* I owe ya one." John closed the door.

Seat-cover my ass. Yet the idea burned like a warm toasty fire in a stone fireplace on a cold winter day when it should feel like searing flames.

Maybe he could just give Carrie a call for a recommendation for a restaurant. John started digging in his pocket for that piece of paper with her cell phone number.

John's number lit up on Carrie's phone and honked his new ringtone. Her heart leaped in her chest with joy but sank. She couldn't talk to him without bawling. The phone shifted to voice mail.

"Carrie, hope you're enjoying the holidays in Cali. Just wanted to let you know I made it to *Bright-lights* and am hungry for some barbeque. If you have any suggestions, give me a call. I'd appreciate it. John."

The fact that he kept her number and the fact that he called, sliced through her like a scalpel opening an infection. Tears of relief brimmed in her eyes.

She just needed to find some way to return his call, suggest a place, and pretend that her entire world hadn't just been destroyed.

Just pretend. And sound all perky, that she was having the time of her life there in Cali. All she had to do was let John believe she was happy. Just lie as she had with the kids.

No. She was done with lying. She had done enough of that all her life. Her marriage had been a sham, and she let her kids believe everything was just wonderful. Well, it wasn't, and she was not going to cover up the truth again. Except she did not want to spill everything out to John.

Her cell buzzed again, flashing John's number. "Hope everything is going perfectly out there. How'd the boys like their blankets? Dammit, Carrie, I wish you were in town so we could grab a bite somewhere. Just call. John."

CHAPTER 10

JOHN TURNED THE key in the ignition of the rental car and his cell phone rang. Carrie's phone number flashed on the screen. After nearly dropping the cell phone on the floorboard, he managed to answer before the call went to voice mail.

"Hey, I came in to service the *rig*." Delight rippled through him. "Didn't you say you knew of a few good places for good barbeque around here?"

"Yeah. Uh, where…are you?"

Like a deflating tire, he sobered. Something itched in Carrie's voice. She didn't sound like her bubbly self. "435 South. Any recommendations? I'm starving."

"There's lots." Silence filled the phone. Carrie cleared her voice. "Want…some company?"

What the hell? Where was she? John swallowed the questions. "Sure. Love some. Aren't you still in Sacramento?" A long pause filled the phone as he drove over the Kansas River.

"Short visit. Frankie had some…business or something."

Something was wrong, and that prick of a son was behind it. "Great, Carrie. I'd love your company. I got a rental so I think I can find that Walter area."

"Walter area?"

"That's where your house is, isn't it?" he asked.

"Oh. You mean Waldo. I'm…not… there. I'm…I'm at the Embassy Suites…on State Line."

Embassy Suites? Why for God's sake? A surge to protect her swept around John like a vice. "No problem. I'm on my way."

The instant John saw Carrie step from the elevator doors, he knew. She wore a fake smile, her makeup was odd, even her clothes hung differently somehow. Funny how much he remembered from their short time together.

He met Carrie in the middle of the lobby. Fury had begun a slow burn in his guts. "Hope you are hungry," he said jovially. "I know I am. Italian or barbeque, whatever," he said and escorted her outside.

She stopped, her emerald gaze sparkling up at him. "Don't you want barbeque?"

He truly smiled. Plenty of fight left in the old girl. "If that's what you'd like, my dear. Just make it good. I'm starving." He opened the car door for her, and Carrie slid in.

The trip to Gates BBQ went easy enough, but not their conversation. Somehow, it was all about the delivery, roads, weather, general crap. He saved his real question until he pulled into the parking lot and shut off the car. He knew from Janis that no woman wanted to cry in public space.

The moment the shadow of the restaurant covered the car, he turned to her. "Carrie, what happened out there?"

She stared at him and then burst into tears. "I can't believe Frank lied to the kids by telling them I was the one who had the affair. Only I didn't. He did. And they believed him. Not me.

"John, honestly, I didn't know. I…I only stayed in that marriage because of the kids. I didn't want to be the one breaking up the family." She fruitlessly dried her tears with the back of her hand. "I…I j-just can't believe Frank would lie… and tell the kids that."

"What did your son tell you?"

"Frankie informed me that was why I stayed with you; that his father told him and Carrianne that I did that all the time. It…it was why I moved into the other bedroom. That… that…" She melted into sobs.

Un-fucking believable. "What an asshole." John dug in his pocket for his handkerchief and offered it.

She took it and swabbed at her face. "John, I couldn't stay in the house, not after finding that out. I just couldn't."

"I don't blame you."

She slumped back in the seat like a deflated balloon. Silence fumed until she calmed enough to stare out the windshield.

"I couldn't walk into that house full of memories," she said absently. "He's all over that place. So, I checked into the Embassy to figure out what to do next. I still don't know."

"Shit, Carrie." John ran his hands around the car's steering wheel. "That would be one hell of a hill to climb."

She looked over at him and smirked. "Is that trucker talk? Hill to climb?"

"Yeah maybe, something like having to gear down to make it up a hill." That came out his ass, but she smiled.

She handed back the handkerchief. "I'm sorry, John. I shouldn't be telling you all this. But it all just spilled out."

Until now, he had no idea how true 'like father, like son' could be. "No problem. Ready to chow down on some ribs?" he asked.

"Oh, John, I can't go in there now. I look horrible. Maybe you should take me back to the Embassy."

"Nope. You look better than anything I've seen over the last few days." He opened his door to the thick smell of hickory smoke. He sucked it in all the way around to her door.

"You just have a case of allergies. Seen lots of truckers with those same allergies in a few truck stops," he said.

Getting out of the car, Carrie asked, "Allergies?"

John held the restaurant door open and waited for her to walk inside. "Yeah, allergies from family."

Following Carrie into the restaurant, he slid his arm around her waist just to let her know, if she needed to lean on him or something like that, he was there. She didn't refuse. That slightly staunched his fury at the little shithead of a son.

"Hi. May I help you?" the clerk behind the service counter asked, startling him. He looked at Carrie for help.

"Mixed plate, beef and pork, and a small order of burnt ends."

"Mixed and a burnt!" the girl announced over her shoulder. "Something to drink?"

"Strawberry cream soda, all right?" Carrie asked.

"Sounds great to me," he answered. Already he could see that Carrie was going to burst apart again. "How about you go find us a seat and I'll get this?"

Released from a trap, she scurried off to the next room. By the time he showed up with the tray of food, she had a line of small white cups filled with various sauces, waiting in the secluded booth.

He set the tray on the table and slid across from her, eager to tear into the pile of meat before him. She took a fry from her plate. "How's Carl?"

He poured hot sauce over enough meat for a week's worth of dinners. "Better. Diane said he's recovering well. Phil is still covering his drivers. But that fool Phil is killing us out there. All the good hauls go to his trucks." After one bite, John died and went to barbeque heaven.

Carrie picked at her burnt ends. "I wish I could do something to help you."

"I wish you could, too. Any ideas of what you might want to do now?"

She studied the wall and shrugged. "No. Except that I can't walk into that house until I do."

He dipped a fry into the sauce. What would it be like to not want to walk into your own house? Maybe it was like not wanting to climb in a cab again. He well knew that one. Every mile he had ever driven for thirty-five years had suddenly been coated with guilt for not spending more time with Janis before she died. He shoulda—

"Ever been to Maine?" blurted from his filled mouth.

"No. But I hear it's beautiful."

"Well, why not go with me and, by the time I get you back here, you'll have something figured out." After all, the road had helped him deal with more than he wanted to admit to.

While holding a fry dripping with ketchup, Carrie stared at him. "Seriously?"

He swallowed and nodded. "Yeah. You like lobster?"

CHAPTER 11

LIGHTNING COULD NOT have struck Carrie with more force. She almost gasped. John had asked her to go to Maine with him. Maine. A thousand years ago, that had been one of her dream trips.

And if she did go with John, she might have time to figure out how to deal with everything. Oh, God. The kids. What would they think of her? Well, nothing worse than they did now.

John poured more sauce over the pile of pork. "Nothing better than real lobster from Maine."

Just the idea of fresh lobster made her hungry. "Maine? Lobster?"

John wiped the last sauce off his plate with a fry, but not the bit of sauce lingering at the corner of his mouth. "All the way to Maine." He sat back like a satisfied pet. "And I'll have you back here in a week."

Adrenaline danced through Carrie's veins. John's familiar scent of Old Spice welcomed her the moment she got back into his truck…no, *rig*. If Frank could, he would be turning over in his grave. Well, do flip-flops, Frank. She didn't care anymore.

After putting her meager things where John said to, she settled in the passenger seat—her seat for the next week—with her laptop and reader beside her. John got in his driver's seat and hung his winter coat over hers on the back hook. He claimed his logbook and information that sparked her curiosity. Putting it away, he asked. "Ready?"

"I am." And she was. Life surged back into her veins as the engine growled to life like a familiar pet, one she had missed. Yet something felt different about the truck. It felt lighter. "Is it my imagination or does the truck feel different?"

"We're *deadheading*." John checked her mirror and frowned. "Traveling empty to Tyson in Warrenton, just past Columbia, for a load of frozen chicken bound for Bangor, Maine."

"That's not good? I mean *deadheading*?"

"I'm not paid driving empty, and we have to cross the state before I get *the pickup*…a load. In this world, time is money. Either you're making money hauling a load or it's costing you."

"There wasn't a pickup somewhere in Kansas City?" Carrie asked, settling deeper into the seat.

"If there was, Phil gave it to one of his drivers." John slowed for the entrance ramp. "I don't have a good feeling about Carl's condition either. My bet is Diane is going to talk him into retiring."

"And then you'll be stuck with Phil?"

John's shoulders dropped with his sigh. "That's a possibility, unless I find someone else to broker for me." He eased into the morning rush hour traffic moving like cold molasses.

A car shot into the lane in front of the truck, passed a car, and whipped back into the passing lane. Carrie gasped. "He's crazy, driving like that."

"They all think they are Dale Earnhardt or something," John said, keeping his eyes on the road and hands on the wheel even while resting his left elbow on the window ledge.

A cloud of earned confidence and experience surrounded him, something younger men hadn't earned. Not movie star handsome, but John was, in his own rugged way handsome nonetheless.

Short sandy hair, dusted with white, lay in soft waves over his forehead. His easy gaze over the road had a steadiness as if he had seen it all. What older women saw in younger men seemed ridiculous. No way was she—

The man driving the car they were passing caught her attention. When she looked down, all she saw on the driver was a white dress shirt, tie, and suit coat atop of two hairy legs. NO slacks. NO underpants. And he was–

"Oh, my God, John! He doesn't have any pants on, and he's playing with…!"

They passed the Mercedes while John laughed. "Just so you know, it's not all pretty out here."

"But, John. I mean, he shouldn't—"

"From down there, he just looks like he's going to work."

"But getting out of the car."

"That's his problem."

John checked the mirrors and slowed for another car. "You wouldn't believe what I've seen from up here. Girls flashing their boobs. Couples doin' it in the seats, front or back, jacking off, or getting a blowjob. It doesn't matter. I've seen it all. What really gets me furious is a kid getting backhanded by an adult."

She was not looking inside another car. However, even as she did, she found herself holding her breath for another horror inside the passing cars, or *four-wheelers* as John called them.

Yet, mostly people texted, put on make-up, or even shaved when they shouldn't be doing any of that.

A little boy pumped his arm in a rear window from his car seat, and John sounded his horn. Joy flashed in the boy's eyes, and then the car disappeared in the traffic.

Occasionally, the highway patrol zoomed by with their lights flashing, or *disco-lights* as John had said. She was starting to enjoy this new lingo.

Carrie had forgotten the rolling hills and beautiful country of Missouri even in the dead of winter. She relished the sight of the passing flat farmland dotted with worn white barns, black ribbons of driveways cutting through fresh snowy pastures.

Mostly, she just rode along in the quiet, giving her mind too much time to think.

✖

As John got off the interstate and turned onto a state highway, Carrie enjoyed how the *rig* grumbled as it slowed down. Further on, a small building appeared. It had two large windows and inside sat a short man. "Hey, Big John. Good to see you."

"Back at you, Sandy. Recovered from the holidays?" John asked and then claimed some papers from the glove compartment.

"Nope. Gained ten pounds from Carol's holiday cookies. Got a few left. Want some?"

"I'll pass this time."

Surprise flooded Sandy's face the instant he saw Carrie. Then, the two men disappeared behind the trailer and then walked back to the small building.

"As usual everything looks good, John. Dock 15's waiting for you. Have a *Happy-Happy*."

John climbed back in and placed the papers on the dash. "Back at ya, Sandy."

He pulled forward into what he called a *yard* filled with more idling rigs that reminded Carrie of a bunch of lazy dogs waiting to chase a rabbit or something.

"A *Happy-Happy*?" she asked.

"Happy New Year," he answered with a smirk.

Then all his attention went to backing up to a concrete dock. A bright, red light beamed and the moment it turned green, John stopped, shut down, and reached for the paper-work papers from the dash.

"Check to see if we need anything at the next stop. Be right back." He climbed out and disappeared into the warehouse.

Carrie went into the rear of the cab and glanced at the neat bed, dismissing the delicious memory of John's arm across her waist. An empty bin on her side of the bed fit about everything she had brought in her suitcase.

She looked through the cabinets for food supplies and found a box of peanut butter crackers, protein bars, and more instant coffee. French vanilla creamer and, oddly enough, a container of honey. The mini fridge had about a quart of milk left in its container. Old butter. Old bread. Old bagels. Yes, he needed this all refreshed. Meanwhile, she felt something going on in the trailer.

'Right back' turned out to be about an hour, and, by the time he did appear, she had a waste bag full of 'old' food waiting for him.

She stopped reading her book on her phone and looked up the moment he swung up into the cab. He immediately pulled out his logbook, entered something on one of the pages, put the paperwork in the glove compartment, and then started up the truck. "Settled in?"

"Yep. And oh, can you get rid of this?" She pointed to the sack sitting like a lost urchin in the back.

"Oh, I see you went through the fridge. Good. But that means we need some things, doesn't it?" he said.

"A few. Unless you're interested in food poisoning." Carrie claimed two bottles of water from the fridge. "Everything go all right?"

"Fine." John checked his e-mails from his laptop. "Aw, shit."

"What's wrong, John?" She slid back into her seat, dropping a bottle in his holder.

"Look!" He pointed to the screen. "Phil has me in Bangor in three days. He knows damn good and well that I can be there in two."

"Can't you just deliver early?"

"No. And the son-of-a-bitch knows this too. First, he deadheads me here, and now this." He threw the pencil on the dash and slouched back in the seat. The trailer shifted with the loading.

"Maybe you can take your time getting there."

"Carrie, out here, time is money. And that money pays for everything else that runs this. I need back-to back loads."

CHAPTER 12

THE ENGINE REVVED and inched forward. Weight fell in behind Carrie and settled in tow. Before long, John had them on the way toward St. Louis or, as he called it, *Gateway-City*.

She had looked forward to seeing the Arch but didn't get to see it. John had to take the *beltway*, or loop, around St. Louis toward Indianapolis, Indiana, or *Circle-City*. Then every city began to look all the same, concrete gray and dirty, industrial areas and skylines on the horizons, and shoulders landscaped with the same trees.

Not to mention that there seemed to be more cars than the population. She couldn't begin to count the number of *four-wheelers* that deliberately cut in front of the truck, expecting John to pull aside just for them.

He took the crush of cars, the slow drag, and the unpredictable NASCAR drivers in stride. He simply let the distance grow between him and the cars and remained alert like a dog on point.

Soon after they had left Kansas City, Frank's lectures faded, to be replaced by other memories of so many more issues that rose like boils. Each struck like lightning, drawing unwanted tears, until, miles later, she had become inured to the memories and wanted to leave them on the interstate to be run over by traffic.

She had done her diligence by staying with that lying, cheating bastard. And, regardless of what her children believed, this could be a new beginning for her.

Nothing about the wintry scenery changed much, except that, when it grew dark, the world became dotted with white headlights, red taillights, and house lights still blazing Christmas decorations here and there.

They passed a road sign announcing Columbus, Ohio, and John pulled onto an exit ramp for an hour break that he said the government required him to take. She read her book while he napped on the bed for an hour, and then they were back on the road.

Time and miles. She was beginning to understand what he meant now, as she watched him log into what he called the *lie-book*. He explained that, when in a time crunch, many truckers lied about the hours they drove. Some drivers even ran two such books. He said he didn't lie, even though there had been times when he was tempted.

Apparently, the government had set controls that he had to deal with. For every eight hours driving, he had to break for an hour. Then, at ten hours, he had to stop for eight hours of sleep. After seventy-two hours of driving, he had to break for thirty-six hours before getting back on the road.

John constantly wrote his driving time on the log sheet each time they stopped for whatever. Couldn't he do that on his laptop?

The Pilot truck stop appeared like a busy beehive where trucks and cars of every kind pulled in and out all around them. The smell of Wendy's hamburgers and diesel exhaust swept inside the instant John opened his door to get out.

While they waited for a pump section to clear, John tried to explain what the different trucks were called. A flatbed—a *skateboard*; a flatbed covered with canvas was a *covered-wagon*; a load of live pigs—a *pigpen*. Not to mention the *four-wheelers* and *crotch rockets* buzzing around like little puppies. The list seemed endless.

Finally, an area opened, and John filled the fuel tanks, logged in the amount, and looked at her with a tired spark of curiosity. "I'm hungry for some real food. How about you?"

"I'm up for it." After all, they had mostly snacked on junk food all day. "Wait here. I'll come around and help you down."

⤸

When he and Carrie came into the convenience store to get the thing on her list, grins erupted and elbows poked ribs to turn heads to see Carrie. That itched like a rash. Obviously, the drivers there approved. But not for the same reasons he knew they were thinking.

He liked having Carrie's company riding along with him. She didn't talk constantly or didn't expect to stop in any of the cities to see the historical sites. Instead, she read local history from Wikipedia about the cities they drove through that he knew nothing about.

When Janis rode with him, she chattered continuously about family, the latest gossip from her two sisters or her mother after each morning phone call. She then would relay every word to him. He loved Janis, but he quickly learned how to tune her out.

Guilt had itched its way into his conscious for even thinking of inviting Carrie to go to Maine with him. But he couldn't leave her there alone. Not in that state.

The road got a little tough for her around *Gateway-City* where he caught Carrie hiding tears and heard her long sighs. Best to leave it to the road to clear her mind. The road was good at doing that. By the time they made it to the Ohio truck stop for dinner, the road apparently had claimed most of it.

"What do you want?" he asked once they were seated in a cafe booth. "I'll go get it."

"Salad is fine. Ranch dressing. Water."

A driver, who resembled a black Paul Bunyan in everything but size, stopped by their booth. "Hey, Big John. Good to see you out and about."

John looked up. "Mike. Hey. Good to see you, too. Where you headed?"

"Bikes to *Guitar-town*." Mike's gaze ventured expectantly to Carrie and came back. "You?"

"Chicken to *Beantown*."

"Just left there in time to miss the snow."

"Snow?" Carrie asked. Panic laced the word.

"They'll have the road clear by the time we get there," John assured and then decided to relieve Mike's misery. "Oh, this is Carrie, a friend who likes lobster nearly more than I do."

Carrie and Mike shook hands. His smile couldn't have been broader. "You won't be disappointed, Miss Carrie. Lobster doesn't get better than up there. And they'll have the roads cleared by the time you get there."

"Thank you, Mike, I'm really looking forward to this lobster I've heard about."

Smiling, he turned back to John. "Heard about Carl. What's the latest?"

John didn't really want to think about that and sat his sandwich down on his plate. "Not sure, but I think Diane is trying to talk him into retiring. God, I hope not. Phil is a pain in the ass. He is brokering for you, too?"

Mike nodded with a grim expression. "Yeah. Screwed me over on this trip. However, hey, I'm getting a few miles. If Diane wins, let me know if you find a broker whose head isn't up his …well, you know." He nodded to Carrie. "Good to meet you. Best get on the road." He looked to John. "Be safe out there."

"Back at ya."

Carrie laid her fork down beside her salad. "What's that about Carl?"

"He's doing better." John dabbed a fry in his ketchup. "Last we talked, Diane wanted him to go on a month's vacation. I really think he wants to."

"You think Diane will win out?"

"Likely." He couldn't eat anymore and pushed away the tray. "I just don't know if I can drive for Phil that long."

"Mike said something about finding someone else."

"Good brokers are like a needle in a haystack. Carl had been a driver and knows what drivers needed. After a bad accident screwed up his knees, he started brokering." John drank to wash the idea of working with Phil down his throat.

Carrie put a hand on his arm. "I'm sorry, John."

"Yeah, me too."

❧

John stirred awake from sleeping deeper than he had in a very long time. Well, at least a few weeks ago anyway. But Carrie wasn't curled up under the covers.

He rolled over to see her sitting in the passenger seat and staring out the side window. "Everything okay?" he asked.

"Just couldn't sleep."

Now he couldn't. He slid into his slippers, walked to his driver's seat, and pulled out his cell phone to check the weather app. How much snow had fallen in Maine? A shadow scurried around the front of the cab and knocked on his door.

"Want any company?" A short girl with curly hair and a thin winter coat peeked into the cab.

"No, sweetheart. Is that your ride over there?" He waved a hand toward the black Navigator parked in the shadows.

"Yes, I mean no. No, it's not." The girl's chin quivered. "G-Glad to do a threesome. W-Warmer for everyone."

"Just a minute." He looked to Carrie, staring at him in shock as he leaned closer. "Can you see that license number? If so, write it down." He leaned back toward the window and handed her a granola bar he'd plucked from the console. He handed it to her. "Not tonight. Don't you want to go home?"

Tears welled in her eyes. "I…I can't. Bye."

John picked up his phone, brought up his contacts, and punched the number. While it rang, he took the small piece of paper from Carrie.

A voice answered. "Truckers Against Trafficking. Can I help you?"

"Not me, but there's a bunch of girls working Pilot Travel Center, I-70, tonight. Can you report this to the *smokeys*? Black Navigator—license number…." As he read off the plate, the car started moving and the girls raced to get in before it left.

"Leaving the site now."

"Thank you, *driver*. On it." The phone went dead.

John slumped back in his seat. "Hope they get that pimp."

"It's hard to believe they are out here in this cold like that," Carrie said.

"That car was their pimp. They work or they get beat. Cold. Hot. Hailstorm. Doesn't matter."

"Why doesn't the police put a stop to this?"

"Some are really trying. Some don't."

"Even truckers?"

"Yeah." He nodded. "We're trying. I just reported it and, hopefully, the *smokeys* will get the bastard before he disappears." He'd seen way too many of these girls over the years. "Even if they do arrest him, there will be just as many back here tomorrow night."

"What do you mean 'we' are trying?"

"Remember the TAT decal on your door? It stands for *Truckers Against Trafficking*. We've become the eyes out here. A lot of us see these girls out here working and call in to report it. Now it's up to the *smokeys*." He shrugged. "We've saved a few, got 'em home to their parents. But it never stops. I just do what I can and hope for the best."

Carrie touched his arm. "God bless you and all the other truckers for trying to put a stop to this horror."

He returned to the weather reports, his arm tingling from her touch. No snow, but plenty of guilt for Maine. He plugged his phone in the recharger and sat back.

He wanted to tell Janis about reporting the pimp. He wanted to feel her hug him and hear her say she was proud of him being a driver for TAT.

He looked over at Carrie who had her eyes closed and her brow furrowed with worry. Her phone lay in her open hand and the screen showed messages from her son.

"Looking forward to lobster?" he asked to break the deafening silence before it smothered him.

A long sigh escaped Carrie's lips. "Is lobster that much better up there?"

"I have actually never taken the time to find out."

She chuckled. That seemed to break some ice inside the cab. "Then we both get to enjoy something new."

"Sorry. Trucking just isn't a vacation?" John muttered.

When she turned to him, a tear escaped her eye. "I've enjoyed being here until this." She lifted her phone in reference. "Frankie is about to have a coronary because I just up and left, disappeared from the face of the earth so to speak."

Her hand dropped the phone back in her lap. "Carrianne wants an explanation. And, I haven't heard from Emily." She studied him. "Why do I feel like I have to report to them?"

"Last I checked this was a free country."

Carrie sagged back in her seat. "I feel like a teenager answering to my parents for being caught in the back seat with my boyfriend at the drive-in."

"That's a blast from the past." He chuckled.

"It was, wasn't it?" She brightened. "And I truly am looking forward to that lobster."

"Well then, let's get on the road so we can get some." He got up and slipped into his shoes.

"Now?"

"Sure. I've had my eight hours of down time." He returned to his driver's seat, pulled out his log, checked his watch, and logged in his time. "Good a time as any."

"This time of night? Really?"

"Time is money. And now is the time."

CHAPTER 13

CARRIE COULDN'T BELIEVE they were leaving the truck stop well before dawn. However, John just eased out of the line of trucks and headed for the road still blanketed by night. And another truck followed.

Trucking was a different world, where miles, time, and sleep were the only things that mattered. Keep rolling. Keep hauling. Just get that load where it has to go and find another to take back.

The night shadows flitted across John's face amid the lights of the interstate flashing through the cab. Snow slushed against the wheels as John drove ever onward, checking side mirrors, reading the road, slowing for morning traffic, and watching. Always watching.

"What kind of coffee do you want?" Carrie asked as she stood before the new Keurig coffeemaker she had bought outside St Louis.

"Regular."

After it drizzled into his black Peterbilt mug, she handed the cup to him. He drank without looking away from the road. She checked the flavor packets, realizing that when they stopped near a Walmart again, she'd have to find more cups.

The fragrance of the French Vanilla trickling into her Garfield mug floated around her like a piece of heaven. Like a sacred pet, the cup had endured everything with her: Frank, the agency, life. She settled in her seat and let the scenery of the rising sun wash her mind with its unique beauty.

Why should she feel so guilty about being on the road with John? After all, she was an adult. She had held down a decent job all these years, paid her bills, taken care of her family, and put up with a lying, cheating husband.

Didn't she deserve to enjoy a trip with a nice person who wanted to take her to Maine for lobster? Did it matter what her kids assumed? No seemed to be the correct answer.

A sign for Buffalo, New York flashed by and what looked like a party of *disco-lights* appeared. At least four patrol cars had surrounded a black Navigator that had been pulled off to one side of the road. Shadows of young girls filled the back seats of the cruisers while the officers handcuffed a man.

"I think they got him," she said, amazed that one simple phone call had saved those girls from any more abuse.

"I hope so."

They slid through a few weigh stations—or *chicken-coops*—where John's logbook was checked.

"Carrianne's message said that Diane and the boys came back, and that Diane and Frankie are going to see a counselor." Her daughter's text message had just spewed out like a geyser. But it felt good to share the news to someone.

"That's a good thing," John said and checked her side mirror.

As a blue SUV slid in front of the truck, she said, "I hope it works, so he'll stop blaming me for her leaving."

"He's just using you."

"Most likely." A huge yawn crawled from her lips.

John grinned and glanced at her. "Go back and get some sleep. Leave the driving to me."

"I think I will."

❦

The snow became deeper with each mile up though New York. However, the road crews had the equipment for snow and obviously knew how to clear roads, so they were making great time.

John checked his watch. He wanted Carrie to see the *Big-Dig* in *Beantown*. He chuckled to himself about how truckers talked, not realizing how it was a language of their own.

But he wanted Carrie to see the underground highway in Boston. Fortunately, he could catch I-95 through there and not eat up much time. Hell, he had enough time to get the load of chicken to Bangor anyway. Thank you, Phil.

His mind settled back to Carrie's bit of news that Frankie was going to counseling. Maybe the counselor could straighten the little shit out about his mother, too, but he doubted it. Many truckers went to counseling with their wives over their constant absence, and a few worked out. Most didn't. The road won.

Freedom lived on the road. For many like him, staying home was more like being put in a cage. A nice cage, maybe, but a cage, nonetheless. Shit, he couldn't explain it even to himself.

Carrie didn't deserve being made to feel cheap by that little prick. Knowing Janis, she would have set the boys straight if they ever tried to do that to her, and he loved that about her. Janis took care of things. She never backed down. However, when things were right, no one enjoyed life more.

He pictured her in her kitchen, fixing something for everyone to eat, always more than enough. "I'll freeze it, so you can take it with you." She'd grin and add, "And you'll come home for more." He could hear those words falling from her mouth.

She always greeted him with a grand smile, open arms, and tight hugs. He remembered her hand sliding into his as the boys came running at him. Somehow, he had managed to hold on and still pick them up.

He blinked at his mounting tears. Damn breast cancer. She had just started talking about going back out on the road with him again when the diagnosis came in.

He had to give it to her because she put up a hell of a fight. All that time, she tried pushing him back to the road. "It's where you belong, John. It's where you have peace. There's nothing you can do here."

The road blurred ahead of him. He swiped at the tears and coughed the rest down his throat. God, he still loved her.

Signs for Niagara Falls began popping up alongside the road. He could still hear Janis laughing as the tour boat took them near the water to get soaked under the thunder and roar of the falling water. He'd heard that the falls were better from the Canadian side, but Janis never wanted to go over there. American soil was enough for her.

But he still wanted to go over to that side to see the falls. He just wasn't sure if he could do it without feeling like a traitor.

Guilt settled over him like a flea-infested quilt. The sign to Niagara Falls whisked by, and the mile sign to the rest stop streaked past. Five miles. When the rest stop appeared, he took it.

Carrie stirred awake. "Where are we?"

"New York. At a rest stop."

❧

The soft hum of the *reefer* unit had begun to add a strange new ambiance that she was coming to like, until John climbed back inside the cab. Carrie could tell something had come over him, leaving him as distant as the Pacific coast.

"You want some water?" she asked.

He took the proffered water bottle. "Thanks. Made good miles today." He took a long swallow and then dangled the water bottle over the top of the steering wheel. His attention stayed just beyond the nose of the truck.

Carrie rested against her door. "You look tired."

"Been worse." He finished the water and then tossed the bottle in the trash bin behind his seat.

"Are we passed Niagara Falls yet?"

"A few miles back."

Carrie turned to stare out at the same spot. "I always believed it would be a great place for a vacation. However, it never happened. Frank said it was like any other waterfall."

John turned to look at her, his blue gaze serious. "It's not like any other fall, trust me."

"Have you been there?"

"Once." His attention returned to the windshield.

"Our neighbors said it's beautiful from the Canadian side." She sighed, remembering her miserable conversation with Frank about crossing the border to go over there.

"Never made it over."

A snowplow charged past on the interstate, throwing snow onto the shoulder like an avalanche. "Someone told me on the American side you get the roar and thunder, but over on the Canadian side you get the beauty of it all," Carrie said, almost verbatim from the neighbors.

"Heard that, too." He turned in his seat. "I'm sorry, Carrie. Wish I could stay up, but I'm beat."

"Don't worry. I can read."

He got up and went to the back of the cab and soon it was full of John's soft snoring and the thickening shadows. A soft ticking noise in the motor added to the quiet.

To keep her mind off what she had to face, she played on her laptop with a new program. It logged miles for a trucker on the computer or their phone, keeping a running tally for them. Just log in the time, place, and a bit more was all John had to do. What was more, it came with five-star reviews. Comments were good, too.

When the truck roared to life, Carrie startled awake in her seat. A kink bit at her neck when she got up. Maybe there was something to do like clean the cab or fix something to eat. She doubted John had eaten anything because if he had, it would have awakened her.

"Want something to eat?" she asked, while standing between both small cabinet units.

"Yeah. Sounds good,' he said without shifting a muscle. Obviously, the invisible barrier remained in place.

She fixed frozen dinners. They ate. John pulled out. He checked mirrors and moved onto the interstate while coffee trickled into his mug. She handed him his cup over his shoulder. He took it without looking back.

"Thanks."

Her coffee finished with the same steamy flourish. She doctored it with cream and sugar and then sat in her seat. The night beyond the windshield was nothing more than blackness dotted with golden fluorescent lights and red and white dots of the few cars also out at midnight. The mounds of snow appeared like gray monsters lurking in the shadows.

She saw it like parallel of her life, a bleak existence filled with dots of happiness and gray lurking issues. The fluorescent lights lining the interstate flickered on John's face like a light switch. On. Off. On. Off.

"How do you do it, drive all night?" she asked.

"You get used to it." He glanced at the mirrors.

She looked out past the nose of the truck at the slushy ribbon of asphalt. "It's really different up here. Towns seem smaller and closer, and the farmland is smaller and hillier than back in Missouri."

John nodded.

Conversation was still stiff. "Where is your favorite place?" she asked.

"Fort Lauderdale."

"Florida is beautiful." She rested her head back on the headrest. "We took the kids to Disney World once. We flew."

"Yeah."

Where this tension came from didn't make sense. Had she done something wrong? Maybe he was starting to regret asking her to come with him.

Well, she shouldn't have accepted his offer. It was a mistake, but what could she do about it now? Just enjoy the lobster and get back home.

CHAPTER 14

CARRIE YAWNED FROM her seat and shut down her reader. "Look. The sun is coming up."

The expression on her face reminded John of his boys the first time they saw the sun come up from inside the truck. He pulled onto the shoulder of an entrance ramp. "You never saw a sunrise?" he asked.

"No. Got up too late."

John picked up his logbook and began entering the time.

"Is something wrong?" she asked. She had to know.

"I have to stop for an hour." He put the logbook up and got out to check the trailer. When he climbed back inside, he went into the back and, in no time, was asleep.

Pulling the curtains closed, Carrie watched the cars zip past the truck on their way to the interstate. John's soft snores filled the cab. She considered joining him. No. Not now.

John murmured his wife's name. "Janis, please…"

Did this Janis realize that she had been lucky to have a guy like John? After finding her fiancé screwing her maid of honor the night before the wedding, Carrie had spurned the idea that love even mattered in a relationship. You only got hurt.

After that, she had thrown herself into the accounting classes at the local college to forget about love or romance. Then she met Frank, and they got married in Las Vegas in a simple wedding, no family, just the two of them.

Frank had been overjoyed at the simple wedding and an instant honeymoon, free tickets to five shows, and a discounted room at the Desert Inn, all wrapped into a nice bundle. She should have seen it then; how cheap he was about everything.

Nevertheless, she was married and was determined to make it work. And she had, even after he destroyed whatever little remained between them with his affair and lies.

A *smokey* raced down the interstate after something. She watched, letting the police car take those memories with it. What would she face once she returned home?

⁂

John didn't dream often, but he just had. Janis was smiling as he came home from their last Christmas together. He was handing her the small gold cross he'd bought for her. She opened it and joy rushed over her face. Then he was hanging it around her neck. "I'll never take it off, John. I love it."

"I love you," he'd promised.

He lay there remembering that after she died; he wore it until a few months back when it just disappeared off his neck one night. He had searched every square inch of the cab, every particle of dirt under, around, and in the cab. Tears clotted in his throat because he still hadn't found it.

Sirens wailed outside, reminding him he had to get to Bangor. He bolted from the bed and fell to the cab floor. In that same instant, he stood, combing his hands through his hair. Guilt rolled over him like a steamroller. And there stood Carrie between the seats, looking at him, worried.

"Just a dream." He stabbed his hand through his hair one more time, while wishing his hard-on would go away. It was in command position. He had to get some fresh air. "I've got to check the trailer."

He grabbed his coat and stumbled out of the cab door. A vicious north wind off the lakes hit the moment he swung outside, slipped on the last step, and almost fell. Something he hadn't done in a long time.

He absently scanned the trailer's undercarriage. Guilt blasted him harder than the wind. Dammit, he wanted Janis back. He wanted to hold her. He wanted to cling to all he had left of her. His memories. Their moments together. Their life. He didn't want to lose any of that. He needed to keep them and didn't want to cloud it with someone else.

Trailer locks were fine. Tires were good. Janis wasn't coming back. Never coming back. Knowing that made the loneliness even darker.

Now he knew that whatever had made him think to ask Carrie to come with him was his mistake. He'd done it because he'd felt sorry for her. He knew she needed to get away from the mess with her kids. She didn't deserve that any more than Janis getting cancer. Still, he couldn't let Carrie ruin what little he had left of Janis.

He pulled out his cell phone and dialed his oldest son's number. Johnny answered almost immediately. "Hey, Pops. What's up? Where are you?"

"Not much. In upper New York freezing my ass off." Just the sound of his son's voice soothed the loneliness that had crept inside his guts.

"You still comin' down in March for the biker run?"

"Plan to. Have the 'Fat Boy' ready when we get there. I'm looking forward to the warm sun."

"No problem. Why not bring that *seat-cover* you have with you?"

Damn, he forgot he told Billy about Carrie. "I doubt she'll want to. Likely, she'll be tired of me by then."

"Never know, Pops. She might take you up on it."

He couldn't shuck the idea of Carrie riding behind him, pressed up tight, arms around his waist. "She has enough to deal with out here."

"Yeah. Billy said you found her along the shoulder in Utah somewhere. Saved her from certain death, I hear. Mom always said you had a soft spot for those in trouble. She's smiling, I know it."

John kicked a block of snow ice from a tire flap, more out of spite than necessity. Janis always said he liked helping people, usually guys struggling with living on the road, driving. Sympathy. A bit of advice. Encouragement.

It was his own damn fault that Carrie rode in his cab now. He'd invited her. Otherwise, she'd be dealing with her mess on her own. And maybe that was the right thing to do.

He'd just take Carrie to Maine, feed her lobster, and take her home. Maybe by then, she'd have her feet on the ground and could deal with her kids.

When he climbed back inside the cab, Carrie was just sitting there staring out the windshield. Warmth swept through him, along with the scent of her perfume, sweet, light, and delicious like a warm spring day, another difference he enjoyed when he shouldn't.

"I shouldn't have come with you," she whispered.

"Carrie, why? I mean…. I've enjoyed you being here." A truth that should have been a lie.

"I should have stayed home and faced up to what I need to do."

"Are you ready for that, Carrie?" He slipped between the seats to make coffee.

"No. However, I don't think I'll find it out here."

"It's only a few hours to that lobster I told you about. After a few more stops, I'll have you home in no less than three days." The sound of that felt more like a sentence than a reprieve, like giving up a comfortable, warm coat.

CHAPTER 15

"THE CENTRAL ARTERY/TUNNEL PROJECT, known unofficially as the Big Dig, was a megaproject in Boston that rerouted the Central Artery through the heart of the city. The Big Dig, the most expensive highway project in the U.S., was plagued by escalating costs, scheduling overruns, leaks, design flaws, charges of poor execution and use of substandard materials, criminal arrests, and one death."

Carrie read aloud about the massive, maze-like tunnel through Boston that they were going through—the *Big Dig*. Tunnel walls gleamed golden from the constant lighting, while sounds of traffic roared off the concrete. The underground maze of arteries shot off like escape routes to somewhere beyond. Frank would have loved…She no longer cared what Frank would have liked.

John's truck shot out of the tunnel like a bullet into the open country of clusters of small towns that were picture perfect for any Christmas card. Silence filled the cab for the next few hours. She pointed to two eagles just sitting in the bare tree limbs. John didn't respond, but then he'd probably seen millions of eagles while driving.

Since he'd been murmuring Janis's name while he slept, she could only imagine what he felt with bringing her along on this trip. Just how many men would be this loyal to their wives even after they died? Frank hadn't, even while she lived.

Regret settled in Carrie's gut like thorns. She once felt it was her fault that he had the affair. She hadn't kept him happy. She hadn't been a good wife. She wasn't pretty enough. Smart enough.

Tears dripped down her cheeks as she shifted in the seat, turning her back, so John wouldn't see her cry. All those years were wasted while other women enjoyed good men, loyal men, and sweet men like John.

"Carrie, everything okay?"

She nodded to the window glass. "Got something in my eye." She faked another smile. "I'm fine."

Lies. She wanted to go home. Just disappear. However, she didn't have a home. She had a house, but no home. Did she even have a family at all now? Her cell phone vibrated an arriving text message. Emily.

"Hey, Mom, how's the trucking going?"

Carrie messaged back. "Fine. Will call." Another lie. She wasn't ready to deal with anyone now or ever.

John slowed to turn into the distribution yard in Bangor, stopping at the gate guard. She went back in the cab to sit on the mattress to remain unseen while John opened his window, letting in a draft of cold air.

"Looking good, Big John. Have a *Happy-Happy*."

"Oh, yeah, back at ya," John answered.

The truck lurched forward. Then he maneuvered the trailer into the assigned dock, red lights turned green. After shutting down, he leaned across to the glove compartment and retrieved the papers for the load. "Be right back." And he left.

Fortunately, John never glanced back to see if she was okay. Maybe she should just have him drop her off at the airport.

The memory of landing in the Sacramento airport sent chills down her spine. The idea of having anything associated with Frankie hurt as much as the idea of returning to her house.

She hadn't confronted Carrianne about any of this, but she'd read enough of the text messages to know her eldest daughter agreed with Frankie. Had she lost her mind?

Her youngest daughter seemed intrigued about everything to do with the truck. Only Emily.

What was she going to tell them? Would they believe her that she and John had done nothing to be ashamed of? But what now? No clue. Who would hire her at her age? But one thing was certain—she had to do something other than face the walls of that house.

The driver door opened and John climbed back inside, startling her. He entered his information in his logbook, wrote a text, to Phil likely, and stuffed the papers into the glove compartment. He shifted across his seat and stepped into the back. Sunlight outside made him appear like a shadow.

"All set to eat lobster? The office suggested a good restaurant that overlooks the river and still serves lobster. They're a bit small this time of year, but good. We can *bobtail* to the restaurant."

"Bobtail?"

He grinned. "Leave the trailer here and come back for it later. Streets are too narrow to take it."

"Leave your trailer?" She had heard how lone trailers were vandalized or stolen. John couldn't afford to lose his trailer and certainly not on her account.

"John, you don't have to risk your trailer to take me some-where to eat lobster."

"It's fine here."

✍

By the time, John dropped the trailer where Ben told him, Carrie had become a new woman. An attractive one at that.

"John, this is the best I could do. I'm sorry."

If this weren't Carrie's best, what could she really do if she tried? He clamped down on that, too, shoving the idea from his brain still struggling to cling to the memories of Janis.

When Carrie had pulled back the cab curtains, she had changed into a red blouse tucked into a new set of jeans sur-rounded with a fancy western belt. She sported a country vest that Dolly Parton would certainly have wanted. Her makeup made her eyes even greener and her mouth lusher.

Oh, God. He didn't need to think of her mouth. His fist crushed the absurdity in his palm. "You look…just fine." Too fine.

He coughed and started the truck. It wasn't a date. It wasn't. Dinner and lobster. It was a promise he'd made. Just a promise.

However, Carrie's sweet perfume tantalized him the entire trip to the small rustic restaurant by Casco Bay. He worked the truck through the narrow streets to the rear parking lot where the brisk wind cut like knife blades. He helped Carrie down to the street and, by the time they crossed the parking lot, it had begun snowing again.

They found the street entrance and scurried inside the busy little restaurant to be bathed in the fragrances of rich beer, heavy butter, and laughter. Christmas decorations still sparkled along banners wishing a Happy New Year.

He helped Carrie out of her coat under the notice of a few lone men at the bar. An inexplainable surge of possessiveness swept over him. What the hell? Carrie didn't belong to him or anybody.

Fortunately, the young waitress shifted his attention to the table overlooking the bobbing pier disappearing behind a blanket of falling snow. They sat, accepting the plastic-covered menus. "What can I get you to drink?" the girl asked.

"I'd like to try the local beer," Carrie said.

Beer? Carrie liked beer? Janis didn't—A stubborn surge burned through him. What the hell was wrong with being seen with an attractive woman who liked beer? He wasn't dead. "Make that two."

The waitress left, and he looked across the table. "You like beer?"

"Love it." Like rich emeralds, Carrie's eyes sparkled from the small candle burning in a plain glass. It even made her face glow in contrast to the blanket of darkness outside the window. "I don't usually drink because of the calories, but I do enjoy a glass of wine or beer occasionally," she added.

He shrugged. He'd quit drinking because the asshole who had taken Janis from him had been drunk and had beat the shit out of her. When she had come back into his life, it made her nervous if he drank. So, he had quit.

The rich, golden beers arrived. Carrie lifted hers toward him. "To lobster. And may you have a *Happy-Happy*, John."

"You too, Carrie. You deserve one."

They clinked the glasses together. She sipped hers and then set the glass down to shift her attention to the boats bobbing in the falling snow.

"Penny for your thoughts?" He shouldn't have asked that, but, like the invitation to Maine, it just popped out of his mouth.

"That's an oldie." Carrie laughed and leaned in. "I was thinking how lucky your wife was to have you. Here's to you, John and Janis." Her toast settled easily around his heart.

"Janis was a good woman. I'll give her that. But trucking is hard on any woman, every marriage. I have to say, I love the road. And I about went crazy staying home watching cancer kill her. Then, I tried settling into retirement. I couldn't do it. Sold the house, bought a truck, and kept my Harley."

Carrie put aside the menu. "I completely understand. I started hating the idea of getting up in the morning to nothing but walls. I ran away…on a road trip." She grinned. "Fortunately for me, you returned to the road, or I'd be an ice cube on the Salt Flats."

"Then, here's to the Salt Flats."

The waitress reappeared. Carrie ordered just about every fresh seafood option on the menu, options which Janis would never like. But Carrie did and with relish.

How long had it been since he'd laughed this much, ate this much, enjoyed a few simple beers? He switched to coffee and watched Carrie push the scoop of ice cream and cherry pie aside.

"I can't eat this. Honestly, I'm stuffed to the gills, and I'm not sure I can climb into the cab. You may need a crane."

Memories of her butt once again in his palms stung with desire.

⬥

She and John walked across the slippery parking lot where snow blanketed the truck, making it look like a cake with white icing. Carrie grabbed the handles, set her leather boot on the first step, and then glanced back over her shoulder. "Here goes."

John's face gleamed with a smile. "I'm ready."

She couldn't remember the last time she felt this dizzy happy. So, the idea of letting John catch her intentional slip almost overpowered her common sense.

Instead, she made the climb into the familiarity of the truck, settled in, and was climbing out of her coat by the time John's door opened, releasing another blast of cold air into the cab. He mounted his side and settled in his seat like a cowboy ready to herd cattle.

Just then, an explosion of fireworks burst like stars into the sky. It was midnight and the beginning of a New Year. Carrie looked out on the black bay at the multi-colored umbrellas flashing like camera flashes on the snow-covered *four-wheelers*. She smiled. "*Happy-Happy*, John. May this be your best year ever."

"And to you, Carrie. You too."

A moment passed when a kiss would have been appropriate, but John turned the ignition and the truck roared to life.

His cell phone rang. He let the truck idle as he checked the caller and sagged like wet noodles. "I have to get this."

"Sure." Carrie sagged back in her seat with disappointment over something that wasn't hers to begin with.

"You have to be kidding me, Carl. I understand. But Phil is a first-class prick. He gives his trucks the good loads and the rest of us shit. I know. I know."

Carrie went to the back for a bottle of water and handed one to John, only he waved it away. She put it in his cup holder.

"Then I'll have to find another broker. Any suggestions? Yeah. Let me know what you find." He ended the call with a brisk poke and tossed the phone onto the dashboard. "Shit."

She sat in her seat and broke open the bottle. "Can I ask what that was about?"

"Carl is retiring. He's not going to broker anymore. Right now, I'm stuck with that piece of shit named Phil." He slumped further in his seat. "I'm sorry, Carrie. I shouldn't be talking like this, but the asshole just gave away my next load. I'm to *dead-head* to Syracuse, empty. And in this weather." He hit the steering wheel with the heel of his hand.

"Can you find a load yourself?"

"I've tried finding loads, but I end up wanting to toss that laptop out the window. Plus, someone has to handle the paperwork. I hate doing that crap."

"You find loads on the computer?" Excitement thrilled through her.

John slowly turned to her. "Yes."

"Can you get the site up?"

"Sure. But I have to get back to the yard for the trailer before they close the gates on me."

§

John worked his way through the narrow streets back to the yard, holding his breath. Meanwhile, Carrie bit at her lower lip as her eyes scoured the screen.

"Can I call Carl?" she suddenly asked. "I think I found something."

He handed her his phone and slowed to keep from sliding into a parked car.

"Carl, this is Carrie Marshall. Sorry to bother you…Yes, happy New Year to you, too. You have a minute? I think I found something for John."

The fireworks paled to the mounting excitement swelling inside John with each mile closer to the distribution center, closed by now. He'd have to wait until morning to get his trailer. But if Carrie got a load, it would be worth the wait.

He overheard Carl explain the graph on the computer screen and a bunch of other things until Carrie said, "I see. Yes. Yes. Enjoy retirement and take care of yourself." She ended the call. "What are we doing?"

John stopped in the lot across from the distribution center. "Gates don't open until tomorrow."

She frowned. "Sorry. But is Saco very far from here?"

"No. Why?"

The frown melted into a grin. "Look. There's a delivery of ice cream in Saco to go to Syracuse. It just came up."

"Tell Carl."

"I just did and it's yours. We got it."

CHAPTER 16

JOHN DROVE THE entire twenty miles to the side parking lot of the long familiar distribution center in Saco, listening to Carrie's frustration.

"I think I get this. No. No, I don't."

Saco had no guard at the gate, so he found the first open dock, backed in and shut down. Only then did Carrie rise from her search. "We're here already?"

"We're here." He claimed two bottles of water from the mini fridge and squatted beside her seat.

"We're going to Syracuse with the ice cream, right?" she asked curiously. Something curious gleamed in her gaze.

He broke open both water bottles. "I believe we are."

"And after that, you need another load in Syracuse. Right?"

"Would be nice."

She pointed to the screen. "There's a load of beer out of Syracuse that needs to go to Trenton, New Jersey."

"Good."

"And here's a load of seafood in Jersey City that needs to go to Kansas City. Is Jersey City far from Trenton?"

"Next door. Get them."

A few clicks later, she announced, "Got it! I'll call Carl to make sure everything is right."

"Carrie, did you know you just paid for this trip?"

The sound of his chuckle sounded devilish, even to him. "And Phil is going to be royally pissed when he finds out."

"Well, in that case, I better get to Carl and make sure you don't lose them."

"Great. I'll take care of the office, so we can get on the road as soon as possible."

Nodding, Carrie brought up Carl's number, never looking up from her pursuit. It released him to take care of business. Had she stood up; he likely would have kissed her for doing all this.

She had no idea that, what she had just done, would never have happened if he'd even tried to find any load. Like all truckers, he needed people like Carl who knew how to get around on the Internet the way he knew interstates. What Carrie didn't realize was it seemed to come natural to her.

He plucked up the full trash bag and began tying it to toss it into the nearby bin. Just then Carrie stood, her face glowing with joy, and stretched her hands to the cab ceiling. "Carl's going to get back to me after he does the paperwork."

John's heart leaped in his throat the moment he realized that he stood close enough to kiss her. And wanted to.

Her gaze warmed, luring him even closer. Then the damn trash bag caught on his foot, nearly tripping him. She took her bottle of water and went to her seat.

What the hell had gotten into him? He nearly kissed another woman and, if Carrie hadn't looked away just then, he would have. He clutched the plastic bag and made for his door.

The only thing that stopped him short was his cell phone whistling. Phil. The asshole was calling. "Hey, Phil, what's up?"

"What the hell, John, those were supposed to be my loads."

"Wish I could say I'm sorry. But I'm glad I got them. You didn't have anything for me anyway."

"Well, don't bother to call me for another load. I won't find you any."

"No problem, Phil. I think I'm covered."

❧

Carrie wasn't sure she heard that conversation right, but John sounded like he wanted her to find him loads. In truth, she wanted to. It had been fun, exhilarating, challenging. Like when she worked—when she had a purpose in her life. It seemed forever since she had felt that way. But could she keep getting John loads?

Well, she had this time. But what about keeping John constantly moving? She really didn't know what he needed or understood what it took to do it. After all, Carl had said he wanted to retire from it all. And now Phil had refused to help John. In some ways, she had an obligation to help him now. If she could, she wanted to… But…

No matter, John seemed pleased with what she had just accomplished. She wasn't sure but, for a moment, maybe he had wanted to kiss her. She certainly wouldn't have refused it. In fact, every pore in her body had wanted him to. But Frankie's voice screamed in her brain, "You whore! That's all you are!"

No, Frankie, I'm not. I'm just a woman who would enjoy being kissed by a very wonderful man who appreciates me for once.

And it was nice to know she wasn't dead. It felt good to defy her son. And if John wanted to kiss her for finding him loads, she had no problem with it.

After all, Carl had mentioned something about her brokering for John, that she could do it. He'd help if she were interested. And she was. However, she knew nothing about brokering. She'd dig into what all that entailed but, for now, she needed to clean up the cab.

While John saw to the load of ice cream, shaking the trailer each time a forklift carried on another pallet, she cleaned the cab, straightened the bed, and had the coffeemaker brewing in less time than it took to get ready to go to work.

Outside, cars and a few trucks pulled up to the docks. One of the drivers recognized John. Her heart stopped at the pure sound of John's laughter. Then coffee overflowed in her Garfield mug, burning her hand. It brought her back into the moment. By the time John climbed inside, she had the cab cleaned and his mug filled as well.

"Here's your coffee." She set his Peterbilt mug in the holder while he started the truck. "Who was that?" she asked out of curiosity.

"Steamroller Spike. Don't get to see him often. He's headed back to *Beantown*. Great *hand* to know. Ready to get on down the road?"

"As ever. What's a *hand?*"

"Another driver."

CHAPTER 17

JOHN IGNORED A KID in the *four-wheeler* who pumped his hand to honk, because if he did, the blast would wake Carrie. He couldn't do that to her, not after staying up all night on her laptop.

He eased the truck into the *granny-lane*, enjoying the delicious weight of a full load tug against the cab and, hearing the reefer kickin'—a beautiful sound. He checked the mirrors and, while Carrie slept, he raced through the *Big-Dig* again and headed west to Syracuse, a route he knew as well as his own driveway.

John tapped his finger on the top of the steering wheel in time with the country music station. He was going to be able to pay the insurance on the truck without going into his reserve funds.

Showing Carrie how to break open the lobster, crack open mussels, and peel crawfish was fun. She had been enthralled by it all, dabbing each morsel in rich garlic butter. He heard her moaning at how delicious the fritters were.

The memory of that moan threatened a round of guilt. Hey, he wasn't a horny kid anymore. Those days were never to return. But the fact those days weren't over settled well.

Yes. Carrie had brought them back with a vengeance, especially after he had thought of kissing her. And for a moment there, maybe she would have let him kiss her.

Thoughts of showing Carrie the country, like the sun rising over the desert or dropping behind the mountains, and the smell of the oceans, only added to the trip.

He doubted that she had ever seen white cotton fields as pure as if it had snowed in summer. So why shouldn't he enjoy being with Carrie? Why shouldn't he like holding another woman?

But did she want him to…in the same way? His palms broke into a sweat. His heart sat on his stomach. Why would she? After all, he wasn't some hunk on *Men's Health* magazine. Not even close. He was just a plain, ordinary guy with nothing to offer but hours on the road and sights to see.

Carrie shut the door to the private shower area and let the hot water fall luxuriously over her body. A sigh of absolute pleasure escaped while she scrubbed her hair and shaved her legs. She would never take a shower for granted again. Ever.

She had traveled more in a week than she ever dreamed possible, Missouri to Maine. She had seen the flat farmlands of Ohio, the snow-covered mountains of New England all the way up to Maine, and the tunnels of the *Big-Dig* in *Beantown*. She giggled at starting to sound like a trucker. And now she was in Albany, New York, headed toward the coast to Syracuse, and then to *Jersey-City.* Then she would be re-crossing the Blue Ridge Mountains back to the cornfields of the Midwest. And she'd be home in almost two weeks.

What then? Her house? Her kids? John? The worst dread sunk to her stomach. She never wanted to face all that. Not now. Not ever. No. She did not want to go home.

❧

John almost dropped the basketful of supplies when Carrie came out of the women's shower area. Maybe it was the way her green jogging suit lit up her eyes, but she was a pretty sight to behold. He smiled.

"Hey." He walked toward her, feeling her smile clear down to his toes. She stopped to look at a Peterbilt model of a semi identical to his truck. "Think Roy might like it?" she asked when he joined her.

"Better get two or Sam will be furious. Here's a red one." He set both toy trucks in his basket. "Let me get them for your boys."

"You sure?" she asked.

"Absolutely. Interested in chowing down at Olive Garden? It's close."

"Are you serious about that? A real restaurant? Not fast food or nuked?"

He grinned. Normally, he never went to a restaurant. He would have nuked something and gone on. "We have the time for some real food. It's only a few hours to Syracuse if the traffic is good."

"And, if we order right, we can have leftovers tomorrow."

❧

Contentment settled over Carrie as she offered John the last bread stick. He shook his head. "I'm stuffed."

She settled back with a luxurious sigh. "John, this has been wonderful. You now have a full load of ice cream to deliver and we can enjoy a great meal with still time to relax." She hoped she was right.

"We'll be in Syracuse in the morning and off-loaded by noon. We'll pick up the load of beer and be on the road by supper. Wish I could take you through the *Big-Apple.*"

"That's New York City. Right?"

"Yep. Wish I could take you through there. Maybe next time."

"Next time?" Carrie's heart bounced like a loose Ping-Pong ball. She wanted a 'next time.' "Uh, yes. I'd…love it."

She studied John stirring his coffee. Did he honestly mean there would be a 'next time?' She hoped he did. She wanted to ask him about brokering for him. She sucked in a deep breath and dove in.

"John, I've really enjoyed helping you find these loads."

A pleased smile floated over his lips. "I'm really glad you did, too, Carrie. I can't thank you enough." His gaze said he meant that.

"I'd love to find more if you'd let me. I mean, since Carl is retiring, and you don't like Phil. Do you think I could do it? I mean, it's a big change, but I promise, I'll try to keep you moving. Seriously, if you think I can and want me to try and Carl—"

"Yes." The answer she wanted to hear came across the table.

John pushed aside the coffee cup. "The way you get around a computer, I have no doubt that you could, Carrie. I'd appreciate it. And honestly, I was hoping you'd want to."

Her heart danced. "I know there's got to be lot more to learn. Taxes and payments. Legal stuff. Paperwork. But being a secretary, I should be able to handle that."

"No doubt." He shrugged and sat back, hands still clinging to the coffee. "Carl said he would help."

"Would you mind if I talked to him, see what he thinks of me brokering for you?"

"I think that's a great idea."

❧

This time, in Syracuse, Carrie had followed him inside the distribution office to see what happened there. John had listened to Carrie's encouraging conversation with Carl. Then the idea of picking up seafood and heading back to *Brightlights* hit him.

He'd be delivering Carrie there, as well as the seafood. Then, he'd be driving empty…even with a load.

Carrie plugged in her charger into the dash as her fragrance of coconut swept around his head like a tornado. Something else he'd miss besides her being in that seat. Damn.

"How far are we from the warehouse?" she asked. "Need anything from the back?"

He jerked his brain back to driving. "Oh, half an hour at most. Or longer in this morning rush-hour traffic. Water."

Soon, a bottle rested on his shoulder. He claimed it. Oddly enough, every time Carrie placed one over his shoulder like that, it unnerved him. In a good way, though. A little thing, yeah, but nice.

"Are you serious about brokering for me?" he asked, wanting to hear that again. He knew she had stayed up for hours last night looking for more load possibilities and searching the Internet for information about brokering. He just had to hear it again.

"Only if you are sure you want to work with a beginner. After all, this isn't an easy job. I can really screw you up with crappy loads strung all over the place."

"You won't. Carl won't let you."

Her lips parted in a smile that warmed through him and settled in the wrong places. All he could think of was kissing her. Fortunately, he was driving.

CHAPTER 18

A S THE *RIG* inched forward, eating fuel like a holiday meal, John kept a wide distance between the cars in front of him. Dealing with Trenton downtown traffic was worse than a colonoscopy. If an accident happened, the blame always fell on the trucker. Every damn time.

A brand-new blue Mustang shot in front of him. He hit the brakes to avoid rear-ending the idiot. Fortunately, the trailer settled down on the cab like a ton of bricks and held straight. He could breathe again. "Damn idiot."

Carrie gasped. "Where the hell did he come from? I'm sorry. I shouldn't have cussed like that."

His heart settled back where it belonged. "Fool kids think they can drive out here like it is a NASCAR track. Goddamn fool. Sorry." Knowing the space ahead would fill quickly, like water down a pipe, he slowed to allow even more for space between him and the cars.

The Mustang veered back into the next lane and then the fast lane. After a while, John had no clue where the idiot went. However, right before his exit, a *smokey* had the Mustang pulled aside and was leaning down talking into the driver's window, granting the driver a *driving-award.*

"*Bears* caught him," Carrie chirped happily.

John smiled, remembering the look she gave him when he had first said that to her. "Speeding, along with carelessness and imprudence. That'll cost him on his insurance."

"Good."

He entered the congested, inner-city streets, where traffic was slower and little better. The light changed, making the turn wide to make the corner, thus stopping a few cars in doing so.

One driver flipped him off. Traffic got tighter and angrier with each block closer to the warehouse. He finally pulled to a stop at the gate and began the ritual of having the trailer checked, papers checked.

"Dock 12," the guard said.

As usual, the docks were lined like cogs on a wheel. He had less than three feet on either side to back into the space. He closed within inches of the concrete dock when the red warning light turned green. He set the brakes and shut off the engine.

"You amaze me. I couldn't have backed a car in here."

"You get used to it," he said, yet seeing pride in her eyes felt damn good. A smile trickled across his lips as he reached for the papers before exiting the cab.

Inside, they waited in line. Finally, the clerk read his papers, pounded each with a stamp, and asked where to send the check. It felt good to give Carl's address again, not Phil's this time.

"Why did you give Carl's address to that clerk?" Carrie asked as they walked back to the *rig*.

"You broker for Carl. Not Phil. It felt damn good to do that, too. And, since you're working as his agent for me, I'll be sure he sends you your check."

"I'll get paid? I mean, I'm not a broker." Her eyes lit up like a Christmas garland.

He jumped down to help Carrie off the dock. "Hell yes. You earned every penny."

Soon enough they were deadheading to *Jersey-City*. Fortunately, the distributor wasn't far, but to his delight, they were too late for the load of seafood.

Cloudy weather had also settled over everything like a thick, wet blanket by the time John pulled into the Penn Jersey truck stop. He glanced at Carrie, who was shutting down his computer. "Learn anything?" he asked.

She grinned. "That I'm in over my head."

He laughed. "You can swim."

"I appreciate your confidence. Do they have laundry here?"

"I think so."

&s;

Carrie stared at Emily's day-old text message as the washer shifted into a final spin. "Hey, Mom, can't wait to hear about the trip. Please call."

Emily picked up on the first ring. "Mom! Where are you?"

"In *Jersey-City*…I mean in New Jersey. We're picking up a load of seafood to bring back." How strange, Carrie thought, to be explaining what she had said. She smirked with pride.

"I can't wait to hear all the details. Where'd he take you? I can't wait to tell Frankie and Carrianne." Emily giggled. "They are going insane with all this. But I'm so glad you went. Seriously, Mom. And I want a T-shirt from somewhere."

Her enthusiasm poured through the phone, bolstering Carrie's desire to make this happen…for her and for John. But she wasn't ready to share all the details, especially about brokering. Too many questions, and she didn't have answers. "Em, you wouldn't believe how beautiful it is up here, even in the winter."

"I can't imagine." Emily's voice melted with envy. "You are going out with him, again, on a trip…not just a date?"

"I don't know." She hoped John didn't change his mind on that. Silence filtered through the phone. "Nothing's happened, Em. John's a perfect gentleman."

"Of course, Mom. But if it did, that's your business."

Yes. It was her business. Their business. Hers and John's business. Carrie barely heard Emily rattle on. "I know I can't wait to meet him. Will he be staying here when you get home?"

They hadn't talked about that, but by the time they got into Kansas City, his 36-hour break would happen. That might give him time to meet Emily, at least.

"I don't know. We'll see."

John strolled into the laundry area with a sack of Subway and two sodas.

"Em, gotta go. I'll be in touch, I promise." She ended the call just as John sat down beside her.

"Hope you are into deli sandwiches," he said. "They make a mean one here. Besides, I figured you'd be hungry."

She started folding the warm load of his clothes. "Starved, but I'll finish this first."

He dug into his sandwich. "Hope I didn't interrupt whoever you were talking to."

"No. That was Emily. She wants to meet you," Carrie said. She fed the dryer more coins again.

"She doesn't seem anything like her brother."

"She's not." Carrie sat and opened her sandwich to the same mountain of pastrami.

Once he finished eating, John helped finish the laundry while she ate. And then, with baskets in tow, they walked back to the truck. He handed her the baskets, closed the door, and went to check over the trailer.

She finished putting away their clothes by the time he climbed in. "You ready to head back?" he asked.

She turned from the bed, empty basket in hand. "No. I have no clue what is waiting for me back there."

His blue gaze sparkled like stolen particles from the midday sky. "And, if you still want to broker for me, I promise to keep you too busy to fret. Whatever you find, I'll see it delivered. How's that?"

His gaze changed from a sparkle to one more deliberate as he walked closer. The basket went to the bed behind her while she didn't turn away, nor did she want to. Both of his hands cradled her head and then his lips touched hers. The touch radiated down to her toes.

Em's words sounded in her brain. *"Of course, Mom. But if it did, that's your business."*

Without hesitation, her arms slid around his waist as he drew her tight against his chest. The kiss held a stronger promise better than any signed contract.

A knock on John's door jerked them apart. "Want company?" the girl yelled. "Be glad to do a three-some."

Somehow the intrusion corrupted the moment. Both melted apart. Carrie retrieved the basket as John settled in his seat, dropping his window. "No. Go elsewhere."

CHAPTER 19

JOHN NEVER LIKED the feel of an empty trailer. It followed like a ribbon in the wind. Scary. That's why he liked to keep loaded. His GPS directed him into a dockside neighborhood where he blocked two oncoming lanes of traffic to get into the only slot available, pissing off every *four-wheeler* who had to wait.

Carrie watched every passing car around the cab as if it were a threat. "They act like this is an insult. How else were you supposed get in here?"

"Yeah, I know." He backed to the dock, shut down, and led Carrie into the office. Somehow, he knew there was going to be trouble. But it was Jersey.

The short, portly man behind the counter had to be one of Phil's guys. John pushed the bill-of-lading for the seafood across the countertop. The guy scanned it. "This isn't Phil's load."

"No, it's Carl's," John said. Damn that felt good to say.

The man's beady gaze seared at him. "Carl didn't send me this."

"No, I did," Carrie stated, drawing the clerk's attention to her.

"And who the hell are you?"

"Carl's agent," John answered. "She filled out the papers for him. And here's the order for delivery."

"I can't give you a full load. I don't have it."

John leaned in closer. "Yes, you do." He poked the contract. "Now give me the full load of seafood that's agreed to here."

The prick's glare hardened until Carrie set her phone on the counter. After noticing the flickering recording light on her phone, the asshole suddenly changed his tune. "I'll check."

"You do that," John said, not knowing why.

While the creep left, Carrie showed him she had recorded the entire conversation on her phone. "Hope it helps."

So that's what changed his mind. "Damn, Carrie, you are good."

∽

On their way out of Jersey, excitement tingled through Carrie. Brokering wasn't that much different than being a secretary. It was mostly dealing with people. It was learning how to do the paperwork. *I believe I can do this. I really can.* And she could stay home and work, maybe make a little office for herself in Frank's…

The thrill of a new future faded like a rainbow. She never wanted to walk into Frank's bedroom or office ever again. In fact, she never wanted to walk into that house ever again. But it was inevitable. A frustrated sigh, as heavy as the load, escaped her lips.

"That was one big sigh if ever I heard one," John said with a quirky grin.

"I don't want to go back…to that house."

He glanced at her, her side mirror, and then looked back to the road ahead. "Got the road fever I see."

"I'll admit, I've loved being with you, John. This has meant a lot. It's beautiful. And fun. But now with brokering…" She let that hang. She wasn't certain about any of this.

"Carrie, I've certainly enjoyed your company, and I'm not in any hurry to deliver you back there myself. I like having my own cocktail waitress." John toasted her with his coffee mug and then drank.

Something more than gratitude wormed around her heart deeper than it should have. Even past the same depths his kiss had travelled. She shifted in her seat.

Yes, she was going to miss being with John more than the freedom of going to new places. She was going to miss waking up with an arm snug around her waist. She grinned. She was going to miss him.

She casually studied his profile as he drove. John was a good and faithful man, and she had been a good and faithful wife.

Still her fantasies entertained her sleepless nights, making her wonder if sex could possibly be fun again. Attraction to anyone had died a slow, cold death over the years since Frank's affair. Yet being with John had rekindled something that she really needed to avoid.

She could only hope they remained friends. Brokering for him could provide a link, but she had to get him acceptable loads. That came first. So better get to it.

Carrie drew out the laptop and opened it. Immediately, the broker pages came up She scoured the list from *Brightlights*. A load of office equipment and desks seemed to pop off the screen at her. She checked the timing. The load needed to be in Tulsa by January 21. It was January 15. "When are we getting back?"

"Coupla days."

"No, the date. When?"

He slowed for the clot of cars ahead. The engine grumbled at him. "Should be back by the seventeenth. Why?"

"You have that 36-hour break when we get to *Bright-lights*, right?"

"Yes. Why?"

"I found a load of desks to Tulsa due for pickup by the twentieth. Oh, you have a reefer. Sorry. Wasn't thinking." She focused back on the screen.

"I can turn the damn thing off. Desks are fine."

"Really. Great!" Damn, she had lots to learn.

John glanced over at her, his gaze twinkling with mirth. "Just so you know, there isn't anything I haven't hauled."

"Would you be able to get it to Tulsa by the 21st?"

He was watching the traffic again, slowing even more as the pile of cars drew closer. "In my sleep."

"I need to talk to Carl and get this set up."

The discussion with Carl went plain and simple. Then, she found John another load of fresh produce out of Tulsa to Wichita and set that up with Carl.

"Keep looking, Carrie. Call me if you are stuck. I'll email you the paperwork," Carl assured. "Is it possible that John will join the rest of the world and learn how to get his emails now?"

"I'll make sure he does."

They laughed, and she tapped 'end' and then plugged her phone into the charger. She sat back, pleased. Something she hadn't felt in so long. "You've got office equipment to Tulsa and grocery to Wichita."

"Sounds good. Ah shit, another *chicken-coop*, and it's open. Damn." John pulled off station and joined the line for the scales with the other trucks.

The idea of Frank's room still itched as each truck rolled onto the scales, moved forward, weighed, and took off like Weight-Watcher members exiting the weigh-in. She would need a place to set up maps, a printer/fax, file cabinets, and storage for necessary equipment. While Frank's office was perfect, it made her sick even thinking of being in that room.

She floated through the rest of her house like a ghost in search of some other place to haunt. The kitchen was too small. The dining room and living rooms were too public. Emily's room would be fine, but she still lived there.

A blast of cold wind shot through the cab, jolting Carrie out of her search for a space for an office. John handed the loading papers to the clerk at the weigh station's window. The man waved him forward. "Later, John. Keep the *sunny-side-up*," the clerk said.

"Will do. Have a good one." John revved the engine, and the truck picked up speed.

"Do they all know you?" she asked.

"I guess. Been here enough," he said as he rolled out.

The truck seemed to settle into its traces as if enjoying the feel of moving again. John put the toll box back on the window, allowing them to breeze through tollgates while cars backed up. Before long, they were on their way to I-270 and finally I-70.

CHAPTER 20

WHILE CARRIE CHATTED with someone on her cell phone, John tampered with the idea of the office equipment going to *Oil-City*, then the produce going to the *Air-Capital*, and coming back to *Bright-lights* with whatever Carrie found for him to bring. If he had good roads, he'd have no problem making those deliveries and being back to take Carrie out for more mouthwatering barbeque within a week.

A voice came over the *squawk-box*. "Hey, Big John, you're looking good after *Circle-city*."

"10-4. Gonna get ugly your way. Do a *brake-check* through *Steel-Town*.'

"10-4. You might do the same through the *Gateway*." John clicked off.

"What was that?" Carrie asked with a grin.

He chuckled. "It's good heading back to Kansas City after we get through Indianapolis. I told him that the weather is turning bad and to watch for *bears* through Pittsburgh. He suggested I watch out in St. Louis."

"Oh." She nodded to the falling snow outside the truck. "Hope this doesn't get any worse."

"Me too." That was a lie. He wasn't wanting to get back to *Bright-lights* anytime soon. Did Carrie?

The eighteen hours from Jersey to Missouri would likely end up being twenty. Still, he could make it before the roads closed.

Right now, more than anything, he wanted Carrie to become his broker. Being rid of Phil felt like getting rid of a bad cold. He had no doubt she could be fantastic once she learned the ropes and he'd help her in any way possible. He owed Carl big time for stepping in when he did because he could have been off on a cruise somewhere warm.

"Okay, $319,000. How long will it take to sell?" Carrie asked. "Sounds great. Sure. Thanks, Ben." She poked her cell phone to end the call and looked at him. "I'm selling my house."

"Seriously, Carrie?" John asked, stunned. "That's a big move on your part. You sure you want to do this?"

"Yes. I can't stay in that house. Not now."

He'd never seen her face more serious. "Yeah, but you must be sure about this, Carrie. If you think Frankie was upset with me, this might put him over the top."

She chuckled at that. She actually chuckled!

"I don't care what Frankie thinks anymore. The only place in that house for an office is Frank's bedroom. I can't work in there. And what's more, this is my life, and I want to do this for me—and for you. I want to be your broker. John. Ben says that, since the house is paid off, I should be able to easily buy a new house once it sells."

"Ben?"

"He a realtor I know from when I worked."

The familiarity struck a spark of jealousy in John's guts. He squelched it. Who the hell was he to care who she talked to? "You have any idea where you might want to move?" he asked.

"Something like a maintained community where I don't have to mow or shovel snow."

"That's why we moved to Florida." He nodded at the heavy snow piled on the shoulder.

She watched it pass and settled back in her seat. "Don't you get tired of the hot weather?"

He shook his head. "How could I? I never stayed home long enough to deal with the heat. Janis and the boys loved it."

Silence filled the cab. Reports said snow on I-70, threatening to close around Columbus. A Love's truck stop wasn't far from where they were. "Might be best to pull in while the crews cleared the roads," he said for himself as well as Carrie. And it delayed the trip for a few hours.

The exit appeared all too soon. When he pulled off I-70 into the parking lot, he obviously wasn't the only driver with that idea. He took one of the few spaces left available and, when he turned off the engine, stress melted into his seat. He sagged back. "They have great country fried steak here."

Carrie looked up from her laptop. "Mashed potatoes and gravy?"

"The works and lots of it."

After quickly shutting the laptop, Carrie climbed in the back and then reappeared with their coats. "Then let's go before they run out."

꙰

"Be right back after I check around the trailer," John said after helping Carrie into the cab and handing her the leftovers, the plastic bags of supplies, and a container of hot chocolate.

When he climbed back into the cab, the fragrance of cinnamon chocolate and just-baked chocolate chip cookies, hot from the microwave, greeted him.

Carrie sat on the bed, staring at her cell phone. A fantasy dashed through his brain of Carrie, naked on the mattress and reaching for him to join her. He choked that image down before it could gain any speed.

"Anything important?" he asked, claiming a cookie off the plate, and sat next to her.

She turned her phone screen to show him a picture of a house for sale. "Ben sent me his MLS listings. There are thousands."

"Wouldn't it be easier to see on your laptop?"

"Actually, it would."

He got her computer and moved the plate of cookies aside to make room on the bed while she poured him a cup of hot chocolate.

"I think a three-bedroom ranch. I don't want stairs anymore. Nice kitchen. Nothing fancy." Carrie bolstered their pillows against the back wall so they could stretch out.

"Sounds good." He nestled deeper into the pillow, desperately trying to keep his mind on the pictures of houses, not of Carrie lounging on the beds in the pictures of the bedrooms. Finally, the images of houses began to blur. Carrie brushed cookies crumbs off the sheet.

He handed her the laptop. "This reminds me of why I got the truck."

"I'll be honest with you." She set the computer on the floor. "I know I can learn how to broker for you but buying a new house…now that scares me."

He shifted to his side to face her. "If you set up the loads, I will see them delivered. That should garner you a healthy paycheck, hopefully enough to pay the water bill."

A smile moved softly over her mouth, giving him ideas of kissing her again. Giddiness of a teenager rippled through him.

"John, you've done so much. Now this." Her smile never wavered. Her hand rested on his forearm. "I'll never be able to thank you enough."

It was like resisting the most delicious treat laying there at his fingertips. "This works for both of us, Carrie." Yes, they had kissed, but that was New Year's. He rose from the pillows to sit on the mattress edge. "Water?"

"Sure."

She stared out the long narrow window beside the bed. Snow fell in a blanket beneath the golden glow of the parking lot lights. "I'll have to get rid of everything. The furniture. The kids' things. And a million memories."

"One thing at a time." He sat beside her. "Just sell the house. Tell the kids to come get what they want. Have an auction. Then move into the new place."

She huffed and took the bottle. "What do I do about the million memories?" She studied her water bottle. "There are good ones."

His hands itched to draw her close. "Then keep them." He lifted her chin so he could read her face. He wanted to add to the good ones. But the concern in her eyes stopped him. "And, just make more good ones."

"You certainly have added to the good ones. Thank …"

He didn't want to hear "thank you" again and stopped it with a kiss. The taste of cinnamon chocolate filled his senses and clouded his reasoning. Reasoning be damned.

He drew her into the pillows to feast, letting the kiss deepen. Until now, memories of Janis had kept him from relishing how delicious this could be. Well, Janis was gone, and he was still alive.

Carrie's hand rose to his face and sank into his hair. Her lips parted, inviting him inside. His mind blurred with the warm wetness of her mouth. A groan he hadn't heard since…

Water flooded between them like a cold slap of reality. She bolted from his arms and grabbed the bottle before it emptied into the mattress. He retrieved the roll of paper towels and began tearing sheets off as if enacting triage surgery.

Outside, the reefer unit kicked in. A truck started up some-where. By the time they were done, the spot was nearly dry. She picked up the crumpled towels and tossed them in the trash like evidence, and then sheepishly started toward her seat. "Charg-ing my phone," she muttered without a glance at him.

He grasped her arm. "Carrie."

She halted and looked up at him with a gaze worth mil-lions of dollars. "Thank you, Carrie…for coming with me."

"Thank you, John." She offered a brave smile and didn't step away.

Before he could pull her close, he dropped his hand from her arm and stepped back. "And for brokering for me."

"You've got a green-as-goats broker agent, John."

"We all start somewhere." He nodded to the awaiting Kindle in her seat. "Better plug that in before you start to thank me for something else and I have to kiss you again."

"Then, thank…."

Damn, it felt good to have a woman back in his arms. Damn good.

CHAPTER 21

S HE DIDN'T REALLY know what was happening in the book she stared at on her phone screen, since her mind kept venturing back to John's kisses.

God in Heaven, it had felt wonderful. Her body had risen from the dead like Lazarus from his tomb, and her insides were still melting. She had thought that all those warm tingles had died long ago. She stopped Frank from so much as touching her, nor had he tried. The old familiar guilt crept in, as if she were a cheater like he was.

Guilt for what? For kissing someone…a man like John? For enjoying his arms around her, feeling her body come alive with desire? No. She was done with feeling guilty. Whatever she and Frank had had died long before he had. So why feel guilty?

One glance toward the back of the cab offered her something to do while John refueled. Cleaning. By the time John climbed back into the cab, the small area was spotless.

"I think this needs dumping." She handed him the Porta-Potty container.

John took it as if nothing at all had happened between them and disappeared in the snowstorm again. By the time he returned with the emptied container, a dusting of snow covered his coveralls.

He climbed out of his coveralls and hung them on a peg by the side window. The delicious fragrance she had basked in the entire trip hit her like an avalanche. Old Spice. God, she loved that fragrance.

"You've been busy. Looks great back there." He turned to start the truck. "You ready?"

"Sure."

Obviously, he hadn't felt anything when they kissed, which left a residue of regret on her conscience. Since they were almost ten hours from home, she needed to get her mind on what she needed to do anyway. Images of a new office blossomed in her mind, along with all the things she would need to keep John on the big road.

"John?"

He settled in his seat across from her and then looked at her, his blue eyes twinkling. "What?"

She blocked the idea of just kissing him, right then, right now. "I have to look for a new house, get packed up, move, and buy a car. But I promise I will keep you moving."

⁂

Carrie managed to get John loads off to Texas, New Mexico, and southern California again. Honestly, him being out there alone on snowy roads really bothered her. When she told him so, John brushed off the threat of icy roads with the usual bravado that truckers professed.

As she set up more files on his computer and connected them to a new cloud that she synced with their phones, John slept his required time. She also set him up with a new online logbook and a GPS so she could find him anywhere.

She figured, when she set up her office at home, she would be able to download everything and be ready to find him so many loads that would definitely end with him returning to *Bright-lights*. She grinned.

Groaning, John moved over as she slid into the warmth of the bed. Absently, his arm glided over her, drawing her close. Sleep claimed her instantly.

When sunlight filled the cab, she woke to find John gone, checking the truck most likely. She got up, made the bed, and had coffee waiting when he returned.

"All clear. The plows have been out all night, so the roads are crystal."

"Crystal as in icy or crystal as in clean?" she asked, handing him his steaming mug.

He claimed the warm coffee with both hands. "Clean all the way through," he said. For a second, he studied her. Then he turned, snapped the seatbelt into its latch, and the truck shivered to life.

She fixed her own cup and eased into her seat to watch the windshield wipers unveil a white wonderland of snow sparkling in the morning sun. A brilliant blue filled the sky with not a cloud floating in it. The airbrakes spewed. The engine hummed, and then John pulled forward. Snow crunched beneath the wheels and blew back like crystal diamonds onto the windshield. With all the magical wonderland surrounding her, a sadness consumed her.

She was going home, and John was going on without her.

CHAPTER 22

A BRISK NORTH WIND assisted in blowing the dry snow from the roads, making I-70 clear and fast. Too fast in John's book. Saturday granted them no rush hour to deal with unfortunately. Now, signs for *Bright-lights* began popping up along with signs for I-435. Then the familiar skyline appeared.

John never wished for a traffic jam, construction, slowdown, or *rubberneckers* until now, to keep from arriving early. But he was. He had the next thirty-six hours with Carrie before he could pick up the desks for *Oil-City*.

He wanted to help Carrie search for a car if she wanted his help. And wondered if he would he be staying in a hotel, in Frank's bed, or with her? His insides warred with his conscience for wanting to sleep with her.

A residue of guilt still tracked into his conscience like mud or something. He knew he'd miss her every night while out on the road. He'd miss smelling her sweet perfume and having someone to hug like a teddy bear.

Carrie's cell phone tinkled its little bells. "Ben? Wonderful… Yes. Tomorrow. Plan on it… The trip is unbelievable…

Sure. Tomorrow at eight. Super. See you then. I can't wait to get all this behind me." Her words stung.

∽

"I'll keep you informed, Carrie. As soon I know something, I'll call," Ben said with a wave and then closed Carrie's door on the new, light grey Ford Fiesta. And she loved the fact John had helped her find it.

The drive home was simple so her mind drifted. She couldn't believe how fast things were moving since she got home last week. Except for the nights, she barely had time to miss being on the truck with John.

Decorating ideas, now, blossomed like weeds for the new three-bedroom house in a maintained community less than ten miles from John's service station. So, when in town, he said he would love to stay with her. So, it wasn't over.

He slept in Frank's room for the two nights they had and enjoyed coffee in the small coffee nook each morning. Then, she fixed him a Midwestern breakfast befitting Paul Bunyan, and, at night, she cooked enough leftovers for him for weeks on the road. Then, time ran out and he had to leave.

Letting him off at the trucking company had nearly torn her in half. She just stood there, watching him climb inside the cab. The engine growled to life. It took a while for it to move. But finally, the truck drove out of the service center parking lot. She watched until John was gone from sight and tears blinded her.

Then, walking into Frank's house without him felt like walking into a dirt pile. Thanks to Emily, she got through it. A young couple had made an offer, and she had accepted it almost too eagerly. She wanted out of there and couldn't have bargained for a better price if she had to.

John had called that first night to report that the delivery went perfectly for the load of desks. A sense of pride swelled inside her along with a sense of urgency.

John had made his delivery to Tulsa, picked up the produce for Wichita, and was well on his way to Dallas with a load of aircraft parts—loads she had arranged for him.

But she had to set up more loads, pack, deal with banks, insurance companies. She heard John's voice. "One mile at a time, Carrie."

She lived to hear his ring, a honking truck, and couldn't answer fast enough. Every eight hours, every morning, each night, she caught herself checking her phone. Then, the moment he hung up, a wave of depression floated over her like a stink.

Except for Emily, she hadn't told anyone anything about the move or brokering for John. Frankie was too busy with work and family counseling to call. Diane had left a text message that, because of the boys, she had decided not to file for divorce…at least not yet. And Carrianne had her hands full with a sick family and the girls' school. Fortunately, Emily had moved back home to help with the move. She would have gone crazy by now without her.

But, with the auctioneer coming to inventory the house, time had run out. Now she had to tell Frankie and Carrianne everything because she needed to know what they wanted of their dad's. Em had already claimed what she wanted, which wasn't much.

After signing papers on the offer of the house, Carrie pulled into her driveway and stared at the back door. No part of her lived here anymore. For her, John's truck had more of her heart than this place. She speed-dialed John's number and he answered.

"Hey, Babe, what's up? I called earlier."

"Yeah. Sorry, I missed it." She lived to hear his voice. "I found a beautiful, three-bedroom place today."

"Any word on the offer?"

She unsnapped her seatbelt. "I signed an agreement just now for full price."

"Wow. That's good news."

She twisted a bit in the seat and imagined herself in John's truck. "Where are you?"

"Headed to *The-Alamo* or I mean San Antonio."

She pictured the long stretches of highway she'd only heard about but had never seen.

"Did you know you're a natural at this brokering? Everything has gone through like warm butter on hot toast, sweetheart."

Babe. Sweetheart! Her heart thundered in her chest.

"G-Great. I'll…I'll work to keep it that way. How's the weather?"

"Lookin' like snow down here, but nothing to worry about, until I get to *The-Flag*."

Flagstaff, Arizona. She grinned that she knew it and he didn't have to tell her. "I will anyway."

He laughed. "You just take care of *Bright-lights* and yourself. I'm getting hungry for some of that barbeque."

She smiled into the phone. "I'm working to get you back here for some. Now, keep *the sunny side up and the greasy side down*, ya hear?"

John truly did laugh. "You're sounding better every day, doll. You do the same."

"Miss you with every mile."

"Same here."

The phone went silent, and so did her heart.

Sitting back in the driver's seat, Carrie stared through the moon roof at the bare tree limbs and listened to the car engine tick in the chilly air. Finally, she forced her feet into the cold, walked to the backdoor, and unlocked it. Shadows enfolded her until she flicked on the kitchen lights. She had to make those calls. She couldn't put it off any longer.

"Just do it. Get it over with." Again, John's voice. It bolstered her enough to punch in Carrianne's number.

Carrianne answered on the first ring. "Mom, I want you to know the girls were finally able to go back to school. At last. What's up?"

"That's great news. I'm glad they are better." Carrie sat down at the kitchen table. "I want you to know I've sold the house, and I'm moving up north."

Silence, thicker than concrete, filled the phone. "You what?" Carrianne asked. "Mom, have you lost your mind? Girls hush. Go in the other room." A chair squeaked when Carrianne sat down. "Oh god, Mom. What's Frankie going to think about this?"

"I haven't told him, but I don't care. This is what I want. At least, Emily is thrilled with the move."

"Of course, Em would be. But, Mom, how are you going to pay for this?"

"I'm a broker for"—she wanted to say John but didn't. In truth she worked for Carl— "a trucking company. I'll be able to work from home."

"It's that trucker, isn't it?" The spite reeked through the phone.

"Yes and no. But I will be helping John with his loads."

"Mom, Papa will likely turn over in his grave, if you do this."

I don't care if he does. She almost said that aloud. "I'm doing this, Carrianne. Now, if you want anything of your dad's or in the house, I must know. The auctioneer is coming tomorrow."

"Mom—"

"Carrianne, I have to go. A call coming in."

She poked the end button and relished the sound of the reassuring voice of the auctioneer. She had barely let him go when Frankie called. Carrianne must have burned the airwaves calling him.

"What in the hell has come over you, Mom? Have you lost your mind?"

"No, Frankie, I haven't." She slouched in the kitchen chair to endure what she had dreaded for days on end.

"Carrianne said it's that fool trucker. He put this in your head, didn't he? This can't be your idea." Something crashed as if Frankie had thrown something. "Dad set you up like a queen, and now you just trash everything for some piece of-shit trucker."

"No, Frankie, I —"

"Bullshit, Mom. I know how this game is played. I see it all the time."

Frankie was just warming up. Before he got a full head of steam, she blurted, "Let me know what you want of your dad's. I have to know this—"

"Everything of Dad's. I don't want that pervert touching anything of his. I'll find a way to get it back here before you trash Dad's things, too."

"I know a trucker who could deliver it." The phone went dead.

Chapter 23

CARRIE LOOKED UP to see Emily walk through the backdoor, stuffing her car keys in her purse and grinning like a happy cat. "I overheard what you just said to Frankie." She giggled. "Good one, Mom."

Carrie almost wanted to cry out in relief to hear that. "You think I'm doing the right thing?"

"Absolutely, Mom. Anyone with a brain cell can see you're miserable here." Emily came around the table and hugged her.

While he had stayed, John and Em had met briefly during dinner the night before he left. They became instant friends, making everything easier for Carrie to deal with.

In fact, they had talked while Carrie cleaned the kitchen, opened another bottle of wine, and filled their glasses. Em was on a roll about her graduation that May.

"How is this broker thing going with John?" Since Emily's major was business, she had become very curious about the whole process of brokering, wanting to know where and what he was delivering.

"He said everything went really well. I only screwed up one thing on one of the docking papers. Taxes. Nothing serious. Carl fixed it."

"That's awesome, Mom. Like he says, you're a natural. I'm hungry. Are there any leftovers in the fridge that didn't leave on John's truck?"

"Uh, no. I sent everything with him."

"Figures."

❧

The next morning Ben's real estate office called. "I'll get to work on the three-bedroom…if you still want it." he said. "I don't see why this can't close sometime mid-March."

"Perfect. And thank you, Ben."

What am I really doing? Carrie's attention drifted along the kitchen counters, the stove, and the pictures of the grandkids on the wall to the dining room. Her whole life had been here, making a home for everyone.

She walked absently through the dining room where memories of past dinners echoed from the round table cluttered with the auction papers, copies of the sales and loan contracts, and bank statements.

She stopped in her bedroom doorway. Her blue bedspread with her mother's quilt laying across the foot of her bed. The white walls. The blue curtains.

She turned around and stared at Frank's doorway. Memories leaked out from under the closed door like bloodstains. After learning of his affair, she had simply gone to work, came home, ate dinner, and left something warming in the oven for Frank.

While he ate, she read or crocheted in her bedroom. He watched sports on the television in the living room and then went to bed without a word spoken. Both she and Frank had performed perfectly to keep the kids unaware.

The sad thing was everything had been a lie. They all had been acting content and happy. Her short time of being with John had been so much more than she ever remembered with Frank. She couldn't remember ever feeling so alive.

Like a siren call, her cell phone honked from the kitchen. *John*. Joy exploded through her. She needed to hear his voice.

"Hey. You're home. What's up?" Once again, he saved her from drowning in doubt.

"I can close in about a month and the auctioneer is coming tomorrow. I told the kids, and they are livid. Except for Em. She says hi. And I'm wondering if I've lost my mind."

His chuckle tickled her insides. "Congrats, Carrie. And yes. You will make it. You know I'll do whatever I can to help. But I don't think you'll need me too much."

"Not true, John." She needed him with every breath. "Where are you?"

"As my broker, you should know."

"Let me think." She checked her phone for his GPS location. "You are in *Cactus-Patch* with the beef, delivery."

He laughed. "Good guess, sweetheart. Right on and on time, too. Offloading now. I'm sitting in the cab, missing my *seat-cover*, and thought I'd call."

Carrie smiled. He still didn't know that she knew every move he made in that truck. But more than that, he missed her.

"Your *seat-cover* misses being there, too. I feel like I'm in the bottom of a dirty laundry basket with everything I have to get done."

That laugh again. "Don't tell me you got the asphalt addiction?"

A teenage giggle leaked out. "Quite possibly."

A pause lingered through the phone. "I have an idea. When do you close?"

He was going somewhere with this question, and she hoped it was where she wanted it to go. "Last part of March maybe."

"When do you plan to move into the new one?"

"First of April, at the earliest."

"Do you think you still can arrange loads and do everything on the road?"

Her heart skipped up to her throat. "I did the last time, didn't I?"

"Want to go again and see the world?"

"Yes! Yes! I'll talk it over with Em. If she is good with me leaving her with everything, sure!"

CHAPTER 24

J OHN STARTED OUT of the truck when Carrie pulled into the parking lot of the service center. Obviously, he'd washed everything, so the chrome gleamed against the long stretch of polished black. It looked like a gift from heaven.

Ideas of racing to meet him played in her mind. Instead, she turned to her daughter in the passenger seat. "You're sure you won't need me?" Carrie asked.

A scowl blazed in her daughter's eyes. "Go. I'll get everything moved and have the office up and running like a Swiss watch by the time you get back. I promise."

John walked toward the car, his blue eyes twinkling with humor. Damn he looked good wearing fresh slacks and a buttoned shirt. Even the Peterbilt ball cap seemed to finish the picture of a "prince-of-the-road"—a *trucker*.

"You live on the road in that? Seriously?" Emily asked with a wave up toward the truck.

John nodded. "Yep and you come can check it out if you want."

"Can all of us get in there at the same time?"

John opened Carrie's door. "Let the tour begin."

John waited for Carrie to join him by her door. Unlike her mother's first attempt to climb into the cab, Emily climbed into the cab like a gazelle. The "oohs" and "ahs" confirmed Carrie's daughter had found the rear area of the cab. The mini-fridge door clicked closed.

"You sure we should leave Em in there by herself?" Carrie asked.

John pulled the ignition keys from his pocket. "Not much damage she can to without these."

"You don't know Emily. What's more, she may get too comfortable." Carrie stopped. "Oh, I left my luggage in the car."

"I'll get it. Go save the cab."

Sitting in her seat felt glorious as the familiar scent of Old Spice that permeated the interior assured her she was home.

"Here's your luggage, Carrie." John presented her two suitcases to his driver's seat and climbed up. Moving them, he settled in his seat. "Well what do you think?"

"This is amazing," Emily said from the bed. "No wonder you guys were fine when you were stuck in the snow. You have everything in here. The coffeemaker, the fridge, the microwave. Shit, I've stayed in larger campers with a lot less."

Carrie turned in her seat. "When was that Emily Marshall?"

"Not tellin'." Em chuckled and then stood to go. Her gaze fell on John. "Well, I'm outta here to let you guys get going. Take care of my mom. Okay?"

"Will do, Emily."

"Call me Em…everyone else does." Her daughter's gaze shifted to Carrie. "You have your laptop and the Internet Hot Spot to keep in touch, right?"

"Yep." Carrie went into the back so her daughter could climb down.

"Well, I'm gone."

They both watched Em leave, then John's voice broke the moment. "Where do you want these?"

"Oh, I'll stash everything away." She got up to begin, but John joined her in the back by the foot of the bed. He touched her arm.

"Carrie, I'm glad you decided to come out with me again. Maybe we'll have time to stop…to check a few places out this time."

She looked into the brightest blue gaze on record. It warmed her down to her toes. "I'll see what I can do on that, John." She rested her hand on his arm. "It feels glorious to be back here."

Their gazes connected with familiar comfort. Was he going to kiss her? She wouldn't refuse if he did.

A breath and a smile later, he asked, "Are you ready to head out?"

"You bet." She cleared her throat of the kiss waiting there. "Any trouble getting the load of computers?"

"Nope. Everything was perfect, thanks to my broker."

Grinning, John took his place before the huge steering wheel and started the engine, a sound she didn't realize she had missed so much. She also missed watching him log-in, check mirrors, and settle in to release the truck forward. The weight of the trailer pulled on the cab, and then everything returned with the comfort of a favorite chair. But it was all there now.

She reminded herself that this was a business trip. She was going to meet people she'd be dealing with, find out more about delivering, brokering. And take the online classes Carl had recommended. If all went well, she would be a licensed broker by the time she got home to that new office Em promised to have ready.

Carrie sank into her air-cushioned seat and snapped on her seatbelt. "Carl gave me a link to an online brokering class so I can get licensed, once I pass the final test of course," she said and fired up her laptop. "He said I should get to it as a soon as possible." Her home screen pictured John's truck. "That should keep me busy and out of your hair."

He stopped at the light at the entrance ramp to the interstate. "And why would I want you out of my hair?" he asked with a grin.

CHAPTER 25

J OHN RESTED HIS arm on the windowsill of his door to listen to Carrie read about the Flint Hills of Kansas.

"Beginning in the mid-19th century, homesteaders replaced the American Indians in the Flint Hills of Kansas. Due to shallow outcroppings of limestone, cattle ranching became the main agricultural activity in the region. However, fire and grazing manages to keep the tallgrass prairie renewed as well as the growth of trees and shrubs…"

When she finished, he smirked at her. "I never believed I would have to admit it, but I've missed you reading about these places. But I have, Carrie."

"Glad to hear that. Kind of makes each place a bit more personal." She changed from the Wikipedia site to the broker-ing site that Carl had told her about. "You ever seen a grass fire?" she asked.

"Once, I'm afraid. Had to pull over because a huge, black cloud of smoke poured in like fog in *Frisco,* I mean—"

"San Francisco."

"Bingo. You got it." John laughed. God, it was good having her back. Once he left Carrie in *Bright-lights,* the miles had grown far longer than he ever thought possible. Every time he stopped, he wanted to call her just to hear her voice.

He really enjoyed Emily. So, at least one of her kids had some sense. And that had changed her mother. Carrie had a new gleam about her he hadn't seen. So different from the woman he found freezing in her car. If he had any part in it, that was great. But he really liked his new *seat-cover*.

He glanced over to see her smiling at the passing plains and rolling hills. "Can you imagine what the pioneers saw when they crossed here?" she asked.

"Not really. But I'm sure there are a few places that are unchanged still." He checked his mirrors and relished Carrie's profile again.

Nearing Manhattan, Kansas, the traffic picked up. Rush hour at Kansas State University left the road a racetrack. *Disco-lights* came like a parade, flickering in his side mirror constantly. Then, the *bear* would fly past him on the shoulder.

"Something happened," Carrie said. "The *bears* are arriving like vultures."

"Yep. *Fender-bender* somewhere, I bet."

Traffic congealed like a blood clot. He slowed, keeping the distance between him and the car in front wide enough for three cars to fit in. Then everything began to shift to the left lane, bringing all movement to a near halt.

The *squawk-box* lit up. "It's a tangle all right. Damn *bear-bait* in that *four-wheeler's gone-greasy* because of a *crotch-rocket*."

"Yeah, parade of 'em is screamin' your way."

"Watch out for the *squirt-trucks* and the *bone-boxes* comin' up on your rear."

"And the *dragon-wagons*. There's a mess of 'em."

The chatter was hotter than most neighborhoods. Carrie looked to him to translate.

"Remember that stupid ass kid driving the Mustang earlier?" She nodded. "Seems he's rolled his car. Bad enough for a bunch of *bears*, fire trucks, ambulances, and tow trucks. It's gotta be a bad one for all this attention."

A car slowed to allow him enough space to change into the fast lane. Then everything became a *parking-lot* real fast. Sirens screamed everywhere.

Time crawled faster than the traffic. Eventually, they came alongside the accident where one car, the Mustang, lay in the median, burning in a ditch. The remains of a *crotch-rocket* were being moved off the only lane open. Blood was everywhere.

They passed the paramedics putting a body in the ambulance. "What do you think happened?" Carrie asked.

"Don't know. But when a *crotch-rocket* is invited to this party, they lose every damn time."

The traffic opened like children released for summer vacation. In no time, the exit for the distribution center came into view. The guard checked him and sent him to the docks. He backed the trailer into the dock and reached for the bill of lading in the glove compartment.

Instead Carrie handed it to him. He had to smile. "Good to have you back, Carrie."

"Good to be back."

CHAPTER 26

WHILE JOHN WASHED his trailer for the load of beef to take to Loveland, Emily called with details of the upcoming auction and about dealing with Carrianne who was coming over to get what she wanted to keep. Which, according to Em, was everything she could put in her car.

She had also dealt with Frankie about the desk and "a few other things" she refused to tell her about. Carrie could tell by her daughter's voice that, that wasn't a pleasant conversation.

"Don't worry, Mom. It's all good. I can handle Frankie."

Carrie dropped the cell phone in her lap and envisioned people milling around the various tables and claiming every part of her previous life, piece by piece. She imagined Frankie screaming at the top of his lungs to stop, Carrianne standing behind him nodding, and Emily ordering the auctioneer to continue with the sale of everything in her life.

Everything hit like the accident they had just passed: her dead car, her empty house, her family. All in exchange for John, her new house, new car, new profession.

An explosion of tears burst from her eyes. Sobs tore from her heart, all of which she couldn't stop any more than she could stop the truck.

John froze in the cab doorway and then shot into his seat. "What the hell? Carrie, what's wrong?"

"Nothing." She waved him away. "Everything. Go ahead. Get the load. I'm okay. It's okay. I'm fine."

"No, you're not." He dug for his handkerchief from his back pocket. "What is it? You didn't get a call from Frankie?"

"No." She laughed through her tears. "I'm fine. Really. Everything just hit me."

John sank back in his seat. "Now? It's all hit you…just now?"

The feeling of stupidity settled over her like a blanket. "I guess so. I don't know. Emily has everything under control. But it's just that everything is just happening so fast."

"Thank heavens for Emily." John glanced at her again and started the truck. "You sure you are all right?"

"Yes, get that load of beef. Time is money. And you are wasting time on me."

They laughed, which had a nice sound about it, but it dissipated like dew when she got back to the lesson at hand.

The loads had them going all the way to California, up the coast, and back across the upper states in less than ten days. Maybe two weeks with his mandatory breaks. So, if she figured right, she barely had time to get licensed and deal with all that.

☙

"Loveland was founded in 1877 along the newly constructed line of the Colorado Central Railroad, near the crossing of the Big Thompson River. The city was named in honor of William A. H. Loveland, the president of the Colorado Central Railroad. The primary crops in the area were sugar beets and sour cherries. During the late 1920s, the Spring Glade orchard was the largest cherry orchard west of the Mississippi River. At that time, the cherry orchards produced more than $1 million worth of cherries per year. A series of droughts, attacks of blight, and finally a killer freeze destroyed the industry."

"Cherries, huh?" John smirked and got off I-70 to cut over to Loveland. The foothills were covered with snow, but the reports said it was all clear. "I've hauled loads of cherries out of Michigan, but never from Colorado."

"Me either," Carrie said without looking at him.

John smirked at her response. She'd never had a load of cherries. But he knew what she meant. The cab got too quiet too fast and he asked, "First, we drop the beef in Loveland, pick up lawn seed and feed and head for *Shaky- Town*, right?"

Without a word in return, Carrie checked the order sheets from the glove compartment and nodded. "That's what I have here." And then back to work on her broker classes as intently as he was driving.

⁂

Carrie forced her attention back on the lesson about expenses but couldn't focus. As usual, John did his nightly check of the trailer, logged in, and then went to bed.

That morning, she woke with his arm across her, an arm she had missed every night. They drank coffee like old friends, nuked bacon and egg breakfast sandwiches, and were on the road before the crack of dawn. It was more like being home than she had ever felt.

How nice it would be to just ride along and enjoy the scenery, talk about nothing, and joke like friends. But she couldn't. Carl wouldn't want to keep helping her forever.

She glanced at John, lost in his driving. The setting sun came directly through the windshield like a fire pit. So, he wore his sunglasses. She'd never seen those on him before. He looked like a rock star.

She opened her phone's calculator app to deal with the assignment on budgeting, when Em e-mailed her that she had settled the expenses of the auction. According to her e-mail, everything had gone well. Another e-mail came from Ben that he'd attached the contracts she needed to sign. On her cell phone of all places. She'd never signed contracts on the phone before, never thought it possible until now. Then she was back to the calculator app to work the figures.

CHAPTER 27

DAMN LAPTOP. CARRIE was either on that or the damn cell phone. Irritation itched in John's guts like a new rash. She had been up half the night working on it, and now she was back on the damn thing.

And she stopped going in the office with him for the delivery or in either of the distribution centers. Hell, he had more chatter on the *squawk-box* than from her. He might as well be driving alone.

He knew he needed to remember that Carrie was doing this for him. After all, he'd introduced her to this game. Like a drug dog, she could sniff out a load better than any broker he'd ever worked with. If this went well, he'd never have to pander to that shithead Phil again.

With his habitual glance at the side mirror, his gaze lingered on the bold title on the screen. 'Loading Forms'. Obviously, she wanted this, or she wouldn't be working so hard to get it done. Plus, she still had a lot on her plate back home.

Guilt coated him like slime. Just shut up and drive.

Night always served *Mile-High* well. No heavy traffic. So, getting back toward I-80 was easy. He pulled into the rest stop for the night and went to bed. Carrie joined him well into the night. Other than mumbling her son's name in her sleep, she slept like a log.

Morning unveiled the beauty of the snow-covered Rocky Mountains where the skies were a radiant blue and the sun a golden yellow. The truck swept down the interstate. Up, down, sweep to the left. Sweep to the right. Signs for St. George appeared, a perfect stop for the night. Nine hours through a beautiful forest.

Little was said beyond the light chitchat about her latest assignment. A question here. Another question there. He could answer most of them. Then, the silence returned with its cold vengeance.

He had welcomed the eight-hour break in a small rest stop. But Carrie kept on with her lesson. All the while, he walked around the trailer, checking things. Then he caught some shut eye, and she was still on it when he started up again.

&

Enduring a brutal north wind pummeling him like a fist, John hunched over the nozzle gurgling fuel into the tanks. Carrie hurried from the stop-and-rob with plastic bags full of supplies they needed. The wind attempted to whip her coat off.

She disappeared around to her side of the cab and, minutes later, he heard her putting things to rights. Yes, she was settling in like a pro. He smiled.

The last few hours had been the best on the road since they left Loveland. She had finally closed that damn laptop and talked about something more than banks and brokering. He had to admit, the beauty of the sunset was something that would stop anyone in their tracks. Fortunately, they were heading right into it, and it had drawn her complete attention.

The fuel nozzle clicked off. After he checked the trailer, he climbed into a cloud of deliciously scented cinnamon and apple. Carrie handed him a full coffee mug and a fresh apple fritter. "I couldn't resist. Gotta sin once in a while. Right?"

This wasn't the kind of sin he'd been thinking about, but it would do. He settled in his seat, filled out the logbook on his laptop, and then bit into the fritter. "Sounds good to me."

He wished he had time to sin, but he needed to get moving anyway. Those thick gray clouds were ready to dump snow everywhere. "Best get moving before it starts snowing."

He finished the sinful fritter, started the engine, and then pulled out, checking all around him.

Carrie set hers on the dash and opened her laptop. The familiar website blazed across the screen, and, once again, she was gone to the world. The fragrance of her sinful fritter simply lost its fragrance into the growing silence.

John studied Carrie's reflection glowing in the windshield. Her cute nose. Sweet lips now flavored with cinnamon chocolate. He remembered one other time like that…after kissing her. He swallowed those memories with his next sip of cold coffee.

The falling snow demanded his attention. The headlights came on early since darkness quickly settled in around them. Fortunately, he was on familiar roads. March snow started falling, but he didn't think it would amount to much.

⁓

As they passed signs for Utah, the world dimmed like theater lights. Memories assaulted Carrie of falling snow, freezing to death, and, flying out to Sacramento to be humiliated beyond repair.

She had to admit, now, that she had been crazy to go on that road trip. But, as insane and unprepared as she had been, she had no regrets. She was in a much better place in her life than ever before. However, she had to pass the final test first. So back to the lesson on weights.

"How's the counseling going for Frankie?" John asked.

Highway lights flashed like bulbs over his face. Seeing John over there driving and feeling the strength of the truck around her, Carrie felt safer there than she ever had sitting at home watching it snow.

"I don't know if Frankie will ever see the light," she answered. "I'm just grateful that Diane keeps sending me pictures of the boys."

"Watching your kids go through something like this can't be easy."

Where was it she had stopped on that chapter? "It's horrible."

"How's the house thing coming along?"

She gave up and closed the laptop. Maybe he needed to talk. "Fine, I guess. Emily won't tell me a thing about what she's doing. But I know she's up to something."

"Just so you know, my boys know you came along with me on this trip and about brokering for my loads. They can't wait to meet you."

"Seriously? They want to meet me?"

"Absolutely."

John sounded happy about her meeting his kids. Nothing like how she felt with him meeting Frankie or Carrianne. That held nothing but dread. Her insides clotted at that thought. "I feel like I'll be meeting your parents," she said, grinning.

"Guess it could be something like that." He glanced at her. "Ever been on a Harley?"

"A Harley? Motorcycle? No!" Her heart leaped to her throat. "But I've always wanted to."

"Well, here's your chance." John's smile was brighter than the oncoming headlights. "There is a bike ride for a trucker friend of mine, who died in a rollover. Every year, a group of us get together to raise money for his kids. The boys and I are setting it up. Want to ride with me?"

She turned toward him. "Seriously, you want me to go… with you?"

He pulled out to pass a car and then pulled in. "Yep."

A Harley. With John. Excitement bubbled like champagne. "When is it and where?"

His mouth tilted in a grin that made her cling to his next words. "All the way to the ends of the earth."

"Where?"

He glanced at her. "Key West."

"Oh, God. Key West. I've always wanted to go there. Beaches. Sun. Ocean."

She had mentioned a trip there to Frank. *Too damn hot for me.* But John was asking her to go with him…on his Harley. Tears blinded her. "If you are serious, John…Yes! I'd love to go. But when?"

She had to consider everything. The house. Setting up a brokerage. Setting up loads. The facts argued with the flashes of sunlit beaches, palm trees, and sand.

"First week in March."

She could barely breathe. "Before we go back home?"

"That's up to you. You're finding the loads. I go where you send me."

✎

When Carrie returned to the broker lesson, she couldn't focus on it. She breathed deeply to regain control, even though she didn't want to. She wanted to hug John, dance, or something other than just sit there, working on weights and loads.

She opened her Excel spreadsheet on the loads so far. They took her to northern Michigan, but no further. She had dreaded that one last load back to *Bright-lights*. Now she didn't have to worry about it. Everything south of Michigan opened for her… all the way to the end of the world.

"Then I need to find loads to Florida."

Smirking, John nodded. "Certainly, would pay for the trip. Though once in Fort Lauderdale, no loads until we leave. Deal?"

"Deal."

CHAPTER 28

OVER THE NEXT few hours and well into the deserts of Nevada, thoughts of taking Carrie out for her first ride snuggled nicely through John.

He was glad his son Johnny had mentioned Carrie coming down there with him. Because, just thinking of her arms around his waist and, well, her lovely chest pressing into his back made his insides smile. Plus, the boys and their families were continually badgering him constantly to bring Carrie home so they could meet her.

At first, he wasn't sure. After all, they had only just met. He really liked her company back then. But now that she enjoyed trucking with him, he wanted her to meet them, too.

Well, she did seem to like riding along with him. And she did make the trip a million times more interesting. When she wasn't on her damn laptop, anyway. And she had never been on a Harley. That only made the idea better.

As she downloaded another assignment on her laptop, Carrie asked, "What happened to your friend?"

Nevada traffic picked up and a car, going well over the speed limit, shot past at least five cars on either side. Once that idiot was gone, he answered.

"Roll over. Not Danny's fault. He tried to miss the fool, like that idiot who just passed us. Bastard likely shot in front of him. Danny tried to miss him and jerked the wheel, and then flipped down an embankment."

The memory twisted in John's guts again, like it always did when he played with the idea of what might happen. "Danny was one hell of a guy. Woulda done anything for you. Since Karen's a beautician, she barely makes enough to keep a roof over their heads, so a bunch of us set this run every year."

The excitement vanished from Carrie's voice. "I'm sure they appreciate it."

"Oh, they do." He slowed to take the exit for the Flying J truck stop near St. George, Utah. "Nice place here. Great showers. In addition, it's nearing ten hours. Gotta stop."

"Oh. There's a Walmart Center. Can you let me off near it?"

He chuckled, glad the painful memory remained on the road. "Not a problem. Just call when you want me to pick you up."

"Will do." Carrie quickly shut down the laptop.

As he drove into the parking lot, he saw a Super 8 Hotel beside the Flying J. Ideas of a long hot shower, fresh sheets, and fresh breakfast nearly made him pull in for a room. But Carrie. How would she feel about that?

❧

The difference in temperature hit Carrie the instant she climbed out of the cab. She stepped away from the truck and felt the warm desert winds greet her.

John slid her cab window down. "Call me, and I'll come pick you up. Don't walk it. Okay?"

"Sure."

The truck left and panic cut through her. He was leaving her…there. She considered chasing after him, then common sense hit like a slap. John would never abandon her. Never.

Emily's ringtone rang on her cell. "Hey. Em, what's up?"

"Mom, thought you would want to know the inside of the house is painted, and we're getting your bedroom set up. Office is going to be perfect. How's the class coming?"

"Great, but slow."

Em refused to send her pictures of what she had done to the new house or of the office. Still, their talk continued through the aisles as Carrie shopped.

"You won' believe it, Emily. John's asked me to Key West with him. On his Harley!"

"Key West! Mom, that's not fair. I forbid it." Emily nearly crawled through the phone. "No. You have to come home. You can't continue having this much fun, Mom. Seriously. Key West? A bike run?"

"Sorry, darling. I'm going. Enjoy the house."

While checking out, she called John, who said he'd be right over. It wasn't long before he appeared in a mall golf cart. She almost didn't recognize him. "Borrowed it from Flying J."

As they scurried past the Super 8 Hotel, the idea of a real bathroom taunted her, but she couldn't make that suggestion. Especially after wondering what it would be like to make love with John. After all, Frank was the mold for the three-minute man. Frank's needs came first and nothing for hers. Newly married, she had believed that was the way all men were, and romance novels made the heroes unrealistic, a fantasy for every other female.

The idea of John wanting to make love to her seemed ridiculous. If he had wanted to play around, he would have tried to by now. They dashed past the hotel.

"Hungry?" he asked.

"Very, for anything not nuked."

He drew up before Denny's restaurant's doors to let her off. "Mind getting a table while I go put these things in the truck?" he asked.

"No. Not at all."

Chapter 29

WHEN JOHN HAD noticed Carrie glancing at the Super 8, hope lurched in his mind that she would mention getting a room. But she didn't. Oh well.

He climbed into the cab and set the bags on the bed, locked up, and started toward the restaurant. One certainty about driving, you never knew the weather for the next day. Last night it was snow and freezing. Now it was desert dry and warm. He loved that about…

The instant John entered the restaurant, he heard Carrie laugh. His steps quickened and then stopped in the restaurant's doorway to see four drivers lurking around her booth like damn vultures. He didn't know the other three, but he did know Brance, that asshole.

Anger crawled through John's guts the closer he came to Carrie. He stopped just outside the circle. "Looks to me like there's plenty more places available than just this one."

A nervous silence encircled everyone. Carrie sat there, dumbstruck. Brance scanned him from his boots to his hard glare. "Yeah, John. There is. I'm sure you can find one."

The other drivers started to laugh, but John stepped closer. "I believe this one is mine. Isn't it, Carrie?"

"Of course. I mean they just came in and, I mean, stopped to say hi."

"Yeah. Is there some sin in enjoying your new *seat-cover*?" Brance asked and turned to Carrie. "Glad to meet you, sweetheart." The man sauntered away, cracking jokes to the others.

John glared at Brance's back. The waitress crossed in front of him with two glasses of water. "Hey, why don't you join your lady and sit down?"

John jerked to life. What the hell had just got into him? He slid quickly into the bench, snatched up the menu, and tried to read it. Nothing looked the slightest bit appetizing, but he was going to eat if it killed him. "Hamburger. Everything. Coffee."

"Cobb salad, ranch dressing," Carrie said to the waitress. "Water is fine."

The waitress left, and Carrie leaned closer. "John, they just stopped by for a second. That's all."

He broke the white tape around the napkin holding the silverware. "It's your business who you talk to, not mine." He drank from the glass of water, trying to get the bile out of his throat. "And just so you know, Frank wasn't wrong about some of these guys."

Green shards shot from her gaze. "I'm aware of that. If I hadn't been, then it's obvious Frankie has tried to make it clear enough."

"Anyway. I left the bags on the mattress. I hope nothing is going to melt. Sorry. I didn't check."

Carrie sipped her water. "Nothing will melt, but I did get a few things to start fixing salads. Something healthier than frozen dinners. Is that okay with you?"

"Sure." He hated salads really, but he would have agreed to dog food to get a grip on what was stirring deep in his gut. Then he nailed it. Brance reminded him of the bastard who had taken Janis from him after high school.

Carrie's hand rested on his arm. "John, it was nothing. They wanted to know if I liked riding with Big John. Of course, I said yes. John, I really do."

The grip on his guts loosened. "I don't know what got into me. But, Carrie, you talk to whoever you want to." He gulped water from his glass and then released a deep breath. "So, how much more of that course do you have left?"

CHAPTER 30

"YOSEMITE IS ONE of the largest and least frag-
mented habitats in the Sierra. Of California's 7,000
plant species, about 50% occur in the Sierra Nevada with
more than 20% within Yosemite itself. There is suitable habi-
tat for more than 160 rare plants in the park, with rare local
geologic formations and unique soils…"

Carrie finished reading about Yosemite forest sweeping
past the truck on I-5, and then she had to force herself to
open her next lesson.

What happened last night in the restaurant still dumb-
founded her. After eating in near silence, they returned to the
truck. She started putting things away while John logged in,
and then he proceeded to fall asleep. Finally, she was able to
finish the prep test on the final lesson and then joined him.

Was John actually jealous? A silly teenage thrill wiggled
through her while the next lesson downloaded. How long had
it been since someone was jealous over her? Well never, really.
She had forgotten long ago how to flirt, and Frank never cared
whom she talked to. So, who else would ever have been jealous
since she never encouraged anyone?

In just a few days, they had gone from snow in Utah to Nevada's hot desert winds that swiftly changed to California's green forests. They had swept through the outside of Las Vegas, allowing her to see the famous skyline but nothing more. Like New York, she had seen it in the distance. Nevada's dust had joined their trip, coating her with grit that only a shower could remove.

"Will there be a shower at Klamath Falls truck stop tonight?" she asked.

"Should be. How about some coffee?" John asked without so much as a glance.

"Want me to get you some?"

He nodded. "Would you mind?"

"Oh. Not at all. Anything else?"

John shook his head.

After carefully setting her computer down, she got up. Fixed him coffee. Placed it in his seat holder. "Anything else?"

"No. Thanks."

She returned to her seat, opened her laptop, and started working on the next assignment, wondering how he managed to get coffee and water when she wasn't there.

Was that why he liked having her there? To get whatever he needed, so he wouldn't have to pull off. That would have been a waste of time. And time was money.

❧

The thickening beauty of the national park fought for Carrie's attention, especially when morning rose in her rearview mirror. She snapped a shot of the view to send to Emily with a cheerful note that she was about done with everything, and that the trip was overall great.

Well, it wasn't all a lie. The trip had been fantastic at first. Now the wall, which had been left in New England, seemed to have returned. John's sullen attitude itched. She had had enough of that expectant attitude from Frank.

"Did you see that?"

She jerked her blind attention off the computer. "No. What was it?"

"Never mind." The truck wound around another curve and downshifted into a valley. "Would you mind getting me a bottle of water?"

"No problem." She retrieved a bottle and then placed a hand along with the bottle on his shoulder to see if he reacted to her touch.

He drove around another curve. Nothing other than, "Thanks."

CHAPTER 31

CARRIE LIKED HOW the truck seemed to float through an immense forest and then glide into civilization with strip malls, farms, villages, and business parks until, finally, the huge, flat distribution center near Fresno appeared. Trucks there swarmed about the lot like short, fat caterpillars of every color.

Before John even asked, she retrieved the papers for the gatekeeper and handed them to him. These were checked, and then they were sent to dock 29. As silent as a wall, John drove to it, backed in, and shut off the engine.

"Comin' in?"

"Of course."

After all, she was on this trip to get to know these people and learn how this game was played. John was already on the dock with a short Hispanic dock worker checking the load papers by the time she had climbed out.

"You know where to go." The dockworker handed everything back to John and noticed Carrie studying how to climb up onto the dock. "Señorita, let me help you." He, not John, offered a hand to help her up. "You go to the office with John, no?"

"Yes. Where is it?"

"This way. I show you," the dockworker said and motioned toward the double doors.

"I'll show her."

The worker stepped away with a grin. "Ah. John. She is a treasure, no?"

⁓

Carrie scanned the room; the usual gaggle of drivers holding their load papers filled the distribution office, each waiting to be helped or were leaving.

"Hey, Big John got a *seat-cover*. Lucky you." A short pudgy driver grinned at her. "I'm still makin' it with Bowser. That's my dog. Found him abandoned at a rest stop few years back. Been together ever since."

"What kind of dog is he?" Carrie asked. Tension radiated from John, which only made her focus on the conversation more delightful.

"Like me, don't know," the driver said.

She could see him enjoying a dog's company. Or anyone's for that matter. "Makes the best kind."

"Thank you, ma'am. Name' s Bill, by the way. And since John won't tell me, you're…?

"Carrie Marshall." She shook Bill's hand, calloused like John's.

"What brought you to ride along with his carcass?" Bill thumbed back at John, studying the papers in his hand.

John jerked his attention away and informed, "She's my broker."

"What happened to Carl? Heard something about a heart attack?"

"You heard right. But he's doing great now." John stepped back to make room for Carrie to join him at the desk.

She didn't accept the offer.

Bill turned his attention to her. "Well, if you want another truck, give me a holler. Like John, I'm an *owner-operator*. Bowser and me never have enough loads."

"John Graham!" a beach-blonde at the desk called out.

"See you on the *flip-flop*, Big John." Bill hurried out the office doors.

John moved to the counter. "Diana, I want you to meet Carrie."

"Nice to meet you, Carrie." The girl had a cheerful gaze and a warm smile. "Carl called and told us you were working with John these days. Maybe you'd like to see what really goes on behind the scenes? While they load *the-box*, want me to show you the floor?"

"I'd love it."

While John departed to oversee a new load of citrus boxes, Carrie followed Diane through glass doors out to a private observation area overlooking a covered space the size of two football fields. Constant motion moved about the floor, taking things to specific spots, only to be moved again to another trailer to continue to its destination. Below, forklifts scurried about like busy ants between stacks of goods, back and forth in a dance of moving pallets and boxes in a pattern that Carrie would never understand. But she could see why being late could bring the entire process to a grinding halt.

"That's John's load of oranges being brought in now." Diane pointed to a load of rectangular boxes with images of oranges and fruit printed on the sides. Obviously, Diane knew every box on that floor and what each contained as it was shuffled about by the loaders.

"Carl sounded excited that you're stepping in for him. Said you're a natural. And in this business, we need naturals," Diane said with a nod of certainty and then pointed to a forklift disappearing out a side door to the docks. "Won't be long before we get you loaded."

Diane led Carrie back through the glass doors into the office. "Keep in touch, Carrie. Call whenever you need a load or there's a problem. We have plenty to keep John busy."

CHAPTER 32

JOHN USUALLY LOVED this drive north out of Fresno, especially since the traffic here was light and easy. Sure, Carrie was friendly, and hell, very easy on any man's eyes. First Brance. Then Jose's imitation of Prince Charming on the docks. Then Bill's plea for her to broker for him. Shit.

He had to admit that most women who made it on the Big Road had to become leather tough. After all, they had to survive out here in this male world. If it wasn't the hours alone, it was dealing with the annoyance of men and breakdowns. So, *seat-cover*s like Carrie were certainly a refreshing sight, which he well knew.

He wanted to protect her from the assholes like Brance. But there were plenty others out there. Jose? Bill? Well, they… they were different. Good guys overall, but still guys.

John steered the truck into the passing lane, checked mirrors, and pulled back into the *granny-lane*. Golden rolling hills changed to small orchard trees, then became taller pines, and finally the higher mountain ridges appeared full of farms and small towns. City smog and exhaust shifted to a scent of dry sage and dirt.

Carrie suddenly closed the laptop and then slid it into its holder by her seat. "I can't work anymore. Can we stop somewhere tonight where I can do some wash?"

He pictured the coming roads and towns in the remainder of California. He had just enough hours left to make it that far. "I think there's one in Modesto. Mind doing mine while you're at it?"

"Of course, I would do yours." She looked at him as if he had grown horns.

Well it was a dumb question. John smiled to the windshield. "Thanks, Carrie. Really. Oh, and make me a list of what we need in the store, and I'll get it while you're doing the clothes."

Hoping to keep from returning to the laptop, he asked, "How's the class coming?"

"The usual. A few more exercises and then the test."

"That's good. Right?"

She shrugged. "I hope so."

And, out came the laptop.

Three hours passed as quickly as the scenery changed. Silence still hugged each curve. Modesto came into view, glowing in the last rays of the setting sun. Trucks were pulling in and out of the stop. Carrie closed the laptop and turned in her seat. "I'll get things ready."

After letting her off at the laundry, he drove straight to the automatic truck wash and sat back to let the sprayers do the work. Then he pulled in with the other trucks settling in for the night and went in to get the things on Carrie's list.

Liz sashayed toward him with that million-dollar grin on her face. "Hey, Big John, I hear you have a new *seat-cover*. Where is she?"

Liz was the *owner-operator* of the cutest pink rig on the road. And, of all the women in the world, there was nothing pink about her. Yet strangely, the color fit her down to her short, sassy brown hair, huge brown eyes, pink cowgirl hat, and leather vest. What's more, she could wear a pair of leather pants that would make any man stand to attention.

One thing certain about Liz that all the drivers knew, don't piss her off. Gossip from the *squawk-box* said she had once been the 'ol lady' of the Hell's Angel's president of some chapter. How she ended up on a truck and not a Harley still had them guessing.

Why would any driver piss off Liz anyway? Underneath that crust of a well-worn trucker, Liz was a sweetheart. If she liked you, you were awarded with a hug that lasted for days. If she didn't hug you, you were shit. Oddly enough, her hugs were right every time.

He walked toward Liz, already looking forward to his hug. "Left her in the laundry."

"Got her trained already, huh?" Her hug was tight and easily worn.

"Hardly."

Liz stepped back. "What's this I hear about Carl?"

"Had a heart attack. Not doing much now."

"Then is that asshole Phil doing your loads?" Liz frowned.

"I hate driving for that son-of-a-bitch, but I really don't want to go back to hauling for a trucking company. Fortunately, Carrie is helping with finding loads"

"So, she's broking for you now?" Interest radiated in Liz's gaze.

John shrugged. "Learning the ropes, I guess."

"Well, she's learning from the best. Gotta go. Keep the *sunny-side-up*, Big John." She delivered another hug that all the drivers welcomed. When she stepped back, her gaze shot over his shoulder. "Oh, shit. I think I just ripped your *seat-cover*."

He craned his neck around to see what Liz meant. There, holding their laundry basket full of folded clothes, was Carrie, frozen into a statue.

Her glare met his, and then she headed for the store's cashier. Liz stepped away from his arms. "Want me to go talk to her?"

He shook his head. "Like you said, time is money. See you on the *flip-flop*."

"Keep in touch. Let Carl know I'll be calling."

"Will do."

He walked to the cashier. The closer he got, the colder it became, like walking into the trailer with the *reefer* going full blast. Shit, he hadn't done anything that any of the other drivers wouldn't have.

Carrie pulled out money for four children's T-shirts for the grandkids and a new folded map of the country.

He motioned to the map. "What's that for?"

"Me. I need it." Her attention concentrated on simply putting her change back in her purse. That done, she claimed the plastic bag and reached for the laundry basket.

"Wait. I'll get that."

"Never mind. I've managed this far." With one harsh glare, she plucked up the sack and then marched toward the outside doors.

⥤

"You obviously enjoyed it," Carrie said as John climbed into the cab with the groceries.

"Carrie, she's just a *driver*. She hugs everyone," John said as he put the food and supplies away. "I…Carrie, it didn't mean anything. It was just a hug."

"Just a hug. Really?" She stepped into the back. "No. That doesn't go there."

Maybe it was 'just a hug', but it didn't help that this Liz looked like an older version of her maid-of-honor whom her fiancée had fucked the night before their wedding.

In an identical moment, her world collapsed and shifted on its axis once again. That time, it had driven her into Frank's arms. This time, she was not going to be that same stupid girl as she had been thirty-three years ago and fall into the arms of a cheater.

CHAPTER 33

"TRAIL OF TEN Falls runs along the banks of Silver Creek and by ten waterfalls, from which the park received its name..."

Carrie read the rest of the information to herself since John didn't seem very interested. He was likely still relishing Liz's hug. They swept through a curve.

"That it about the Falls?"

Carrie started over. "Trail of Ten Falls runs along the banks of Silver Creek and by ten waterfalls, from which the park received its name. Four of the ten falls have an amphitheater-like surrounding that allows the trail to pass behind the flow of the falls. The park's most visited waterfall is South Falls. Double Falls, however, is listed as the highest waterfall in the park...." Carrie continued reading it like an advertisement.

"Sounds beautiful," John said.

"I'm sure it is."

One click and she escaped to the last question of the exercise on the psychology of a driver, not sure she was believing what she had read about them.

Yet the beauty outside halted any concentration. The scenery passed, growing lusher by the mile. She wished, just once, John would stop long enough to enjoy something, even if it were nothing more than the fresh air. But time was money.

However, those words were becoming very lame lately. Maybe they could at least stop to see Rushmore, a place she had pleaded with Frank to go to.

Then again, maybe she should just forget about Rushmore, about the bike run, about everything, and just fly home. And just work from her new office instead.

⌁

Oh, for God's sake, Liz hugs everyone. Well most everyone. At least, I'm not on her shit list. But Liz was right. Instead of just ripping his *seat-cover*, it was more as if she had torn out the whole damn seat itself.

If Carrie got any colder, he could use her and turn off the reefer to save money. She finished reading the piece about the Falls as an expectation and then immediately went to work on her damn laptop. Now, he was back to fixing his own coffee, getting his own water, and going outside to take a piss.

Even so, Carrie had turned into a trucker's miracle worker. He'd asked her to set up a delivery to Rapid City, South Dakota. Some of his friends in the distribution center there wanted to contribute to the bike run for Danny. And he now had a load of bike parts to deliver in Michigan.

He checked the right mirror. Carrie was staring out the windshield instead of working on her laptop. "We're getting close to Puget Sound. Do you have any history to read about this area?" he asked, hoping that might help warm the cab a bit.

She went to work on the search engine and started reading the information as if it were a recitation or something. "The Puget Sound region was formed by the collision and attachment of many microcontinents to the North American Plate between about 50 to 10 million years ago…" When done, she clicked a button and went back to the lesson waiting for her.

The eternal hours together since Liz's hug had just about fried his nerves. At least, the distribution center was not far from the Portland airport. If she wanted to head home and skip going to Florida, fine by him.

⚬

While they went through the same ropes as every other distribution center, Frankie messaged Carrie, saying he needed to talk. "Right now."

Carrie ignored it. Then Em e-mailed her that the Internet was giving them trouble. "We'll get it. I promise, Mom."

No Internet? She had to have that.

Then Carl left a message that he had a few new ideas he wanted to discuss. "If you are serious about brokering."

Ideas of catching a flight out of Portland plagued her. Did she really want to go back to a house without Internet and deal with family issues? Not really.

The bike run really bothered her. She had looked so forward to that. Em would never let her live it down if she didn't go. But how could she, with John acting this way?

It still aggravated her that it was all right for him to get furious over a few men who had done nothing but talk to her. Yet he couldn't understand why seeing this Liz, giving him a full body hug, was something to be upset about.

She was being ridiculous, and she knew it. Even so, her heart had been ripped apart …again. No matter how she tried to convince herself that she and John were just business partners and not in any kind of "exclusive' arrangement"—as Emily called it—it didn't take.

John backed the trailer into the dock, claimed the bill of lading from the glove compartment, and headed for the dock.

Simmering, Carrie climbed down from the cab. One of the men on the dock helped her up, while John just stood there. He started toward the office, but she stopped him in his tracks. "I'll take care of this."

"Fine." He handed her the papers and turned back to the dock crew.

The office staff was exceptional to work with. Carl had called and they were glad to finally meet her. They chatted about the years they had worked with Carl and Big John. Everything was easily dealt with, and Carrie returned to the truck by herself.

John must have been inside the trailer, checking the load of tires. When she got in the cab, it felt messy. If she was flying home, she wasn't going to leave him with a filthy cab. She changed the sheets on the bed, put the dirty ones in a laundry bag, cleaned the kitchen area with bleach spray, and ran the handheld vacuum over the carpet.

She was back on the next lesson by the time John climbed in, filled in his paperwork on the load of tires for *Rapid-City*, and entered his time on the new program that she had uploaded to his laptop to make things easier. This time, he managed without asking for any help.

If he had, she could already hear herself spewing, "Figure it out."

He said nothing about how clean the cab was, nothing, but started the engine as if she wasn't there. Thank heavens Em called.

"How's everything going?"

"Great," was her biggest lie ever. She started reciting all the places they had been through and how the lessons were going. "Tough."

Frankie called and left a message. "Mom, you there? Mom, I know you are. Shit."

She returned Carl's call, but got no answer, and the idea of leaving him a message seemed impossible. A plane flew in for an approach. "Have we passed the airport?"

"About thirty minutes ago. Why?"

"Nothing. Never mind."

CHAPTER 34

JOHN HAD TO watch these *lumpers* loading the trailer like a hawk, and then he had to pay them while they nearly punctured his trailer wall with the pallet of tires.

Simmering, he climbed into the cab. By the time they were back on the road and he had settled down enough to thank Carrie for taking care of everything in the office and cleaning the cab, she was, once again, lost on that damn computer.

Eight hours across Idaho and into Montana went with the sun. Now his time app on his cell phone went off, announcing he had to stop for the night. Fortunately, a truck stop wasn't far. He'd pull off there. About an hour later, the app went off again, just when he started off the exit.

Carrie looked up abruptly from her screen. "Eight hours already? I can't believe it."

"Almost ten." He stopped behind the *stop-and-rob*. "Need anything?"

She shook her head and returned to her laptop.

After the longest truck wash on record and taking longer to inspect the trailer, exhaustion forced him back inside. Dread made the climb his longest ever.

He logged his time. The warm, setting sun poured through the windshield as a reward. Carrie was right about the login program making the procedure easier—now that he understood it. Gratitude made him attempt to penetrate the cold barrier lurking beside him. "How's the class coming?" he asked.

"Fine."

"Anything I can help you with?"

"No."

He plugged his phone into the dash and got in the back. "Gonna hit the rack."

She didn't say a word even when he pulled the curtains closed. The only thing that woke him was hunger that hit in the dark of the night. When he opened the curtains, Carrie was asleep against her door. *Stubborn woman.*

He touched her shoulder, startling her wake. "Climb in the back and get some real sleep."

Without argument or a word, she settled in the back. Meanwhile, he grabbed a cup of coffee and a sandwich from the *stop-and-rob* and then pulled out. Before he knew it, the first rays of dawn began to burn away the black shroud of night, something he always loved. Janis had said she loved watching the sun come up.

Just the memory of Janis cut like a knife, enough to draw tears. He shouldered them away and drove. Now more than ever, he knew Janis and Carrie were two very different women.

Janis would never have kept her mouth shut. If she were pissed, she'd say so. He remembered a few of their arguments, not in a good way. However, afterward, the air was clear, and the matter dealt with. There was no harboring anything with Janis.

Apparently, Carrie simmered, and he had no clue how to deal with that. Still, he just didn't want to ruin what he had with Carrie. She was a damn good broker. But he had enjoyed her company. Until this thing with Liz blew up in his face.

But was it all Liz? It could be that damn son of hers, or the move, or the brokering class, or something back home. Fantasies of her going on the bike ride had entertained many a mile until now. But now, he wasn't so sure if that was even going to happen. Nor did he care. Explaining that to the kids bothered him though.

Carrie stirred awake. "Where are we?" she asked from the back.

"Just past Helena."

"Making good time, I guess." She made a cup of coffee. "Want some?"

"Seems that way. Sure." It felt good to talk.

The fragrances of tempting coffee and warming breakfast biscuits filled the cab. Soon, she placed his steaming mug and hot sandwich on the dash console. He prayed it was a sign that whatever had pissed her off was gone.

He picked up the warm breakfast biscuit. "Thanks. And thanks for cleaning the cab yesterday."

With her biscuit on the dash, Carrie settled in her seat with Garfield in one hand and opened her laptop with her other hand. "Oh, thanks for noticing."

The brokering screen popped up instantly and, without another word or smile, she was back to work.

∽

The classes were coming along well. Not as difficult. Mostly, they were on accounting and management, something she could do in her sleep. Ben had answered a few questions she had to e-mail him about. That was done. Carl had sent her a problem with the load of buffalo meat to Michigan.

Should she call Emily and ask about the house? Call Diane and ask how counseling was going? But if neither weren't 'coming along' well, Carrie wasn't sure she could handle knowing that. Ignorance was bliss at times. The feeling of becoming insignificant in her kids' lives threatened with possibility.

John's eight-hour break came just in the middle of a quiz on one of the lessons. So, she couldn't get out with him and walk around the rest stop that displayed why Montana was called the "big sky country."

She saw John out there, alone. Very much alone and staring off over the vista full of a sky as blue as his eyes. Unfortunately, that gaze had become a stormy blue lately.

She didn't care who John hugged now. He was his own man and a good one at that. Problem was she couldn't get her heart back to where it belonged.

Maybe she'd pushed too hard with getting the broker class done. Maybe it was everything changing in her life. Maybe she just couldn't get past the clot of memories that these last few days had dredged up. But whatever, it had filled the cab to the point of suffocating both.

The quiz finished uploading and she needed to get back to that. John climbed back into the truck, ready to get going to *Rapid-City*. They quickly returned to the "normal" silence again.

A city limit sign of 6,600 population appeared just after another sign that advertised the Harley shop barely five miles farther down.

"Aren't there more people than that here?" Carrie asked.

"You don't want to drive through here in August. Trust me. Sturgis isn't too far from here and hundreds of thousands of bikers ride in for a couple of weeks. Even *Shaky-Town's* rush hour is nothing in comparison. The boys came one year and returned with some wild stories."

"You never came with them?"

"Nope. But drove through once. Never again." He shot her a knowing glance that had been torn from the Montana sky. "Trust me on that one."

He pulled into a *stop-and-rob* on Lazelle Street and waited for a pump to open. According to John, his friends, Herb and his son Harvey owned the small company that made or repaired parts for every kind of bike ever made. "Any biker that comes here knows Herb knows bikes. So, during the rally, they manage to make enough for the rest of the year. They're stocking up tires and parts now."

"What do they do after the rally?" Carrie asked.

"Not much." He laughed softly and pulled in to fuel up.

Carrie looked back at the laptop screen covered with more about percentages and only saw the smile she had missed for so many miles. Or, for so many states actually.

For a breath, the cab had cleared as if a window had opened to a breeze that just blew everything away. Then that window closed, and the suffocation returned the moment John got out to fill the tank.

⌇

John pulled into the gravel parking lot of a wind-blown, sun-dried garage and backed up to a rising door. The young man, about Frankie's age, waved him closer to the dock and then closed his fists to stop. Brakes hissed, and John turned off the truck.

"'Bout damn time you got here. That check is burning a hole in Pa's pocket. Best get the hell in there and get it."

"Will do, Harv. Good to be back."

After man hugs and slaps on backs, John led Carrie into the garage. With all the dirt and grime outside, with the weather-worn façade of the what appeared as a rickety shop, the inside was as spotlessly clean and organized as any she had been in during the entire trip.

But the smell of stale coffee assaulted her the instant she stepped inside the office. An older man, wearing "Herb" on his shirt, got up from his wooden desk chair. "Where the hell have you been, Big John? We began to think you forgot how to get this far north."

John and Herb pounded shoulders in a hug. "Phil. That should explain it," he said.

Herb backed up and motioned to his son for more coffee. "Want' some?" He noticed Carrie with interest. "You, is that the little lady I've been hearing about? Want some?"

"No. I'll pass on the coffee." Was John and she the chatter of the country now? Were truckers greater gossipers than women, she wondered.

Herb shot a glare at John. "Well, you gonna introduce me to this *seat-cover* of yours, or do I have to do the formalities?"

Setting the hot cup of coffee down on the glass counter, John turned. "Sorry. Harv and Herb, meet my new broker, Carrie Marshall." John then looked to her. "And these are the two I've been telling you about."

"Don't believe a word he said," Harvey said with a smirk. "Nice to meet you, Carrie."

"Yeah, likewise," Herb said, shaking her hand. "Heard about Carl. How's he doin'?"

"Headed for a cruise soon enough. So, he's recovering." John said and drank from his coffee mug.

"Good to hear that. But you ain't getting me on one of those boats." Herb barked, waving hands as if to remove that thought. "Not me. Flatlander through and through."

From the tanned, leathery cap, covered with a Harley-Davidson insignia, to Herb's worn work boots, Carrie wondered if the man had ever left *Rapid-City*? She doubted it.

Harvey, a younger twin of his father, slid the load papers across the glass counter filled with an arrangement of dusty paraphernalia for bikers. "So, she's gonna be your broker from now on?" he asked.

"I hope so." John said with a smile. "She's a good one."

"But, Big John, can she find us on a map?" Herb asked.

"He's here now, isn't he?" Carrie answered before John could. Something had made her want to stand up for herself and not let these men exclude her.

"Yeah. I guess. Can you see this goes where it belongs?" Harvey handed her an envelope. "Don't trust either one of those bastards with this check. Just you."

Carrie pulled out a check, donating a thousand dollars to the bike run for Danny. She slipped it in her jean pocket. "Consider it safe and secure."

Herb rose. "Son, have you lost your mind?"

"She looks safe to me." Harvey set his hands on the glass ledge and studied her. "Now, what I want to know is, you goin' on that ride with John?"

"I hope to." She looked at John, wondering what his answer was going to be. "If he wants me to."

"Of course, I do," John answered, his gaze trying to read hers.

❧

John had forgotten how much work it took to offload, but the tires were now in Herb's warehouse. *Lumpers* earned their wages, for sure.

Carrie had disappeared into the cab, likely to finish another lesson or whatever. Little more was said until the job was done, but Herb had given him final approval on his choice of *seat-cover*.

"Got you a good one there, Big John. A real keeper."

"Yeah."

Herb and Harv loved sassy women, and Carrie had held her own with them. He grinned at that. But he wasn't so sure if Carried wanted to ride anywhere with him again."

John leaned against the garage and scanned the horizon. When he could, Carl always gave him this stretch of road on the 90 or 94. He loved driving it, even in winter. Occasionally it got brutal, and he had to pull off somewhere to wait it out. But he still loved it here.

"Well, best get goin'," he said to Harv who appeared from inside.

The young man was busy wiping grime onto his pant legs. "Yeah, I get it. Time is money up here, too. See you on the *flip-flop*."

"May Sturgis be kind to ya both."

Fortunately, the wind settled down while they *deadheaded* the half hour to Keystone, South Dakota, to the meat processing plant for buffalo meat that Carrie had set for delivery in northern Michigan.

As John headed toward the darkening horizon, signs for Mount Rushmore flashed past. He needed to take a break. An exit appeared so he pulled off on the shoulder, logged in his time, and then climbed back.

He had no idea when Carrie had joined him, but he woke with his arm over her waist, something he tried to stop doing. After all, once she got in her new office, he didn't know if she would ever be going out with him again. Hell, he wasn't sure if she wanted to go home now and forget about meeting his kids and going on the run with him. That was really starting to bother him.

The loads ended in Michigan. So, she could head back to *Bright-lights* or she could decide to go on with him to Florida. He was leaving that up to her.

A tortured sigh escaped Carrie's lips as dawn rose on a vista that somehow had sprouted hills exploding with trees. Now, a totally different landscape surrounded the Black Hills National Forest where Mount Rushmore lay hidden in its depths.

Mt. Rushmore. She sighed. Was that to be only a distant vision like all the others? A passing view? Over the last month, she'd learned so much about trucking goods across a continent that deserved every word of the song "America the Beautiful."

She was starting to feel like a functioning part of the *rig*, a real *seat-cover* that found loads, delivered bottles of water or cups of hot coffee with a side of your choice of sandwich or frozen dinner.

And she was dreading the time she had to spend on the damn computer, learning to be something she was starting to even question. Did she want to be a broker now? She missed being able to read a book, talk, even laugh again.

Brokering was quickly becoming a senseless blur of forms, distributors, miles, loads, and calculated numbers. Everything was melting back into the same routine as with Frank. Work, fix dinner, watch television, or read.

But John needed her. He needed a decent broker because Phil wouldn't help him now. And Carl wanted to retire. Who else did John have but her?

Truth was she wanted to be more to John than just his broker. She wanted to be a friend. She wanted what they had when they had traveled through New England, when she felt important, and they had laughed. She leaned against the side of the cab window, not seeing the passing scenery. At first, it was exciting and new. A true escape. Now it was becoming the new normal.

John walked past the window after checking the trailer. Wind buffeted the collar of his coat, the same coat he had zipped up when he got out of the cab to save her from freezing to death. Again, his sandy-colored hair lifted in the wind, blowing about his face. Then, he disappeared, and the driver's door opened. He logged in and touched the ignition. The truck grumbled to life. "Ready to roll?" he asked.

Let's get this over with. "Sure."

❧

"The Mount Rushmore National Memorial is a sculpture carved into the granite face of Mount Rushmore near Keystone, South Dakota, in the United States. Sculpted by Danish-American Guzan Borglum and his son, features 60-foot sculptures of the heads of four United States presidents: George Washington, Thomas Jefferson, Theodore Roosevelt, and Abraham Lincoln."

Reading about Rushmore was harder than any of the other towns and cities. More than ever she wanted to just get out of the truck and spend time sightseeing, even if it amounted to only half an hour. John had a long break coming. So why couldn't they?

The question blurted out like puss. "You have a long break coming up. Is it possible to visit Rushmore?"

"Won't know until I get this load in."

&

"No need to come in. I got this," John said, after he backed up to the dock, and then exited the cab with papers in hand.

Was John that tired of her company? Well, she could rent a car, go to Rushmore by herself, and drive back to *Bright*… Kansas City, and finish the damn broker class there.

She had found a car rental site on her phone GPS just as John climbed up into his seat. He had a jubilant air about him while dangling a different key fob from his fingers. "You still want to go see Rushmore?"

Her heart leaped into her throat. "Yes, but… Those aren't your truck keys?"

"Nope. They're car keys. Stan assured me they won't be able to load for at least two hours." He jingled the keys. "So, he loaned us his car."

Carrie was starting to breathe as John drove the car along the twisting highway sweeping around the hills. Joy danced just beneath her skin, making her want to giggle, her gaze vigilant for the first glimpse of the stone faces.

Only a hint of the Presidents appeared until they pulled into the parking lot. A sudden gust of cold wind greeted them, pushing them along a walkway lined with snapping state flags.

The unbelievable sight of the huge faces cut into the rock of that granite mountain appeared more impressive than she ever dreamed possible.

John pointed at the bird soaring over the stone faces. "Look. An eagle."

As she began taking shots of the eagle, the mountain, and the flags, she felt John's arm slide around her waist, tugging her closer. She glanced at him to see for sure it was not a dream.

The hard, stone faces had claimed his gaze, so he was totally unaware that she snapped a picture of his profile, one she'd keep when she was home.

"Unbelievable that anyone could do that, isn't it?" John muttered.

"Yes, it is." She slipped the phone back in her pocket. "I bet your truck would be a pimple on their noses."

He looked down at her, stars gleaming in his eyes. "If they could get it up there."

"Would you like a picture?" a park photographer asked.

❧

Carrie gazed at a forest of trees that surrounded the concession area near the snapping flags. An overhead patio heater burned nearby, and the surrounding walls kept the chill and wind gusts at bay. Clouds drifted in the clear blue sky behind the presidents' heads. On the table lay three photos with their arms around each other, each smiling at the camera as if they were just another happy, contented couple.

Yet in one, it was the way John looked at her—the way Carrie wanted a man to do. Soft, happy, glad. The idea of a rental car blew away with the next gust of wind.

John slid onto the concrete bench across from her and set two cups of hot chocolate on the warm patio table. He pushed one toward her. His gaze lifted to the stone faces. "They say it's even more impressive at night with the lights on."

She nodded. "I bet it is even more so when it's snowing."

"That too." His hair blew across his eyes that were as brilliant blue as the sky.

She asked, "Have you ever stopped here?"

"Been through here, but, no, never stopped. You know—"

"Time is money." Carrie smirked.

He toasted her and then drank. "You got it, Carrie." He sat the cup on the table and studied her. "Thank you for understanding all this."

She hadn't been that understanding at all. "I'm learning."

"You are a lot better than most." He played the cup in circles on the table. "Are you almost done with that course yet?" His voice sounded pained as he spoke.

She sipped the hot liquid, scorching her tongue. "A few more exercises and then the final test."

The flags stole his attention. "Good. I've really missed your company." He glanced back over the table to read her reaction.

She choked on the hot liquid. "What…did you say?"

That familiar low-throated chuckle sounded across from her. It seemed forever since she had heard it. "I hope to never see that laptop in your lap ever again."

She stared at this man with disbelief. She was doing this for him! "I've really missed your company, too."

Just then, layers that had built up between them seemed to melt away. She blinked away tears. "John, I'm sorry. I shouldn't have reacted the way I did when I saw you hugging that woman driver. I was wrong. It's just that…it just brought back old memories I thought I had buried long ago." She looked to the flags behind John, "I know that was a thousand years ago, but all I saw was my fiancé…" She couldn't go there again. "It was just suddenly happening all over again."

John shrugged and looked down at his chocolate. "I totally get it, Carrie." Then, their gazes connected. She saw pain in his eyes and knew he did.

"The same thing hit me when I saw the guys talking to you at Denny's." He stared out at the trees. "Before Janis and I were married, Janis broke up with me and went off with an asshole like Brance. I thought that was buried, too."

She touched his forearm, welcoming the feel of his strength. "I guess you never really forget, huh?"

He took a deep breath and let it out. "Look, I'm sorry for being such an asshole, Carrie. I should have been more understanding about all you are doing for me. I really appreciate it." A plea emerged on his face. "But truth be told, Liz hugs everyone she likes and expects one in return. She never settles for halfway. You'll find out if we run into her again."

"You want me to meet her?"

He laughed. "Of course. If you do, you'll find she's a sweetheart and one damn good *driver*." His fingers entwined with hers. The warmth went deeper than her palm. "And just so you know, Liz can drive circles around me any day. But don't piss her off, or you will be sorry."

"And John, I'm doing this for me, too. And thank you for the chance."

Sparkles lit in his blue eyes and suddenly he started telling her about everyone he knew on the road. The names all became a blur, but she enjoyed listening to every word. She enjoyed watching how he talked about them even as they strolled, arms around each other, out to the parking lot and, after one last glance back at the Presidents, they left.

When they pulled out of the parking lot, John turned in the wrong direction. "John, don't we go back that way?"

He smirked. "Crazy Horse isn't far from here. Let's check that out while we're here."

CHAPTER 35

JOHN TAPPED HIS finger on the steering wheel to George Strait singing on the radio. Traffic was good. Weather was even better. Carrie was herself again, even if she was back on that damn laptop again. Driving out of Keystone with a full load of Bison was like riding in a new cab.

Best thing he had ever done was accept Stan's car keys. He had nearly screwed up the best thing he'd had in a long time, and he had forgotten how bad stupid he could feel.

Yes, he had been stunned over Brance, yet nothing compared to what must have hit Carrie when she saw him hugging Liz. Carrie had handled it with more class than he had in the restaurant. That was for sure.

A tingle of excitement thrilled through him. Carrie said she still wanted to go on the bike run to Key West. That was a relief.

All he could think about was getting her down to warm weather, in the salty air, and on the 'Fat Boy.' He'd see to it that she enjoyed every moment.

Love's truck stop near Sioux Falls, South Dakota came into view, and he pulled in to fuel up. Carrie closed the laptop. "They have showers here?"

"Good ones."

"Great. I'll get things ready." She claimed their bags and began gathering and separating the toiletries and clothes.

He hesitated, wondering if she wanted to get a room at the Econo Lodge next door. He had to ask because every pore in his body begged for a long, hot shower and a solid bed to sleep on. And maybe company.

"Interested in staying in a motel with a real bathroom?"

Carrie stopped mid-pack. "Do you mean a real shower with a real tub?"

He nodded.

"Oh, God. Yes."

◅

Like all other Econo Lodges, the bathroom was immediately on the left. Two double beds with white comforters lined one wall. A window with blue curtains draped the outer wall and, straight ahead, was a dresser bearing a television. After the truck, the room felt like a mansion to Carrie.

She poked John's chest as she strode into their room. "I get the tub first, Big John."

"Deal. Just be sure to leave me enough hot water." The door clicked closed. John lifted their small suitcases as an offering. "Which bed do you want?"

He had his, and she had hers. And after the one bed in the cab, it was like separate rooms. "Either," was her answer.

◅

Carrie sank below the water nearly lapping the edge of the tub. Why don't they make tubs deeper? The bubbles barely covered her. But it still felt like heaven. She had no idea a truck could make her appreciate such small things, but it certainly had.

For the first time in days, she felt happy about her future. That felt better than the bubble bath. Things were good with John again, and then, hopefully, she'd be a licensed broker in a few days…if she passed the test.

Chilling air greeted Carrie the instant she left the cozy bathroom, wearing her nightgown, nothing more.

John stood by the window, adjusting something on the furnace. "Is it…" he started to say, then stopped the instant he turned around. The heat from his gaze warmed every ounce of her flesh. "…chilly in here?"

"Umm, it's all yours." Somehow, she had managed to step back and wave toward the fog-filled bathroom, even though part of her wanted to slither across the bed like a wanton child.

✍

Finally, the water shut off and Carrie knew John was climbing out of the shower. Steam flooded under the bathroom door, filling the room with thick humidity. Images of him naked and toweling off played over her fantasies.

He appeared wearing flannel lounge pants and pulling a tee shirt over his head. For a man his age, he had a great body. Okay, there was a bit of a paunch, but she'd seen a lot worse on men half his age.

She had to stop this. Now. Yet no part of her wanted to end the fantasy of running her hands through the silver hair covering his chest.

"That felt amazing."

Ideas of seducing him tantalized Carrie. "I totally agree. From now on, if there is a motel, I suggest we do this. I'll pay my half."

"No way. You are my broker." He put a plastic bag in the ice chest and then picked it up. "Going for some ice. Want anything from the drink machine?"

"Surprise me."

He grinned and headed for the door. "Pizza should be here any time. If it comes, use my credit card." He pointed to his billfold on the dresser.

"Got the room key?"

"Oh, yeah. I'll need that."

He returned with the ice before the delivery boy knocked on the door. Carrie began pouring the orange soda into plastic cups when the pizza delivery appeared in the room. She let John take care of paying as the small room filled with the scent of pepperoni and cheese.

She met John midway in the room with his soda in hand. "Here. I'm starving."

Maybe he'd need another shower, John thought, as he exchanged the pizza box for the bubbling drink. Either Carrie was sexy as hell in the long nightgown, or he was just horny as hell.

Then the weather report on the television intruded like a slap of cold reality. They both turned to see that snow was moving across Canada into Michigan with an unpredictably brutal forecast for this time of year. They looked at each other with the fact that they really needed to get to the center before the damn thing arrives.

CHAPTER 36

"THE TAHQUAMENON FALLS ARE TWO different waterfalls located near Lake Superior in the eastern Upper Peninsula of Michigan. The water is notably brown in color from the tannins leached from the cedar swamps that the river drains. The upper falls are more than 200 feet across with a drop of approximately 48 feet, making the upper falls the third most voluminous vertical waterfall east of the Mississippi River."

While Carrie read about their next stop, John watched the dark clouds blanket the sky, coming in like a plague.

He prayed those fat, gray clouds weren't filled with the forecasted snow. But never-the-less, he just needed to get across the Mackinaw Bridge before they broke loose. The load of medical supplies barely weighed enough to keep the wheels on the asphalt. Too light meant he needed to slow down even more. This was one time he wanted a heavy load of anything.

The large body of radiant blue water of Lake Superior appeared around the next turn along with the pristine view of the bridge that joined the upper and lower parts of Michigan. The fact that the bridge could be covered with black ice twisted his guts into a fist. No traffic on the *squawk-box* about it. That much was good.

A lazy snowflake fastened itself to the windshield. Shit.

"John, it's snowing."

"Yeah."

Nodding, he gripped the wheel to feel every turn of the tires, every shift of the trailer, every rise. He couldn't breathe. Just feel.

He had to focus his attention on everything about how the truck moved, how the bridge felt beneath the tires, and how the trailer followed. A gust of wind could push the trailer off track, taking them over the railing and into that freezing ass water. He'd seen enough trucks dangling off the side of a bridge because of that.

Suddenly, an explosion of snow blinded the world before him. The bare specks of bridge were his only guide. Knowing the bridge was straight, he had to drive by feel now. He didn't want to slow down to a crawl, but he had no choice. What he wanted to do was *put-the-hammer-down* and get across this damn bridge.

⁘

Carrie held her breath. John had turned into a white-knuckled *trucker*, nothing like the man she knew, confident and unshakable. Always in control. By the time they left the bridge, he had become riveted to the steering wheel. Sweat lined his forehead. He was so tense that if she so much as touched him, he might shatter.

"We're going to have to pull over. I really don't want to. We have to," he muttered more to himself than for her.

Carrie looked out of her window and couldn't see the side of the truck or where the shoulder of the road was. *If John pulled over too far, if the trailer slid...oh, God.* Her heart made a slow climb in her throat. She'd seen rollovers on the nightly news. "John, there's...there's no shoulder."

"I know. I know."

Snow held them in a white cocoon. Inches passed instead of miles. The air inside the cab thickened like cotton. A snow-coated sign showed only bits of its wording '...est St...'.

"Rest stop. Did you see it?"

"No. How far?"

"Here." She prayed she was right because if she was wrong—No, she didn't want to think of that.

He eased the truck right toward a parking light barely glowing like a dull, distant star. Then the truck seemed to die in place. John turned off the engine and just sat back, staring outside at the white frozen world beyond.

"John? Want something to drink? John."

No response.

She retrieved a bottle of cold water, broke the lid loose, and placed the frigid object on his shoulder. Only the fingers of his right hand somehow managed to pry from the steering wheel as he accepted the bottle.

Simply resting her hands on his tight shoulders explained how tense he had been. She dug her thumbs into his muscles. It was like digging into dry clay. Slowly, his flesh gave way and began to relax.

His left hand dropped onto his thigh as he sagged forward and melted into her hands like putty. She nudged him to rest over the steering wheel so she could work down the concrete wall of his back.

Still, she didn't have room to work. The angles weren't right. "John, come back here and lay down. Okay?"

He extricated himself from his seat and then slid face down on the mattress. "God, Carrie, this feels good."

She pulled the bottom of his shirt out of his trousers. "Take this off."

Like an obedient child, he rose and peeled free of his shirt. She poured drops of her almond oil onto his skin. Gliding her hands over his bare flesh, relishing his deep-throated moans.

A long sigh of contentment vibrated through his chest. He rolled over and slid his hand along her arm to the side of her neck and drew her down to his lips.

The instant her lips settled on his, something different, something ancient, and long forgotten stirred. She eased alongside him as if drawn, sliding her hand into that carpet of silver covering his chest.

The delicious kiss lingered for a thousand heartbeats while everything she had shoved back on the shelf of life resurfaced.

At any moment she expected to wake up and find this a dream. A fantasy. Well if it was, she wasn't going to waste one moment.

When John's hand ventured beneath her top, her world toppled and gloriously slipped off that shelf into the hot energy diving between her legs.

She gasped at the memory.

He jerked away, ready to apologize. His mouth open. His hand tangling in her knit blouse as he tried to retreat. She halted his words with a kiss of her own, clamping his hand exactly where it was.

He didn't have to ask twice.

CHAPTER 37

THE DELICIOUS ESSENCE of warmth snuggled around their entwined bodies as Carrie drowned in the fragrance of Old Spice. However, something about this didn't feel like a dream. It was real. And, when she opened her eyes, she knew being there was real.

John was asleep beside her, and as naked as a jaybird as she was. Memories of the night floated down like rose peddles. A long-forgotten contentment sank her deeper into the mass of wrinkled sheets they had torn up the night before.

He shifted and his hand rested on her breast. She welcomed the caress and brushed her leg against his thigh.

John's eyes struggled to open. "Good morning, Beautiful," he said with a lazy smile.

"Good morning, Handsome." She giggled and glanced outside where falling snow curtained the window. "It's still white out there."

He stuffed a pillow under his head, leaving their faces only inches apart, and brushed strands of hair from her face. "Good. Maybe we'll be stuck here for three more days."

His kiss drew their bodies close, flesh to flesh, heart to heart. It could only be better if it became soul to soul.

❦

Feeling better than he had in years, John forced himself from the bed. "Coffee? After all, you're always getting it for me." He slipped into his shorts and filled the coffee carafe with water. "What flavor?" he asked.

Carrie stretched beneath the blankets with a soft happy smile. "Caramel mocha."

"Why'd I ask?"

Her giggle sounded like music to his ears.

Carrie sat up, clutching the sheet over her as she had during another snowstorm that he could easily remember. But, this time she wasn't wearing any clothes.

Coffee drizzled into her Garfield mug, while he watched Carrie settle back into the pillows like a satisfied kitten. He'd never seen her hair in such disarray, but it only made her cuter.

Cup filled, he drizzled creamer, sprinkled sweetener into it, dropped a plastic spoon in the caramel-scented brew, and handed it to her. "Here you go."

Eyes closed, she sucked in the scent. "Ah. This is delicious," she muttered. A teasing grin appeared on her lips with a taunting grin in her gaze. "Thank you."

"You're welcome." He dropped another plain flavored cup in the coffeemaker.

How last night happened played through his brain. He'd never driven through such a storm, one snowflake, and then it was white. He'd never been so scared in his life. He still wasn't even sure where the truck was parked. But it was parked. Not dangling off the bridge or laying in a ditch.

But he felt as if he were dangling off something. And whatever it was, it was one fantastic fall. Yet he felt more alive than he had in years. Nothing could wipe the smile implanted on his face now.

John carried his mug to the bed and then sat beside her. "No. I believe I have to thank you, my dear."

"Oh, I think you did."

CHAPTER 38

JOHN WATCHED THE *salt-shaker* cut into the three feet of snow and blow past the rest stop as if it didn't exist. Early morning sun beamed down on the single lane of roadway in the snowplow's wake. Fortunately, the wind had blown most of the dry snow away from around the truck. Even so, the tires had to claw their way forward.

Carrie was already on her cell phone with the Rite Aid Pharmacy Center in Cedar Springs to let them know they should there by noon, roads permitting. She ended that call and went to her laptop.

"Cedar Springs, Michigan was named for the fine springs bordered by a massive cedar grove. It was established as a lumber town in 1856 and boasted numerous lumber and shingle mills. It then became the northern terminus of the Grand Rapids and Indiana Railroad and the crossing point east to west for the Toledo, Saginaw, and Muskegon Railway, later becoming the Grand Trunk Western Railroad that was built in 1888…"

Exquisite snowdrifts lined the reasonably dry highway. They would make good time to the distribution stop. Even so, this was a storm he would never forget. For more reasons than snow.

Janis had been a wonderful person and wife. Until now, he always believed her the most willing and responsive partner anyone could have in bed. But Carrie went well beyond all that. It was as if both were starving for flesh. Well, maybe they had been. He chuckled. Maybe so.

A glance at the city signs for the truck stop-Petoskey showed Carrie's reflection in the windshield as she worked on another lesson. That old simmer stirred.

"How many more of those damn things are left?" he asked.

She looked up and smiled. "I'm on my last one and then the test."

That fact, coupled with the roads feeling better by the mile, made the drive even more pleasant. "Then what?"

She sagged back in her seat. "Well, if I pass, I'm finally done." A long sigh seeped from her. "And I can get back to living again."

Relief peeled from him, too.

GPS directed them to the Fifteenth Street exit. He drove through the sleeping town with streets already cleared for the morning traffic. He turned into the parking lot of the Rite-Aid center. Even so, the warehouse looked closed and no one had opened the dock doors. Yet, they knew they were coming.

Once backed up to the dock, John started from the cab. "I'll take care of this." As he trudged to the office door, Carrie followed like a bundled Eskimo. His pounding on the office door provided nothing. Finally, someone answered, "We're closed."

John showed the short, blond-haired man the bill-of-lading. "I have your fucking delivery."

"What delivery? We don't have a delivery," the man muttered sleepily.

John stared at the man. "What the hell? We called."

"I didn't get no a call. Who'd you talk to?"

"Stan," Carrie answered.

"Stan left an hour ago."

John waved the papers at the fool, and he finally opened the door and looked closely at it. "Well, go ahead. Off load. I'll tell him when he gets back."

Shit and son of a bitch. He had to off-load this! "When does this Stan get back?" John asked.

"No telling when. I'll unlock. There's a loader inside."

Carrie's hackles rose. "Excuse me. You want us to off load this…load?"

John left it to her, not sure if it was self-defense or to let her have at this oaf. But he'd been down this road enough times to know they expected him to either off-load it himself or pay a *lumper* to do it. And obviously there was no *lumper.*

Following him like an angry terrier, Carrie spewed her fury all the way back to the dock. "John, you're not—John, you can't. You shouldn't…I mean…What are those…those…?"

"*Lumpers.* Home asleep, all snug in their beds." He wasn't looking forward to doing this, but ideas of warm sun and warmer beaches made it easier.

"You can't be serious, John."

"If we are going to make the schedule, I think I am." He opened the trailer doors. "Happens all the time. If we want to get that load from Wolverine this afternoon, what other choice do I have?"

He pulled the pallet loader away from the wall and pushed it into the trailer for the first pallet. He'd hustled heavier loads without a loader before, but it wasn't getting any easier.

Carrie marched back toward the office. By the time he started dragging the second pallet out of the trailer, the man burst from the office doorway like a scared rabbit. "Holy shit, man. We'd better get this load off your trailer if I want to keep any flesh on my body."

⸙

Still simmering, Carrie waited in the cab. She couldn't believe what just happened. Of all things. John had no business offloading anything. This was their order. If they needed the stuff, they should be the ones to unload or hire it done. She was going to see to it this never happened again.

The thud of the trailer doors vibrated through to the cab as John closed and locked the now empty trailer. It wasn't long before he climbed in the cab and he hung up his winter coat. Sweat had soaked his shirt.

"You won't ever have to off-load anything here, because I'll never get a load for them again. Or, I will make it clear they are responsible to unload the trailer. Not you."

Smirking, he started the truck. "You don't think this is the first time a *driver* has had to off-load his own trailer, do you?"

She looked at John with total disbelief. "Are you serious? John, you deliver the damn loads. They should unload it."

"That would be nice."

While John headed across town to the Wolverine distribution center, she snapped pictures to send to Emily of the crystal forest of some fairytale that lined the short drive through a lovely part of the small town.

John backed into the leather-manufacturing parking lot cornered with mountains of new snow. Men, wearing winter jackets appeared on the dock, motioned for him to stop. Like always, they both got out and headed to the office.

"Glad you guys made it after that storm," the man behind the office counter said, while taking the proffered paperwork.

John unbuttoned his light jacket. "Came in fast, for sure."

"You were lucky getting through." The office clerk signed the papers. "Heard the roads were impassable up there."

"We were lucky to find a rest stop near Gaylord Forest Area," Carrie said.

The clerk stopped and looked at her. "Gaylord? No rest stop up there. You sure that's where you stopped?"

That was a night she would never forget. "Yes. Saw the name on the outbuilding."

The clerk finished the paperwork and then handed the clipboard to John to sign. "I go hunting up there all the time and never saw a rest area around Gaylord."

"Well, there definitely is one, and it's a great rest stop," John added with a grin. Obviously, Carrie's and his minds were in the same place. He claimed the papers and opened the door for her to leave with him. "Look for it."

CHAPTER 39

CINCINNATI HERE WE come. John pulled away with a full load of shoes and boots. He'd checked everything, adjusted the weight, and got on the road in no time. Even with snow piled everywhere, he could feel the warmth of the Florida sun already. He couldn't wait to share a beer with Carrie on a Key West beach where the palm trees swayed.

The familiar brokering screen popped up on Carrie's laptop like an unwanted rash. "You do that test yet?" he asked.

"Just about." She just stared at the screen. "I can't do this right now. You want some coffee?"

"Love some."

"I wish it were done and over with too," Carrie said, filling the coffee carafe with water. "Frankly, I'm tired of having this in my face all damned day." He heard the familiar buzz of the coffee maker. "But to get what we want; I have to do it." Something dinged in the microwave, smelling sweet and cinnamon.

Taking the proffered Peterbilt mug from her, John sighed. "I just hope you have it done by the time we get to Ft. Lauderdale."

A heated pop tart appeared next, and then Carrie returned to her seat. "Me too. I hope I'm your official broker by then." She grinned. "If you still want me."

"Oh, I want you for sure, as well as for my broker."

A smile lit up her face. "I really didn't think taking this class would be so hard. You know, more than once I considered quitting."

He passed a car full of teenagers swerving all over their lane. Praise God in heaven they shot off the next exit. "And?"

She sipped her coffee. "Along with the many idiot drivers out here *like them*, I never realized how much there is to trucking."

✖

After getting fuel at a stop near Lansing, John climbed inside to the smell of microwave cookies and Carrie handing him a cup of milk and a pile of cookies on a paper napkin. He put the treats on the dash to pull out to the open area, shut down, logged in his time and fuel, and then relished the warm treat.

Carrie turned toward him with her cookie in hand. "Tell me about your sons again."

He settled back in his seat. "Little Johnny is bigger than all of us put together. He took after Janis's side. He's married to Barb. I think I told you they have two kids, Eli, ten, and Barbie, eight. Johnny's an electrician for a private company. Billy is more like me and manages a distribution center for Walmart. He is married to Sally, who is pregnant with their second. Sarah is seven and all princess."

Carrie broke off a crumb and ate it. "I'm still surprised neither wanted to haul like their father."

At times, that bothered him. It meant the time he was on the road had hurt more than he wanted. "Said they didn't want to miss out on their kids growing up like I had to. I don't blame them. It is tough being out here. But, believe me. They can't wait to meet you."

Treats gone and memories alive, he started out of the parking lot to end the conversation.

"I look forward to meeting them." Carrie said as she resumed the online class and lost herself to that world.

A weigh station appeared. "Shit. A busy *chicken-coop*," he grumbled as he pulled into the rear of the line of trucks waiting to be weighed and released.

❧

Not only did the line stretch endlessly in front of John's rig, it amazed Carrie at how quickly more trucks lined up behind him.

The clerk inside the so-called coop weighed each axle and then, as if shot out of a cannon, the truck took off like members of a weight-loss program. But then, if their weight wasn't right, they were pulled aside for some correction or fine.

Finally, John was allowed onto the scales. Carrie thought of removing her shoes just in case. The man from the window of the small office eventually smiled and waved them through "Looking good, John. Keep *the sunny- side- up.*"

"Count on it." John handed her the paperwork and geared up to leave. She scanned each one through the new portable scanner she had picked up at a Walmart, filed them electronically and then manually filed the papers in the expandable folder wearing the dates of the deliveries. Then, Carl was gifted with copies of the papers in an email. That done, she was back to her broker screen. Her last assignment zoomed off into cyberspace as the emails had and now for the final test.

By the time they were heading south on the interstate, the test loaded. When they arrived in Cincinnati, she was well into the middle of it. She handed John the needed papers for him to deal with the distribution office and went back to the test.

Fortunately, the load of shoes was off-loaded with the help of lumpers this time, and cases of sodas were jarring the cab with mini-quakes as the boxes were loaded. Once done, they would be off to Gatlinburg, Tennessee to make that delivery and to pick up golf balls.

Pausing to give her brain a break, Carrie sagged back and realized that, in three months, she had tasted New England's fresh lobster and travelled west to California. Memories of going through Sacramento floated over her like mud, but that vanished with images of the lush scenery around Portland, Oregon. And Mt Rushmore. She smiled at that. Then, she had left snow-buried Michigan, bringing a smile to her lips. And now was heading to the warm sands of Florida. And, she had a new house, a new car, a new job, and a great friend in her life now.

"How's the test coming?"

His question jolted Carrie out of her reverie as John swung into his seat with the new delivery papers for her to file.

"Fine." She took pictures of each load page, filed them as before and sent a copy to Carl. Then John handed her a chilled can of soda. "Here. Compliments from the office staff." He went in the back to put the rest of the six-pack in the mini fridge.

After a few moments, he said, "Apparently, we need a grocery stop?"

"Wouldn't hurt." She tried to find her place on the final test before losing the program all together. Finally, it reappeared.

He checked his phone app. "I have enough hours to get us to Gatlinburg. Love's has a great rest stop there."

"Sounds good."

⋑

After a driving break, John focused on the road while Carrie went back to the test. Whether she knew it or not, she had timed her loads to perfection. Few brokers ever came to grips with that very important factor, leaving *drivers* to report their required breaks or simply log as lies on their *swindle-sheet*.

The first star popped out in the night sky when, "There. Done!" burst from the other seat. "Now, to send it."

He glanced at Carrie with her finger poised on the enter key.

"What are you waiting for? Hit the damn thing." If he could, he would have hit the key for her.

She punched the key, releasing the well-known *death wheel* as she called it, to go round and round. Six exits passed as they both held their breath.

Carrie waited with closed eyes, until "bing" and she saw the words on the screen. "YOU PASSED! 87% WELL DONE" scrolled across her screen.

Carrie's screech tore through the cab. "I did it. I passed." John pulled the cord on the horn, blasting the news to the world.

CHAPTER 40

"GATLINBURG, TENNESSEE. DESPITE the town bearing his name, Gatlin had arrived in the small town around 1854, and was known for constantly bickering with his neighbors. By 1857, a full-blown feud had erupted between the Gatlins and the Ogles, probably over Gatlin's attempts to divert the town's main road."

John checked mirrors and asked Carrie, "Seriously, that's how it got its name, over wanting to divert the town's main road?"

"I guess so," she said. She finished the blurb and then rested back in her seat to relish the changing scenery. Delight danced inside her. She was a licensed broker. Carl had sent her a virtual bouquet of roses with a note of congratulations. "John's one lucky trucker for sure."

She needed Carl until she got on her feet. Fortunately, he was glad to continue helping her, at least until she got home.

In Cincinnati, they had pulled into Loves', and, when she came from the women's shower area, John presented her with a dozen real red roses that now filled the cab with their musky fragrance.

He'd found a small, but lovely, Italian restaurant in a strip mall. They dined on wine and delicious lasagna—most of which chilled in the mini fridge. When they returned to the truck, he had even given her another night she would well remember.

Never in all her years married to Frank had he ever made her feel this wonderful, this wanted, or this beautiful. However, she had never expected anything more than what she had then.

Now, she realized that had been her mistake, settling for something secure. She also knew now, that nothing in life was ever secure. It could change in a moment's notice, like a car dying on the side of a road, or the hundreds of other accidents they had passed.

The beginnings of a warm southern breeze floated in through the open windows, stirring the fragrances of John's roses and Old Spice aftershave.

What's more, the familiar sparkle once again danced in John's eyes. His face, in fact his entire body, seemed more at ease. This same man, who had first saved her from the snowstorm, from going mad, and took her to Maine for lobster, now felt like a true friend. One she could truly trust with everything in her life.

Her phone lit up with a call from Frankie. To avoid answering, she looked to John. "What kind of Harley do you have?"

"A Fat Boy," he said with a taunting grin. "Know what that is?"

"A fat, motorized bike with two big wheels and a handlebar."

"Close enough."

⋘

God, Carrie was beautiful. If he didn't have to drive, he'd just watch the wind whip her hair against the headrest. Everyone was going to love her. And, by every force in nature, he counted on being right about that. He only hoped Carrie loved being on a bike more than Janis had. The death of a friend on a *crotch-rocket* had kept Janis from enjoying any part of being on a bike.

He jerked his attention back on the road and listened to Carrie read about their next stop. "Myrtle Beach, South Carolina. Prior to the arrival of Europeans, the Long Bay area was inhabited by the native Waccamaw Tribe. As the American colonies gained independence, the area remained essentially void of any inhabitants. However, George Washington had scouted out the area and stayed a night at Windy Hill. Want me to keep going?"

"Not really."

"Good. I didn't want to either." She put down her cell phone and gazed out at the continuous display of landscaped golf courses breezing past. A light chuckle drew his attention. "I think they really like golf down here."

"Just by the number of golf balls we're carrying should prove that point," he said. The little suckers had filled the trailer.

Traffic forced them to move over due to road construction. "You know what those orange cones are called?" he asked.

Carrie grinned. "No, but they've followed us everywhere we've gone."

"*Schneider-eggs.* Go figure."

A stink drifted into the cab as John slowed down behind a *bull-hauler.* "I don't know how drivers do it, but I can't haul livestock. The idea of leaving them in the slaughterhouses bothers me." John glanced seriously at Carrie. "They know what's about to happen."

Carrie nodded. "Kinda makes you think of becoming a vegetarian, doesn't it?"

He shrugged. "Until I get a delicious steak. Which, in fact, we will be enjoying tomorrow night. Billy called earlier and said they are planning to grill his famous steaks when we get there."

Carrie looked out at the passing golf greens. "I feel like I need to bring something."

"Just your beautiful self."

Closing the curtains for privacy, John heard her moving about, taking care of matters. When she reappeared, Janis's necklace dangled between them. "I found this under the bed, near the Porta-Potty. Something said it was important. Is it?"

His heart crashed against his ribs. Janis's cross! He was almost blinded with tears by just seeing it. But he was driving. "I thought I lost it. Uh, it's Janis's."

"It's beautiful. Want me to put it, where?"

He opened his palm and let her drop it there, and he stuffed it in his pant pocket. *Why now,* played in his mind for miles. He had scoured the cab, looking for it.

CHAPTER 41

"JACKSONVILLE, FLORIDA. THE area was originally inhabited by the Timucua people, and in 1564 was the site of the French colony of Fort Caroline, one of the earliest European settlements in the United States. Under British rule...." Naval jets blasted overhead, drowning every word Carrie read about the naval base. "...The town was established there in 1822, a year after the United States gained Florida from Spain; it was named after Andrew Jackson...."

He didn't like the sound of the reefer unit kicking in constantly. A glance at the reefer gauge said the temperature was holding. A sigh of relief escaped, because if it didn't, he'd have to pay for the load out of his own pocket.

Checking the mirrors, he noticed Carrie's eyes, a darker green than usual. "I always enjoy driving through here," he said to break the thickening silence.

"The pictures don't do it justice. Coffee?"

"Sure."

She disappeared into the back. Traffic picked up, slowed down, and picked up again. Navy jets flew overhead.

"Can't wait for you to meet the grandkids." A long pause opened, and then his cup of steaming coffee appeared over his shoulder.

"I'm looking forward to it." She sat and proceeded to stare out the windshield. Then she was up again, getting something from the back, and then reappeared with a bottle of fingernail polish.

⁓

The closer they came to Ft. Lauderdale, the less Carrie could search for anything to keep her nerves in check. Nails were multilayered. Her wardrobe chosen. Cab spotless. Mail answered and sent. Now what.

Lush plants bloomed everywhere along the highway and all the other beautiful landscaping on golf courses, ramps, and even streets. Every brush of warm air tingled with the salty scent of the ocean and swaying palm trees caressed her face. It was far more lavish than she expected for February.

Her gaze caught John again caressing his pant pocket that held Janis's necklace. Images returned repeatedly of his gaze when she showed to him. It was as if he were staring at the Hope diamond. Was Janis reminding her that John still belonged to her?

Well, if his wife were, she would honor that wish, but only if John agreed.

"I can see why everyone moves down here. It's beautiful," she said to break the silence.

"Janis…well, we loved raising the boys here," he said as he passed a car and then settled back into the *granny-lane*." His right hand went directly back to his pant pocket.

Fortunately, Emily provided distraction and called with news that her boyfriend Scott was installing a "state of the art office"—whatever that meant. And her mind raced to learning what that meant.

❧

John had loved coming home until Carl had called while he was in *Shaky-Town*, telling him to call home immediately. Carl never did that unless it was an emergency.

He had called Janis. She started out bravely. "Just hurry home. Yes. Everything is fine." It wasn't. That's when she broke down into tears.

He *deadheaded* home on the same stretch of highway he was on now. Nothing mattered, not even speeding tickets. The whole way, he heard Janis crying.

When he pulled in the driveway, she came out of the house with a brave face and open arms. He had clung to her like life itself until tears consumed both.

Then, it was hospitals, doctors, chemo, her losing her long hair that he dearly loved, holding hands, making jokes that made no sense. Then, it was watching her dwindle away, each day a little more. It was like his soul was drying up.

"John, don't stop living. John, be happy. John, take care of the kids."

"I will, darling. I will. Don't worry. I will."

Then, it was hospice, dealing with the boys, the grandkids who always came with hugs for Grammie no matter what. He just sat at Janis's bedside, holding her hand, waiting for the doctors to be wrong, yet knowing they were right.

Then came the practiced answers with the funeral home, the kids, and the grandkids who wanted to know where Grammie went. "Heaven, sweetheart."

And then came their questions he didn't have practiced answers for. "Why?" "Where's heaven?" "No, Grampa, I want her back. Now."

Then there were walls that grew thicker each day. He had gone out on his bike to escape and came home to get drunk worse than he ever had. He had smashed everything that reminded him of Janis until he found her coat hanging in the back of a closet—the same damn coat she had picked out at Walmart.

His legs just gave out and he sat on the floor hugging it. Johnny found him, helped him leave that room and go outside. A few more beers and he agreed; he had to get back on the road. He sold the house to Billy and got the truck.

Now, he was bringing a new woman back home. A woman he really cared about. A lot. More than he dreamed was possible.

He hadn't figured on bringing Carrie into his past like this. All he'd wanted was for her to meet his kids and for them to meet her. He hadn't planned for the painful memories that were choking him.

"You have to send pictures, Emily," Carrie demanded. Her call ended cheerfully, and silence resumed.

"John, is something wrong?"

"No, nothing's—."

Like a gift, a small fist appeared outside a car window and pumped up and down. So, he blasted the horn a few times. It staunched the wound pouring into his soul.

CHAPTER 42

"G RAMPA!" MATCHED THE decibel sound of screeching jets roaring through the open cab window. Images of Roy and Sam running toward her in the airport hit like a tornado. Tears welled in Carrie's eyes. That had been the beginning of the end or the end of the beginning…whatever—everything had changed.

John stopped in the gravel driveway of the modest suburban house outside the city limits of Hollywood, Florida. The familiar spew of airbrakes filled the evening air, as the kids broke from their parents' grips. By the time they reached the truck, John shot out of the cab, squatting down to hug them with open arms.

"You're here! You're here!" they all yelled at once.

He stood up, holding a girl clutching a drawing of a horse in her fist. She had to be Little Barbie. The one hugging his leg and wearing a tiara had to be Sarah. And that had to be Eli racing out with an oversized ball glove.

"Grampa, see my new glove? I've got one for you, too, so we can play ball now."

"No, I got him first," Sarah yelled after John had set her down. She tried shoving the boy away.

"No, you didn't. I did," Barbie snapped.

"Hey. Hey, you guys. Not all at once." That had to be Little Johnny who, as John had said, was not little by any means. Everyone had left the porch and followed the kids.

After delivering a huge hug, Billy asked, "Weren't you leaving the *rig* at the shop, Dad."

"Couldn't wait. We'll take it over tomorrow morning."

Carrie scanned the crowd surrounding John. This was his family. Sally, the pregnant one. Billy, who looked like John, and the girl beside Billy had to be Barb. Seeing them with John and knowing Janis's necklace lay in his pocket kept Carrie in the cab.

Little Barbie pointed up at her "Is that her, Grampa?"

"Yep. That's her. Come on. Let's go meet her." John carried the girls around the chrome bumper as she forced her feet to climb down. Eli stopped long enough to reset his glove and then raced to catch up.

John sounded happy and proud, but his gaze said he was struggling. And why wouldn't he? Carrie could feel Janis in every shadow.

John put the girls down and stepped closer to her. "Everyone, this is my new broker, Carrie Marshall." He turned, his gaze a dark blue. "Carrie, this is my bunch."

The wives took over from there. They surrounded Carrie and took her toward the house, leaving the boys and kids with John. "I truly hope you are ready for the chaos that is coming," Barb said with a grin.

"Yeah. I think I am. I wish I could have brought something."

"Oh, no need. We have everything ready."

During dinner, everyone talked at once, introducing themselves, apologizing for something, and laughing at taunts.

Jokes abounded about why she ever wanted to broker loads for their dad, of all people.

Carrie put her glass of sweet tea on the table. "I guess it was because he needed one, and I needed a job."

Johnny, then, draped an arm over his father's shoulder and asked, "Well, Pops, you ready for the big ride?"

"Can't wait to get out and take Carrie on her first ride on that bike."

No one believed she never was on a bike.

Everything began to blur. The grandkids refused to leave John, which he seemed to appreciate since he was on the floor with them. Sarah already had a crown on his head. Barbie's fury exploded when John ignored her new horse statue and tossed Eli a ball.

Carrie wasn't allowed to help with dishes or anything. "No. You've put up with enough just being on the truck with Pops," Little Johnny ordered.

Laughter turned to Sally's pregnancy because they still refused to tell what the child was even though they knew. It was as if she were caught in a whirlwind, one that could easily have happened each time John came home.

Obviously, John and Janis had been a very blessed family. A sense of envy started to enfold around her. Carrie forced it away and enjoyed watching the grandkids consuming John with absolute joy. It radiated from his face.

"Grandpa, can just you and me sleep in the truck," Eli begged. "Please?" The boy clutched John's arm.

John ruffled his hair. "Sure, Eli. We can stay in the truck."

"I want to, too. Momma, can I? Pleasssseee?" little Sarah begged, only to be echoed by little Barbie. "Me too. I wanna stay in the truck too."

"You all can't sleep in the truck," Billy said, standing up to defend his father from this assault.

The girls snuggled around him like frightened urchins also in need of protection. Eli braced at his side while glaring at the girls as invaders.

"Sure, they can," John said.

Billy shook his head. "No, Pops, you sleep in here, and I'll stay with them." Cheers turning into fury from the kids.

John shrugged. "Out voted. I'm sleeping' with my grandkids." He looked at Carrie. "Mind?"

"Of course not."

Everything shifted into a flurry that erupted again. Her luggage was claimed from the truck and the grandkids' toys, sleeping bags, teddy bears, My Little Pony bears, and teapots overtook the cab.

One yawn from Carrie and Sally directed her to Sarah's room decorated in princess pink. "Sorry, the bed's only a twin."

"It will be fine." Carrie motioned to the bathroom just across the hall. "That truly has become a luxury these days. I don't think I will ever take a private bathroom for granted ever again."

Sally giggled. "Then, when the boys are gone tomorrow morning, plan on a long soak with bath salts and lavender bubbles, as long as you want."

Billy motioned to the bartender for another round of beers. "Mom would like her."

Hearing Billy say that and seeing Johnny nod loosened the vice around John's heart. Tears started to well in his eyes.

He choked them down. It had been tough letting Carrie handle getting to know everyone on her own. But, like the distribution offices, she had done so easily enough.

But for him, no matter the extent that Billy and Sally had redecorated and remodeled, the house remained the same. He knew those walls too well and the memories were still there. Janis was still there. The grandkids wanting to sleep in the truck had granted him a reprieve from the misery cutting at his heart.

"Good to hear you say that." John couldn't say any more.

"Seriously, Pops, Carrie is perfect for you."

"She's a good woman. Different, but…good."

John didn't like thinking of just how good Carrie really was. "All I can say is she's a natural at finding loads."

"Yeah, so I hear." Johnny lifted his beer as a toast. "So, here's to you, Carrie, and trucking."

Billy did the same. "To new adventures, Dad."

They drank and then Johnny leaned in close. "Seduced her yet, Pops?"

John spewed beer over the bar. "What the hell kind of question is that? It's none of your damn business."

Billy laughed and then downed the rest of his beer. "You owe me, big brother."

John stared at both sons. "You two had a bet on…on that?" Suddenly he could breathe. Life felt good. But he wasn't telling these two shitheads that.

"Of course, Dad," Billy retorted with a toast. "But the real question is, was it recently or back on the Salt Flats?"

John focused on his beer. "Like I said, none of your damn business."

Johnny pointed to his mother's necklace rustling around in John's hand. "See you found Mom's necklace."

"Yeah." He didn't want to think about that just then, but it burned on his chest.

"What's Carrie think of it?"

"I don't care what she thinks of it." But he did care. And they hadn't talked about it.

CHAPTER 43

CARRIE STROLLED AROUND John's Harley, running her fingers across the fuel tank and then over one of the two mirrors on the handlebars bearing the gold insignia of a flying eagle and the words "Live to ride. Ride to live." The motto seemed to fit John because he did…in a *rig* or on a Harley apparently. "So, this is a Fat Boy?" she asked.

John stood by the bike while both boys leaned against the doorway of the shed. "Yep."

The metallic silver and red bike wasn't fat in any way. In fact, it seemed smaller than some Harleys she had seen. It certainly wasn't the *crotch-rockets* that raced through traffic like bats fleeing hell. She pointed at the skull on the belly of the fuel tank. "Why a skull?"

He walked to the side of the bike like a protective parent. "Came on the bike when I got it and, well… Looks good, don't you think?"

She touched the handlebars, the brake grip, the black leather seat, and then pointed at the leather packs for personal belongings. "So, where are you going to put your things?"

Before John could answer, Billy burst out laughing. "Guess you'll just have to wear yours, huh, Pops."

Ignoring them, he handed her a blue biker helmet. "Want to go for your first ride?"

"Any time you are ready."

"Have you ever ridden a horse?" he asked and slid the helmet over her head.

"Once, as a kid. A pony ride." The helmet's tight fit muffled his answer. "What?"

"Wait a minute." He slid his helmet on and plugged in the wire somewhere. She heard him clearly. "Did you fall off?"

"Almost."

"Good. You can hear me." He swung his leg over and adjusted the bike beneath him. "Hop on."

"Oh yeah, just hop on. Sure." She grinned.

John held her arm as she sat behind him. Adrenaline swam through her veins like a drug. She snuggled close, wrapping her arms around his waist.

"Hold on."

John took off out of the garage like a bull from a rodeo cage and laughed at her screech. They were down the driveway and had swerved onto the road before she could catch her breath.

"Doing okay back there?"

Giggling like a schoolgirl, Carrie answered, "I think so."

She gripped John's waist even tighter as the bike tilted and swept around another curve in the road. By the third curve or so, she relaxed.

Speeding down a road with nothing around her but the wind and the sun left a strange sense of freedom she had never felt and easily explained why so many loved bikes. That was until a bump jarred her teeth like an insult.

They came to the first intersection where another biker passed and then dropped his hand down, pointing two fingers toward the asphalt. John returned the gesture.

"What's that?"

Stopping for the light, John supported the bike with one leg. "That's called 'tipping the deuce'—saying hi."

"Can I do it?"

"Absolutely. Whenever you see another biker."

The light changed, and he took off up an entrance ramp to the interstate and merged into traffic zooming around her.

In John's truck, the speed was nothing, but out here on his bike, it felt insane. They came alongside an *18-wheeler* that seemed to suck them closer. As if for the first time she saw the hoses, the tire flaps, so close and so real. She knew they were hoses that were behind his cab, the flaps over the wheels, of course. But never so close that she felt she could touch them.

John swept down an exit, slowed to blend into local traffic. Concrete and asphalt changed to beachfront properties, sand, and the symbolic palm trees. He pulled into a beach parking lot, came to a stop, shut off the bike, and took off his helmet.

"Ready to check out the water?" His eyes sparkled brighter than the ocean beyond.

Carrie struggled out of her helmet. "Sure."

The crashing waves, the brilliant sun, screeching seagulls, and hot, smoldering sand swept away all else. Only the essence of warmth and peace surrounded her.

As John took her helmet, he asked curiously, "Like riding?"

There was no hesitation. "I love it, John. I see why people love it. I really do. But I don't see ever wanting to ride alone."

"That's good news." He claimed her hand and led her to a postcard perfect beach scene where people meandered or dodged incoming waves. Dogs chased thrown toys while children piled sandcastles and dug pits that the waves destroyed.

John scanned the vista before them, sparkling, curling waves, rolling over in a crest. More waves swelled out in the distance that also basked in the afternoon sun. People wearing sweatshirts, cargo pants, and flip flops spread out beneath palms rattling in the sea breeze.

"Seems impossible, doesn't it? Barely a week ago, we were caught in a snowstorm," John said to the vista.

Sand gave way beneath her shoes as they strolled toward the water. "Impossible. But everything has seemed that way since Christmas."

He looked down at her, his gaze sparkling brighter than the diamonds covering the waves. "You have to be careful, or you'll get addicted to these extremes. Beautiful sunsets, sunrises, mountains, and deserts. Rivers and farms. I could go on, but I think you know what I mean."

"Oh, I do, John. Not only that, but days of sleeping and nights of driving. You have to be a bit crazy to do it."

The smile on his face made her want to drown in it. He leaned closer and kissed her, releasing a ripple through her insides. It lasted barely a breath but seemed a lifetime. He pulled back. "Want to head back?"

No part of her wanted to leave. She wanted to feel this wonderful forever. However, nothing lasted forever. She knew that well enough. "Let's walk in the waves first."

⋘

John laughed when the first wave wrapped Carrie's foot. She jumped away. "Damn, that is cold. I see why there's not too many swimming this time of year."

After that, Carrie simply enjoyed letting the waves play around their legs. Bits of seashells carpeted the way. He and Janis…

John looked up at the sun, letting it warm his face. She was up there somewhere, watching. Did she care that he walked the beach with Carrie? *Do you?* he asked.

As they walked, he let his heart float out to the heat, hoping for an answer. If the answer came back yes, what would he do? He didn't know.

Of course, he'd take Carrie on the bike run, enjoy her company, and then take her home. What they had would turn into what he and Carl had—a business arrangement.

If the answer was, she didn't care, what then? *Yeah. What then?* That possibility nearly suffocated John.

Suddenly Carrie asked, "I bet being here with me hasn't been easy, has it?"

He chuckled. "I'd be lying if I said it wasn't. You can't cover up memories with paint."

She walked in front of him and studied him. "So, spending the night in the truck made it easier?"

He smirked. "Easier in one way. Impossible in another. You aren't going to believe what the kids did to the cab last night. There is not a storage bin untouched."

He went on telling her about making what seemed like hundreds of cups of chocolate, putting things back on shelves, answering questions about dials and knobs, while letting Eli pull the horn to wake up the neighborhood. All that, to cover up where the conversation was going.

"I hope you know it that you're blessed," Carrie said out to the waves.

"I like to think so."

She looked at him again, her gaze never greener. "Do you think she's okay with me here with you?"

John pulled Janis's necklace from his pocket and let it dangle off his finger. "I don't—"

Suddenly, the chain broke, and the necklace slipped into the sand. A wave claimed it and took it to sea before either of them could reclaim it.

It was his answer that he had been wanting for. "I think she's okay with it."

CHAPTER 44

CARRIE COULDN'T BELIEVE the number of bikers who came to help Danny's family. It seemed thousands were swarming into the Harley Davidson parking lot like busy, rumbling bumblebees. The loud, puttering engines brought with them the excitement of one massive reunion of friends.

Not too far away were Barb and Johnny on their bike chatting with friends. Billy swerved alongside John, alone. Everyone was busy talking and taunting as if they hadn't seen each other in a long time.

John handed her a patriotic bandanna like the one he wore around his head. "You may want to put this on to keep your hair from blowing in your face."

She was wrapping it around her hair when a biker stopped in front of John. The guy seemed as comfortable on his bike as John was driving a truck. "Big John, dressing up your bike I see. No wonder you look better," the guy said with a smile that was infectious.

"Carrie, this is Wild Bill. He always put this run together for us."

"Great to have you, Carrie. Ever been on a run?" Wild Bill asked, while revving his bike.

"This is my first one."

"Then, here." He offered a bottle of sunscreen to Carrie. "I know John didn't think of it."

"I didn't."

After covering her face, Carrie handed the cream to John. "Think I'm covered now. Thanks for thinking for us."

Wild Bill's face lit up with delight. "Well, you couldn't be in better hands than John. Hope you enjoy this."

"Me too."

Everyone started putting on helmets, checking around them, and revving the bikes. John made sure Carrie's helmet was on right. Like before, she was caught in a silent world until there was the click. "Can you hear me?" he asked.

She nodded, but then added. "Yep."

"Ready to see Key West?" he asked through the helmet.

"As ever."

He helped her onto her seat behind him and then revved his bike, adding the blast of his bike to the cacophony of rumbling motors. It vibrated through her.

Wild Bill appeared before John and nodded. "Let's make this ride happen?"

"Let's do it." John nodded and the bike moved beneath her like an anxious racehorse.

"Then let's roll." Wild Bill took off.

They surged after Wild Bill and bikes began to peel off like an obedient herd.

Carrie glanced back over her shoulder at the two, long, staggered lines of bikes that stretched down the street and stopped traffic at every intersection. She couldn't believe it. They were on their way to Key West, Florida, the southernmost point in America. Hemingway's country. How many romance novels were set down here? More than she could count. She had always wanted to come here, but never in a million years would she have believed she'd do it riding a Harley.

⤚

John collected her hand with his fingerless leather glove, drawing her closer. It made their world more personal than she had ever felt inside the truck. It also made it clear that he wanted her there with him.

While they roared through Miami and onto the interstate, the air gradually changed from exhaust to salty. Every mile farther south lost its touch of the city's concrete and metal to become filled with sand dunes and wispy grasses. Buildings became smaller and beachy, some even hiding in the lush groves.

They passed a sign for Florida City when Wild Bill lifted his left arm and pointed into an upcoming gravel driveway to an island bar and store. A sign that read, "Welcome to the Keys," caught her attention.

The long line of bikes followed the leaders into the parking lot. Each pulled up, backed in, and shut down until the parking lot was lined with a chorus line of bikes. Never had Carrie's butt felt so perfectly numb. She personally knew every bump in the interstate. Still, she was in love with riding with John.

Pulling off her helmet, she asked, "Why are we stopping?"

John removed his helmet and wiped his face with the patriot "dew-rag." "Pulling in for a bathroom break and a draw."

"A what?"

"Forgot to tell you. This is a Poker Run." He put their helmets on the seat. "I entered you. Here's how it works. At each stop, you get to draw a card. By the time we get to Key West, we'll make five stops to make a complete poker hand. The winner with the best hand will be announced in Sloppy Joe's and win the prize."

"And that is?"

"No one knows yet."

Walking felt wonderful. The chat at the bathroom was fun and light, especially when all the women complained that their butts were as numb as hers. The cold bottle of water tasted beyond delicious. Best of it all was John's arm around her while they waited to make their own card draw.

John drew from Wild Bill's deck of cards. Three of hearts. He handed the card to Billy, who wrote "John-3 hearts on a pad, punched a hole in it and, then gave it back to John who slid it into his back pocket.

Carrie drew the king of spades. Again, like John's, it was entered on the pad, punched, and returned. Soon the bikes followed Wild Bill onto the highway again, to a place named The Tiki Bar, and then Big Pine Key, each time everyone drew a card.

Then they started across the Seven Mile Bridge over the longest vista of blue water Carrie had ever dreamed possible. It seemed endless. Yet, there could not be a picture that could capture the beauty of the water or sunlight, or the fragrance of pure salty air that floated everywhere. No wonder pirates had loved this area. The line of bikes made her wonder if they were not part of that history. It looked like it anyway.

"It's beautiful," Carrie said through the microphone.

"And it only gets better from here. Are you doing okay back there?" John's muffled voice came through the headset.

"Butt's numb. Not sure if I'll ever walk again after this."

He laughed. The sun bled red over the waves as it seemed to set in the water. He asked, "What cards have you got?"

"Not telling."

"Oh, come on. I'll tell you mine if you tell me yours."

"Sorry."

"We have one more stop before Key West. Maybe I can talk you into telling me then."

"Don't count on it."

He squeezed her hand in answer. She answered with her own.

CHAPTER 45

JOHN LOOKED FORWARD to any excuse to ride to Key West where no one hurried to do anything. After keeping track of miles and time, this felt like heaven. The entire line of riders slowly paraded into the sun-bleached, lazy town that just made you relax whether you wanted to or not.

Having Carrie riding with him only made it better. In the *stop-and-robs*, she managed to charm everyone, but refused to let him see her cards. He couldn't lure her to show him even one card, no matter how he begged.

The ride seemed too perfect. She fit up against him as if she were made to. Her laugh was more delightful in the headphones than he had ever heard from her.

By now, he'd seen her about every way possible but now in jeans and a leather jacket really turned him on. He had to smile to himself, excited to see her reaction to the surprise he had planned. Oddly enough, she hadn't said anything about this being Valentine's Day.

They pulled into a sandy parking lot outside the streets of Key West where John swept up beside Wild Bill, backed in, and shut down behind a bar with a huge sign—"Sloppy Joe's."

Billy pulled up next and then Johnny and Barb. Everyone followed suit and climbed off their bikes, shedding helmets as if they were suddenly filled with bees. At this point, Carrie assumed the ride was over. Some would head back that night or stay a few nights. But no one left until the winning hand was announced.

"Ready for a frosty beer?" John asked as he helped Carrie off the bike and out of her helmet.

"Yes," she said. "This was Hemingway's favorite bar?"

"That it was, my love."

Billy and Johnny looked curiously at him and then smiled, shoving each other into the back doors of the corner bar.

The antiquated building blended in with all the other bars and stores along the infamous Duval Street, where doors and windows remained open to the fresh air year round. Caribbean music, blasting out the many open doors, greeted everyone.

Carrie followed everyone inside and saw the infamous horseshoe bar that the bikers gravitated to and started calling out for beers. A stage, across from the bar, boasted a silver and white motorcycle with a sign stating it was a Heritage Soft Tail Classic.

With a frothy beer in hand, Wild Bill bounded up the side steps of the stage and walked over to the bike. "Okay, get your beers and cards ready," he announced. "Let's see who wins this beauty."

⌒

Excited murmurs rippled around the room while the punched cards hemmed the stage like lace. Jeering commenced as Wild Bill examined each set, insulting the cards' owner before moving on. John didn't bother showing his hand. He already knew he wasn't winning anything. Besides, he and the Fat Boy had too much history to be replaced.

Carrie spread out her cards, face down, next to his, still refused to let him see it. Then Wild Bill picked the cards up and seemed impressed. Like everyone, he waited, as their illustrious leader took his sweet time inspecting her hand, checking against the pad of paper, looking for the punch holes. "You know what you have here, Lady Carrie?" Wild Bill asked.

"No. I've never played poker."

He revealed a full set of spades, 10 to Ace, for all to see. John stared at it as did every other biker as they crowded closer to make sure it was a full hand of black spades.

"I believe, Lady Carrie, you win the bike," Wild Bill said as he displayed Carrie's hand to everyone. "Anyone ready to challenge this." Nothing but grumbles. "No? Then, Lady Carrie, you win the bike."

∽

"Oh, my God, I won! I won!" Carrie wheeled on John, wrapping both arms around his neck, surprising him with a kiss. The entire bar booed, swooned, whistled, and cheered.

"Way to go, Carrie. Too bad it wasn't the lottery." Billy whooped beside her.

"Maybe John can teach you to ride it," someone yelled.

"I doubt that's possible," Carrie retorted, still in shock.

Hands lifted her onto the stage, pushing John to join her. "Get on your bike," John said with a sweep of a hand and then proceeded to hold it from falling on her.

She straddled the soft leather seat and then grasped the handlebars as if she knew what she was doing. Photos broke out like a rash as she posed like a movie star.

Before long everyone settled back into their own lives and Carrie climbed off, letting people come by to admire the bike and congratulate her.

"What the hell am I going to do with this?" she whispered to John. "I can't handle this thing."

"Whatever the hell you want to, Carrie."

"You want it?"

John shook his head. "I don't need it."

"Would your sons?" she asked, pointing at Billy and Johnny caressing her new bike as if it were a newborn.

"Ask them."

The answer she got was the same as their father's. They liked the bike, but preferred their own already broken in. She felt as if she had won a prize elephant.

She grabbed Wild Bill by the arm. "This is fantastic. It's beautiful. But, Bill, I don't know what I'm going to do with it. Is there any chance I can give it to Danny's family to sell or just give it back to the ride for another draw?"

He stared at her. "These guys would give their eyeteeth for this bike."

"Then auction it or something."

Wild Bill's gaze turned serious. "Well, yes, we could do that. But, are you sure?"

There was no doubt she wanted rid of the beautiful thing, however, one glance at John said he had not changed his mind. "Yes. Auction it."

Wild Bill threw a leg over the bike and whistled for everyone's attention. The entire room silenced to hear his announcement. "Miss Carrie wants to give this to the club and ride with John. So, let's have an auction. Anyone interested?"

Cheers and whistles pummeled the walls, bringing the place back to life. Wild Bill tried to keep up with the bids. Finally, one biker, obviously an auctioneer, stepped in and the bike quickly went for a ridiculous price.

People crowded around, offering to buy drinks and taunting John for not bidding. Then he whispered, "Want to leave?"

"Yes."

When John spoke to Johnny, his son handed him something, and then gripped her hand. Then he led her onto Duval, bathed in the late afternoon sun. Streets basked with every fragrance and stink floating from the buildings and alleys. Happy music of every kind pulsed from every bar they passed. A menagerie of people, with dreadlocks to the latest style, filled the sidewalks. All clothing had one thing in common—simple and cool. Her jeans and shirt felt like furs as she walked beside John. Still, it was fun strolling the varieties of stores and avoiding the roosters strutting around the various benches.

John told her the Sunset Celebration was winding down on Mallory Square, a plaza at the edge of the city. Jugglers and performers gathered their coin bags and waved goodbye to the lingerers. Music, drifting from restaurants, blended with the lazy slush of waves against the wharf. Not far away, boats bobbed about a marina, ready to take people fishing or out on a cruise to maybe some fantasy island nearby

John stopped at a Sunset Key shuttle boat marina and handed something to a young Jamaican man who stepped forward.

His dark brown eyes looked up with a happy sparkle in them. "Ah, Mr. Graham, yes. Please let me help you on board. We have already delivered your luggage to your room."

"What? Our room?" Carrie's heart clambered against her ribcage. "John, when–"

"I'll tell you on the way over."

Grinning like the cat that finally ate the mouse, he helped her onto the boat. She no more than sat down on the side bench than the driver handed John a bouquet of a dozen red roses.

"Carrie, thank you for everything and happy Valentine's Day," John said as he presented them to her.

Tears burst from her eyes. "I forgot."

John's gaze sparkled with delight as he sat down beside her. "I almost did too. But the boys made sure I didn't."

The puttering motor smacked the boat into the small waves as it crossed to a lonely island an easy distance from Mallory Square. Old Spice competed with the heavy fragrance of the roses on the voyage to a fantasy island nearby.

John leaned close to whisper, "The boys suggested that maybe we might like to stay a few days. So, while they were auctioning the bike, Johnny checked us in at the Sunset Key Cottages."

"They know…know about this?"

He nodded. "Not that their dad needs his kids' permission, but they granted it."

"I don't have any intention of getting pregnant here, just so you know."

He chuckled. "But we could try, couldn't we?" He lifted her face and pressed a kiss to her lips.

"Oh, yes. Absolutely."

Chapter 46

ALL THE WAY from Mallory Square, across the water to Sunset Key Cottages, John basked knowing Frank had never wined and dined Carrie as he planned to do now.

That only made everything sweeter. He watched as she smelled every flower, caressed each leaf, and gazed at him with stars. Her giggles tickled him enough to keep him grinning.

He kept his arm around her shoulders and basked in her sweet fragrance that lingered on his pillows in the cab now.

The shuttle boat slowed and bumped against the dock that stretched out before a bunch of cottages that faced the water. One of them was theirs.

The hotel attendant opened the door, allowing them to pass inside. "Your luggage bags and helmets are already here. If there is anything we can do to make your stay more pleasant, let us know. Do you need anything for the roses, ma'am?"

"Yes, please."

"I'll send a vase up immediately." The bus boy scurried off with his tip.

Fantasies popped in John's brain when he saw the four-poster, canopied king-sized bed covered with a white bedspread and a mass of feather pillows. He wanted Carrie stretched out naked over that.

He followed her outside to a private veranda with two white rocking chairs with blue cushions, and surrounded her waist with his arms. There, he kissed the base of her neck. "Beautiful, isn't it?" he whispered.

Carrie turned, glowing. "Unbelievable." She clutched his shirt and began pushing him backward through the patio doors. Once flat on his back on the bed, she began unbuttoning his shirt.

Piece after piece fell on the floor, as she spread kisses over his chest down to his stomach. He pulled her back to his lips so he could finish what he'd started, the removal of her jeans.

∾

A dozen roses and now this. Carrie couldn't believe all that John had done. All these years, she had convinced herself that all her romantic desires had dried up or died. That she could never want this again. That she was too old. Who would want her? Why would any man want to touch her or even kiss her? Make love to her? Thank God, she was wrong! No part of her ever wanted John to stop. Nor did she want to stop either. It was mind-blowing and glorious.

Gasping, Carrie fell back onto the lush pillows, drowning in the long forgotten or never known sensation feasting through her. John's arms and face were well tanned. But, like her, the rest of his body was creamy white. A feathering of white hair lay between his nipples that, by now, she had done forbidden things to.

"I never believed I could ever feel this wonderful," she whispered. Her gaze lowered to a taunting flirt. "Thank you, John. Thank you. Thank you. Thank you."

Laughing aloud, he clasped her face with both hands and kissed her. "You know, Carrie Ann Marshall, those are dangerous words. Keep that up and you know what I'll have to do."

Giggles erupted as she released a swath of tongue lashes over his skin. "Thank…"

∽

John stirred cream and sugar into a mug and then spread a thick layer of cream cheese and chives on a toasted bagel.

Last night had been a long, slow banquet of sensual pleasure he never thought possible. Feathers from the pillows were very stimulating. He'd never been in a bubble bath before, but he'd never refuse one with Carrie now.

The hotel had delivered champagne and chocolate strawberries along with their dinner eaten out on the veranda in bathrobes.

They had curled up on the bed to watch a movie, but it ended up with a long slow seduction of kisses and caresses. It was better than in the snowstorm in Michigan when they had made love like desperate teenagers.

Contentment flowed through John as he carried the breakfast plate into the bedroom. "Hey, beautiful."

"Hum?" Carrie stirred awake and struggled up from the pillows. He was getting addicted to seeing her wake up, disheveled and sleepy. "Want this in bed or on the veranda?"

"What time is it?"

"Nine-thirty."

"Seriously?" She sat up. "I slept that long?"

"Guess so."

She took a bite of the bagel. "John, you didn't have to do this, you know."

He sat on the bed and put the plate on her lap. "Figured I owe you for waiting on me in the truck."

"Tha—."

He kissed her in hopes of capturing the gratitude. A giggle escaped when he drew back. "Where's your coffee?" she asked.

"Out there." He motioned to the rockers where he had enjoyed the rising sun.

"Give me a few seconds, and I'll join you."

She appeared in the hotel bathrobe, hair brushed back, lipstick on, and carrying two steaming cups. She handed him a second cup and sat in the other rocker, trying to cover her cleavage. He put that to a stop with a kiss.

"John, I don't want this to end. Can we stay here forever?"

"Anywhere with you would be perfect to me." The words slipped out, but he didn't regret any of them. "I mean it, Carrie."

Tears glistened in her eyes as she smiled. "It was a good day when I met you, John Eli Graham."

He drank coffee. "Even if you believed I was a mass murderer?"

"Yes. Even that. And, all I can say is thank you for everything." She moved so the bathrobe opened with a grander invitation. It took the rest of the morning before they could leave the room to the hotel maid.

He'd walked Key West many times with Janis and the kids, but never had he laughed as much as he did with Carrie. They had pictures taken at the marker of the southernmost point of the continent. Souvenirs were bought for the kids. Slivers of key lime pie were relished along with piña coladas.

Beers and fresh chowder out at a Jimmy Buffet Bar fed them until he knew it was time to be heading back.

⋘

No part of her wanted to return to the real world. John had completely changed her, heart and soul. He had made her feel more than beautiful and special to the point of being truly loved. She loved him. But the words weren't shared even though she wanted to say them.

John handed her the helmet, but she couldn't put it on. Instead, she held it by the chinstrap while he mounted the bike, adjusting it beneath him, and then looked expectantly up at her. The rumbling motorcycle made her turn away from the golden sun in the afternoon sky filling with exquisite thunderclouds.

John revved the engine. "You comin' with me?"

She looked back at him. "I don't want to go."

"Me either."

He made room for her to climb on the bike. She started toward him and froze, dropping her helmet with a clamor. She turned away, not wanting him to see the tears climbing up from her soul.

He shut off the bike and, moments later, enfolded her in his arms. She turned and leaned into his chest, hearing his heartbeat. "You really want to stay here, don't you?"

She nodded against his shirt. "I do…with you. This has been beyond perfect."

His body slumped against her. "Oh, God, you're pregnant then."

That shot her off his chest. "What? I don't think so."

He dried her tears with his hand. "What if I promised to bring you back?"

"That would help." She rested in his arms.

"Then look forward to it."

In that moment, she knew that spending the rest of her days with him would be beyond belief. She didn't care where it was, on the truck, on the bike, at a rest stop, or in a snowstorm. She simply wanted to be with this man wherever he was.

She sucked in a deep breath and climbed onto the bike. She stopped. "The roses. I'm not leaving them here."

"I had them mailed to Johnny's."

John revved the engine and adjusted his helmet. He had to admit. He didn't want to leave any more than Carrie did. "Can you hear me?"

"Yes," Carrie answered through her microphone. She drew ever so close. "Can you feel me?"

He groaned. "Loud and clear." Before he changed his mind about staying, he gunned the bike toward the main road.

Silent hours flew by as quickly as the bike sped back across the Marathon bridge, along the coastal highway to the interstate through Miami.

John slowed and pulled past his parked *rig*, washed, fixed, ready to hit the road. He stopped in front of the shed and waited for Carrie to climb off the bike. "Go on in. I'll get everything," he said.

She went inside the house with Sally, leaving him alone to store the bike. As he closed the doors, he looked at his rig and realized this was the first time that he didn't want to climb back into that cab.

Oh, there were birthdays and holidays that left him dreading to hit the road again, but he had a purpose then… provide for his family, pay bills. This time, he was dragging his heels, dreading to take Carrie back home.

CHAPTER 47

"A NOUVELLE-ORLÉANS OR NEW Orleans was founded May 7, 1718, by the French Mississippi Company and Jean-Baptiste Le Moyne de Bienville. It was named for Philippe d'Orléans, who was Regent of France. Later, during the American Revolution, New Orleans became an important port to smuggle aid to the rebels, transporting military equipment and supplies up the Mississippi River.

"Oh, John, you'll like this," Carrie quipped. "It handled huge quantities of commodities, which were warehoused and transferred in New Orleans to smaller vessels and distributed the length and breadth of the vast Mississippi River watershed. The river in front of the city was continuously filled with steamboats, flatboats, and sailing ships."

Listening, John worked his way through the city's highways that had been submerged by Katrina, a sight he would never forget. He had delivered loads of sheet rock and building supplies to help rebuild the devastated town.

When he turned onto an exit to a major highway into the Garden District, Carrie pointed at the passing trees. "What's that hanging all over the trees?"

"Mardi Gras beads. They are all over this town, especially here." He drove under an overpass. "They are everywhere here during Mardi Gras."

"Oh."

As if they went into automatic pilot when the CSX distribution center came into view. Carrie handed him the load papers for the gatekeeper, who directed them to Dock 23. The driver at Dock 24 had barely left him room to back in, but he made it.

While Carrie dealt with the office and met Melissa, he oversaw the offloading of cases of wine that Carrie had arranged in Tallahassee, Florida. He washed the trailer and then moved to pick up a load of frozen seafood for Memphis, Tennessee.

"Everything okay with the load?" Carrie asked.

"I suppose. Yeah."

"I'll go check the cab and see if we need anything." She jumped down from the loading dock and climbed into the cab like a weathered pro.

John grinned, remembering her lush butt resting in his palms the first time she attempted to climb into that cab. Now, he had even better memories of just how good her butt felt in his hands.

"Looks great, John. Everything checks out." The dock manager's voice jolted him out of his reverie as he closed the trailer doors. "All set."

"Yeah. All set."

Before John knew it, they were back on the *Big- Road* toward Tennessee, the warmth of the south slipping back into the chill of the Midwest.

How easy it was to shift back to normal. Pick up and deliver. Pick up and deliver. In some ways, it felt good, in other ways, the old familiar trucking routines returned like a bad rash. Frankly, he never wanted to go near Missouri. He just wanted to keep on going anywhere but there.

✍

John pulled into a rest stop just outside Memphis, shut off the engine and, like every night of his life, climbed out to check the trailer. Promises of spring surrounded the bustling parking lot. Buds of daffodils and tulips peeked from the mulch on either side of the sidewalk as he walked to the men's restroom.

When he climbed inside his truck again, a spicy, sweet scent greeted him. Atop the checkered tablecloth blanketing the bed perched three plastic plates. Two were heaped with spaghetti. The third plate held a flickering candle. Brownies slowly revolved in the humming microwave and a bottle of wine chilled in the ice-filled sink.

Yet only Carrie captured his gaze. Stretched out on the bed like a Victoria Secret's model in black lingerie she whispered, "It was the best I could do."

"Looks fine to me." He pulled her to her feet and ran both hands under the silky lace. His palms drifted down to that lush bottom of hers to hold her tight enough to prove he liked what he held.

She pulled off his jacket and let it fall to the floor. Next was his shirt. When she reached for his fly, the microwave dinged, releasing the fragrance of chocolate brownies.

"Let's eat first." He glanced at the flickering feast waiting on the mattress. "Then have dessert."

She giggled and slid back onto the mattress.

✖

As the miles ticked off ever closer to Memphis, Carrie's thoughts returned to Key West where her romantic fantasies had been unleashed, thinking that would never happen again. But she had guessed wrong.

When she had walked through the Walmart Supercenter, the idea came to her to give John a late Valentine's present and something to remember each time he stopped for a break. It became a night they both would never forget. Never had she done the things, wanted to do the things she had done with John.

Now, no plate of spaghetti or brownies would ever be eaten with such abandon again, nor would wine be tasted in ways that were nearing sinful. If she saw that same gleam on his face as she had last night, she would make it happen again…and maybe, again.

But for now, John was checking the trailer and she was back to fixing coffee. Her gaze drifted over the bed she had made. The sheets were smooth, pillows in place, and the blue comforter tucked with precision. She considered stretching out on it to see if he would decide to forgo the delivery and join her, but she knew John wouldn't. There was a load to deliver. He had bills to pay. Now, she did too.

Tomorrow, they would be back in *Bright-lights* with the load of tissue products. And she would be moving into her new home and officially beginning her new job as his broker. He would be back on the road without her, and they would be left to calling each other. She missed him already.

CHAPTER 48

EVERY MINUTE AND mile of the eight hours through Missouri weighed heavy on John. Especially after Arkansas and the signs to Kansas City appeared. The last week had been unbelievable. First, the bike run, then the resort, and, holy shit, last night.

He never dreamed he could love someone as he had Janis. But he did—Carrie—and in a way that he couldn't explain. He knew he wasn't abandoning his love for Janis. Never in a million years. Yet, this was totally different. He wanted to tell Carrie. However, the words stuck in his throat.

Their conversations rambled around small talk about his next loads, her house, almost anything except what was about to occur. He was heading out, and she was staying.

Everything that had happened between them felt real. It really did. But was it? Maybe that was why he couldn't tell her he loved her. After all, she could still find someone else who was better than he was, someone who came home every night.

Carrie's cell phone sounded Emily's tinkling ringtone. She answered and put it on speakerphone. "Hey, you on your way back?"

"Yeah. With a trailer full of toilet paper."

"Good. We need some. You guys getting close?

"Closing in on Springfield. We'll make the delivery and then we'll be there."

"Can't wait for you guys to see the house." It sounded like Christmas in Emily's voice. "Everything is going great. So much to show you."

"Looking forward to it," Carrie said, grimacing. Hope pleaded in her gaze that John would understand.

He shrugged and kept driving. After this long break, the seat beside him would be empty, and he would be seeing the same view he'd seen every day of his life.

After Em's call, he admitted, "Wish there was some way you could come out with me again."

A painful smile appeared on Carrie's lips. "I do, too, but you heard. Em can't do any more until I get home. After all she's done, I can't let her down. Besides, she doesn't know a thing about brokering, and I have to set that part up."

"Makes sense." And it did. Nothing good ever seemed to last long enough. John slowed for the ever-present traffic in Springfield on I-44. "Heard from Carl?" he asked.

"He wrote. Said the last loads I set looked good to him. No complaints. No suggestions."

That was terrific. Just wonderful. Dammit! He just kept driving. Carrie had a great office right here with him. After all, she'd managed perfectly this far. There was no reason for her to not go back out with him again.

"Why not just keep working it from here?" he asked, as he slowed for traffic. He hated I-44.

Carrie melted back in her seat. "Like I said, after all Em has done, I have to stay. At least for now." She turned a pleading gaze toward him.

"Yeah, I understand."

March winds slugged at the truck. Week-old dirty snow lay in clumps along the shoulders like forgotten trash. A cold wind found anyway it could to penetrate the cab. And the wintery view only looked bleaker with each mile. A longing for warm winds and sandy beaches ate at him.

Why didn't he just turn the truck around and...? His cell announced an e-mail from his insurance company. It was like a siren call that answered the question for him. Time was money, and the bills just kept rolling in.

Thanks to Carrie, he figured he just had enough to make it now. With a few more good loads, he could even get ahead. Like it or not, the old John, the responsible one that he'd lived with all these years, had returned, and had taken the place of the new one.

"We'll make this delivery by late afternoon, and then I'll take you home. Will that work?"

"You have a break coming so I want you to stay over with me before you have to leave."

Oddly enough, it sounded like a command not a request. John had to grin at that. "If you're asking, I'd love to stay."

Carrie's hand touched his elbow. "Of course, for as long as you want to." Her gaze grew serious. "But, one problem, I have to remember how to find this place."

John enjoyed the familiar laugh together. Then she went back to searching for more loads, and he went back to driving.

He took the exit that he'd taken more times than he could count, to drop off the load at the distribution center on Front Street. Once that was done in pristine time, they were deadheading toward Kansas City Peterbilt to have the truck serviced.

"A friend said he has a car we could use. Want to stop for some barbeque first?" he asked, stalling.

"I'd love to, but Em's message said she's expecting us."

❧

John turned off the engine and started out of his cab door. "Be right back. Okay?"

"Sure." She watched him head into the service center, leaving her to get packed to stay home. John's world was returning to something she understood. His world was freedom with a purpose, delivering something the country or the world wanted or needed, something that might save a life or bring a smile to a face.

Her part in it was to find him the loads, and his job was to deliver it. So, while he returned to the world where men lost themselves to the road, she had no clue what awaited her, except for finding loads.

Looking back at the desperate woman who had decided to escape across country to see her grandkids, Carrie realized she wasn't that woman now. She had become a secretary to escape an unsatisfying marriage, and now, because of John Graham, she was a licensed broker with a new future ahead of her and no longer desperate. It felt good.

Carrie climbed in the back and, after putting her things in her suitcases, she sat on the bed she and John had shared, staring at the gift bags she hoped would appease the kids. She should be excited about going home to a new start but wasn't.

Her life was shifting yet again. John had said she could go out with him again. And, by every bone in her body, she wanted to. But how could she if she wanted this brokering thing to be successful, she needed an office at home.

She knew the routine she was going back to—the one that had once kept her sane. Get up, drink coffee, go to the office, go home. Now that world had expanded to finding deliveries, filling out forms, and keeping John moving. The nights would find her eating alone, watching a boring movie, going to bed, and getting up to do it all over again. All without John.

CHAPTER 49

"GRANDMA! GRANDMA! YOU'RE home."

John pulled her new *Navigator* to a halt in the drive of her new house all ablaze with lights. The front door burst open, releasing her princesses, Annie and Mary. They raced down the snow-lined sidewalk toward the car, followed by Carrianne, her son-in-law Dan, Emily, and her boyfriend, Scott.

Joy raced through Carrie's heart at the sight of the girls, who looked so much bigger now. Stepping out of the car and wrapping them in her arms broke the lingering sadness that had followed her.

After a round of adult hugs, Carrie led everyone over to meet John. He slipped out from his side of the car. She braced and turned to face her small audience. At least Frankie wasn't among the small crowd.

"Everyone, I want you to meet John Franklin, the man who saved my life." Heads nodded greetings. "But first, let's go inside first. I'm freezing," Carrie said as Emily claimed John's arm as if to lead him inside.

"You are going to love this, Big John," Em whispered as they walked toward the house.

All the reasons she fell in love with this house hit Carrie immediately. The wide entry opened to a great room, an open kitchen, and a dining room stretching out to an alcove off the deck. A happy fire snapped in the corner fireplace next to the large windows that opened onto a huge deck.

And Em couldn't have decorated it any better. Gray green paint covered the walls, bronze paisley curtains hung at the windows, and a new leather sectional circled in front of a new television.

Coats were claimed by Scott while John gazed around at the view. "Wow, Carrie. This is nice."

"I can't wait to show it to you. But first." She turned to her family. "John, this is Dan, Carrianne, and my little princesses, Anne and Mary. You know Emily. So, I presume this is Scot?" Carrie asked the young man still holding her coat.

"That's me."

Unlike Carrianne's husband Dan, who hosted a good gut and a half bald head, Scott was shorter, leaner, and held an eager gaze beneath a crop of curly brown hair.

"Momma said you drive a big truck," Mary said. "That's not a big truck. That's a car."

John squatted down as he had with his own grandkids. "I left it in the shop, but it is a very big truck. If your mommy says it okay, I'll show you sometime."

Anne snuggled in beside her sister. "Can I see it, too?"

"Sure thing."

Both girls wheeled to their mother. "Can we, Mommy? Can we go see his truck? We wanna see John's truck that Grandma got to ride in. Does it have a horn? Can I honk it?"

Carrianne hesitated a bit too long to respond. Too much of Frankie obviously lingered in his sister's gaze. "Maybe some time."

Anger cut through Carrie. She'd had enough of Frankie's attitude to deal with. She didn't need it from her eldest daughter as well. She knelt and pulled the girls to her.

"I'm sure you'll get your chance." She looked up at John. "Any time and I'll go with you."

The girls immediately started arguing who got to be the first to honk its horn. Retrieving the gift bags from Scott, Carrie shot a glare at Carrianne and pulled out two princess teddy bears and two new games from Key West. The girls clutched them with joy.

Dan directed the girls into the formal dining room off the entry. "You can play with them in here."

"By your suntans, looks like you guys had a great time in Florida," Emily said as she moved toward the kitchen bar.

"I did. I just hope your mother did too," John said. A happy spark returned to John's face, allowing Carrie to breathe. But the fact that Carrianne had retreated to the kitchen after a "nice to meet you" burned in her guts.

"Em, I can't wait to see what else you did to the place."

John followed Carrie toward the open kitchen and took a proffered paper plate from Carrianne, who was not her mother's daughter, but must have claimed her father's critical attitude. He studied the bowls and platters of food on the bar. Barbeque meat, potato salad, coleslaw, and fries.

Annie pointed to a bowl of potato salad. "Momma calls this 'tato salad and this is cold slaw. Want some?"

"Sure." All he could think about was little Barbie and her tea party.

He had barely filled his plate and sat down at the dining table when the doorbell rang. Everyone there seemed to freeze even as Carrianne raced to answer the front door. A gust of cold wind blew in, followed by footsteps, muffled voices, and then came… "Mom?"

There was no doubt that the man in the entry all bundled up in a thick winter coat and knit hat was Frankie. John put his fork on his plate and looked at the little bastard radiating a vulture's gaze that scanned everyone and slithered to a halt on John. It shifted and raked over his mother, who sat there like a deer caught in the headlights.

John quelled the instant rage and gulped some iced tea. Dan shuttled the girls back into the play area while Em started toward her brother.

"Well, Frankie, looks like you're just in time to eat."

"I'm not hungry." Frankie walked across to the dining room and stood arm's length from Carrie.

She stood. "Frankie. I'm glad you're here. I want you to meet—"

A hard gaze skewered John from head to foot. "You must be this trucker I heard about, first from my mother, and now from my little sister."

"Last I checked, I am."

Their gazes latched together as solid as any trailer and truck. Then Frankie shifted his attention to his mother. "Do I get a hug, Mom?"

Even though the hug didn't last longer than it took to light a match, the room seemed capable of breathing again.

Carrianne hugged her brother and then led him off in the direction of the back bedroom. Dan shooed the girls after their mother and hefted Frankie's luggage from the entry. Scott was still eating while Emily stared in her brother's wake.

Carrie stood there, looking at the entry, until Emily ordered Scot to help her cleanup. "Scott, help me. Mom, go on, show John around. Oh, and there is dessert and champagne."

Carrie turned to him, her gaze the dark green he now knew was not one to mess with. "Want to…see the place?"

"Sounds good."

As Carrie led him about her house, void of her touch but nice, he had to ask, "Did you know anything about Frankie being here?"

She shook her head. "Em never said anything." She pointed to a closed door of a room behind the kitchen where Frankie and Carrianne's little family seemed to have escaped to. "That's Em's bedroom, I think."

He grinned. "Good idea. Wouldn't want to intrude right now."

"No. Not a good idea." She smiled and touched his arm.

He brushed a hand along her cheek. "I can already see why you fell for this place. But what I want to see is your room."

"Oh, I'm saving that for last."

Carrie's familiar spark had returned until Carrianne appeared in the kitchen hallway with her coat on. "Mom, the girls are tired, so we're leaving. Oh, and Frankie is staying with me tonight to spend more time with the girls. Okay?"

Once the front door thudded closed, she took John's hand and led him toward the bedroom. "It's way too big. For me. Really. I mean…"

She blustered on about the room as he looked at the massive dresser with an even bigger mirror that fully displayed the king-sized bed covered with a white bedspread. He could turn his cab around in here. Or run after Carrie and never catch her. He grinned.

"Even though Em did a great job, this still needs something."

"You'll figure it out."

"I hope so." She claimed his hand to continue the tour. "After you see the bath, maybe you won't leave."

Seeing the double shower, footed bathtub, double sinks, and a private toilet, he did consider staying. "Carrie, I think that tub alone is bigger than my entire cab."

Her giggle was filled with nerves. "When you are back, I want you to stay here. I mean if you want to. I mean—"

John pulled her to him and kissed her to stop the rambling. "I'll gladly stay here if that is what you really want, Carrie."

"Hey, you two, cake's in here," Emily yelled from the great room. "Champagne's getting warm."

They left the bedroom and joined Emily who was holding two wine glasses filled with bubbling wine. Scott appeared by the table.

"Where'd everybody go?" Scott asked.

"Home, to be with the girls," Carrie informed as she took a glass.

Em chinked glasses with Scott. "More for us then."

John enjoyed hearing Carrie tell about the bike run as did both kids. Then Emily set her empty wine glass on an end table. "We're outta here, so you two can run around naked. But I don't' recommend eating any cake in bed. Too messy."

"Emily Sue!"

Her daughter burst out laughing and climbed into her coat. Scott smirked as they both headed toward the garage. Suddenly, the house felt vacant.

"More wine?" John asked.

"Absolutely. And I think we should find out if Emily is right. About the cake in bed. Agreed?"

❧

Carrie relished lounging in her new bed with John's arm stretched across her waist. Dawn barely brightened the closed curtains, so it was too early to get up. However, she couldn't sleep. And it wasn't from the cake crumbs in the bed. Em was right.

Once again, her life was about to shift on its axis. She had an office to set up, a house to make livable, and more loads to find for John. And, with all that, he was leaving, opening a large hole in her heart.

"Good morning, beautiful," John whispered in her ear as he drew her to him, resting a kiss on her lips that curled her toes and washed her mind of everything.

She drew back to see the man lounging like a satisfied male lion beside her. "It is now, handsome." Her hand played in the nest of hairs on his chest. "I don't want to get up."

"I don't either, and so let's stay here and see where it ends up." He drew her lips to his for a morning kiss that lingered longer than expected.

John's hands and kisses amazed her in how they found places that melted her insides and then sent skyrockets through her brain. Ending up in the new tub, they feasted through another sensual adventure. Their giggles and laughter melted into swoons and sighs.

He drew back with a groan. "Carrie, go out with me, work from the truck. Whatever you need, we can get it."

Reality plopped into the bubbles between them, destroying the delicious moment. "John, you have no idea how much

I want to. But I need to set up…here. A base of operations or something like that. You know that. Right?"

He brushed her face with his hand. "I guess."

CHAPTER 50

JOHN'S CELL PHONE buzzed. The service center showed on the screen. The truck was ready, and there was no putting this off any longer.

The last two mornings with Carrie had been unbelievable, even down to drinking coffee while she made enough breakfast for the next five days. They laughed over nothing. Touched every chance possible. Now they stood outside in the freezing cold. He drew her close for another kiss. "I already miss my *seat-cover*."

"I already miss getting you coffee." She brushed her hand down his cheek and left it on over his heart. "Call me each night, or I won't sleep. Promise me."

He opened the driver's door of the rental. "Every chance I get. I promise." He captured her hand and kissed the palm. He really didn't want to do this, but a load was waiting for delivery.

❧

Letting John leave was like cutting off her arm. Carrie backed toward the garage as he climbed into the car seat. There was that moment of hesitation and then his car window lowered. "Carrie."

She raced back to the car. "What?"

"It's not too late."

"I wish it wasn't, but this is for us."

He lifted her hand from the windowsill and kissed it again. "Then have the cake and sheets ready when I get back."

"Oh, trust me. I will." She pulled her hand free and rested it on his shoulder. "And thank you for everything."

He pulled down on her sweater, easily drawing her lips to his. "I'm taking that with me."

She giggled. "And just remember, there is more where that came from. They're yours for the taking."

The grin on his face radiated through the closing window. He waved and drove off with her heart.

⋙

Carrie turned back toward the garage and noticed Frank's desk sitting alone against the garage wall. She walked to it. Papers, pens, desk pads and his phone normally were spread across the top. Now, it was bare and collecting dust, like her memories of life with Frank.

As the garage door shut, she wondered if this was why Frankie had come? Not for her, but to get his father's desk. She could only hope. She wanted that piece of furniture gone, out of her life now. A life that included one very special trucker.

A car drove up the drive. John! He'd forgotten something. *Her.* She raised the garage door only to have her heart sink to see Frankie getting out of Carrianne's car.

"Hi, Mom."

Her heart clogged her throat. She was alone with no one to help defend her. No. She wasn't taking his crap anymore.

Frankie could say what he pleased and leave. She was moving on with her life whether he liked it or not.

She waved toward the back door. "There's some coffee left. Want some?"

"Yeah. Sounds good."

The kitchen felt a million miles away as she walked through the laundry room with Frankie on her heels. Her only reprieve came when he stopped to peel off his coat and leave it on the dryer.

She poured coffee into a Peterbilt cup and handed it to him. He sat at the counter and scanned the dirty kitchen. "I see you made enough breakfast for an army. I hope he appreciated having a normal one."

"John did, like always. And yes, I made enough until he gets back in town for more."

She poured coffee into Garfield. "Have you eaten anything?"

"I ate already."

The coffee had somehow turned into battery acid in her stomach. "Roy and Sam, how are they?"

He sipped coffee. "Growing up…without me."

"They do that with or without you." She leaned against the counter. "I guess by that remark, Diane hasn't decided to come back."

"She refuses to stay at home like you."

Carrie swirled the cold liquid and looked at her son. "Well, if she's not happy, why expect her to stay home?"

The inherited patriarchal glare surfaced. "I can take care of them just like Dad did us."

"Nevertheless, Diane should be able to do what you and your father enjoyed, making a living doing what she loves doing. And you know full well, she loves nursing."

"I've heard enough of that shit from her. I don't need it from you, too." He swirled the coffee. "So, how are you and… your friend doing?"

Get it out, Frankie. Get this over with. The sudden shift in conversation irked her, but she let it be. "I've never been happier in my life. So, if you have a problem with that, Frankie, I don't care. I don't want to hear it anymore."

He stared at her, and then shook his head. "Nor do I want to believe what Emily told me, that she caught Dad going into a hotel with that other woman. And that was the real reason why you moved into the other bedroom."

Em? Carrie drank that fact down and walked out to the dining table to where John sat last night. "Frankie, well, I guess that proves that he cheated on me and lied to you and Carrianne."

"Yeah, I guess so." Frankie's shoulders wilted into tears. "Mom, I'm sorry. I'm so sorry. Mom, I don't understand. Everything's gone to shit."

She turned, holding onto the back of John's chair. "Frankie, you can't control everything in your life like your father tried to do. You can't. Diane really cares about you, but she can't take being dictated to, any more than I could. I wish I hadn't put up with it."

"But Dad fixed everything."

"No. He destroyed more than he fixed. I went to work to get away from him. Then he destroyed what marriage we had."

Walking to the bar, she sat down and claimed her Garfield cup like a lifeline. "Don't get me wrong, your father, in his own way was a good man, but he made the same mistakes you're making. Don't do it, Frankie. Give Diane a chance, and work with her. Please?"

"I don't know." He looked at the cloudy sky hovering over the deck. "I'll try."

The garage door opened and a few minutes later, Emily appeared in the hall. "Hey, you're dressed. I guess John had to…Oh, Frankie, you're here." Em presented an envelope with Carl's return address. "Bet it's a paycheck from Carl. Open it."

⸎

Carrie didn't hear a word of what Frankie and Em were saying, because she held a paycheck for $4,000.00.

Congrats, Carrie, on getting your broker license. You did a great job setting up the deliveries. John is a very lucky driver to have you. When you have time, give me a call. I have something I want to discuss with you. Don't mention anything to John… not yet. Not until we have time to talk. Carl.

"Mom? Earth to Mom, are you there?"

Emily's voice finally broke through her shock. *Don't mention anything to John just yet. Not until we have time to talk.* Why?

She tore her attention from the check and handed it Emily. In an instant, her daughter burst into a happy dance with the check in hand. "Wow. Frankie, look at that. And she was only gone a little over four weeks."

When her son saw the amount, his eyebrows raised, impressed. "Not bad, for a road trip."

Carrie walked into the dining room, picturing it arranged with a desk, monitor, and computer. All she saw was John standing by the window before he left. Why couldn't she tell John about whatever Carl wanted to discuss?

Frankie walked in behind her. "You really think you can do this, Mom?"

"You saw the check."

"That's only one check and one driver. You're going to need more than that." He looked exactly like his father just then, superior and arrogant.

Carrie faced him as she had Frank the day that she had informed him she was going to work. "This house is mostly paid for with the sale of the other. Car insurance mostly paid for my car. My retirement from the agency and your father's will pay the bills. I'm fine."

Her son's face burned red with fury. "Dad's rolling over in his grave that you sold everything for all this."

"I don't care, Frankie. I'll do what I have to, to make this work." She was not letting John down.

CHAPTER 51

JOHN CLIMBED INTO his cab and started the truck. Normally, the sound of the engine surged through him like an energy drink. All he had to do was get on the road and make the delivery happen.

Only this time, his little speech didn't work. It was all there—the power, the purpose, the need, the everything—but not Carrie.

It was like the day he walked out of his house for rodeo camp to learn to be a rodeo clown. After his high school friend, Jake, had told him that Janis had just married that asshole, he had figured, "May as well be a clown as feel like one." He shut his mind down from that memory.

Get with the program, he ordered. He had deliveries to pick up and move as he had all his life. Only difference now was the way he felt about leaving. What would Carrie think if he just pulled up in front of her house and honked? He could easily see her race to the truck and climb in. *"John, thank God you came back. I can't stay here. I'm going with you."*

No. She wouldn't.

Carrie had him set up with enough loads to pay all the expenses coming in the next two months. All he had to do was make Carrie's deliveries. He looked at her itinerary that started with *Oil-City* and then south to *Big-D* to *Hotlanta*. From there, the deliveries lined up to *Philly*, to *The-Peg* in Canada—that was going to take time getting across the border—and back through *The-Dirty* and *Gateway-City* to *Bright-Lights*. And Carrie.

Time wise, with all the breaks and shit, he'd be gone nearly a month. A whole month without her. Damn. So, the sooner he started, the sooner he'd be back to bubble baths and wine.

While he waited at a stoplight, he punched in Carrie's speed dial, only to listen to it ring. And ring. Frankie. What did that little shit do this time? He fumed until Joplin, Missouri, and Carrie finally called.

"John, I'm so sorry. We were busy picking out office equipment. I can't believe the sale on office equipment that we found. We're on our way home now with more stuff than you would believe. Oh, and…uh, Yes. And, John, we found a perfect desk, too."

John noted the hesitation. What was that about? "What's Carl think about this?"

"Oh, uh." Another pause. "He's great with it. What? Oh, Emily needs me. I'll call you later. Okay?"

"Sure."

⚘

Emily leaned against the doorframe. "Mom, you have time to talk?"

Carrie tore her attention from the two monitors on the wall that Scott had just connected to the wireless Internet. One was for tracking John and the other for keeping a scrolling list of loads that needed delivery. Another smaller one showed the weather and road reports.

"Sure. Just a minute." She closed everything with a sigh. "I need a break anyway and something to drink. What is it?"

After claiming bottles of water, Carrie sat down at the bar, across from her daughter. She had an unusual gleam in her eyes.

"Mom, I was thinking you need a partner, and maybe, can I be that?"

"What? Emily Sue, do you mean you want to broker? What brought this on?"

Her daughter moved closer. "I found out there are damn few jobs out there for graduates, even with a degree in business. But I did some research and found out that there really is a need for brokers. The trucking industry is practically begging for them. And there's good money in it obviously."

"That remains to be seen." Carrie only hoped Emily was right. But she was only thinking of doing this for John. "Are you sure about this?"

"With rejections racing through everyone I know, it's worse than the Black Plague. I don't want to go through all that, not when there is a perfectly good job right here. I figured, if we do this right, it could be great." Em sat on the next bar stool. "Here's what I'm thinking. What about we call this 'Marshall Brokerage' with a sheriff's badge as a logo? Scott and I have already worked up a website banner. Look." She uploaded the banner on her phone. "What do you think?"

A brokerage? A real brokerage with more drivers? No. She couldn't handle that. But with Emily's help, maybe she could. She should check with John and see what he thought about this. "Sounds interesting."

"We can get business cards, and John can put them up at truck stops. He could tell all his trucker friends too." Emily continued as if everything were already accomplished.

John…pass out the cards for Marshall Brokerage? Carrie couldn't see him ever doing that. She remembered his reaction with Brance. Images collected around her as the restaurant flashed in her memory. No. She couldn't see John doing that.

And Carl had said not to say anything to John. Maybe she should have anyway. But, damn, she'd forgotten to call Carl back to find out why. She wanted to ask him about Em's idea anyway.

Yet the idea of Marshall Brokerage sounded feasible. More trucks paid more bills. If Em really wanted a future in this, they would need more drivers. As John said, "Time was money." And, well, other trucks were money, too…or could be. She remembered so many saying they were willing to work for her. They hated Phil.

Carrie toasted her daughter. "I think I have partner. However, I must warn you, brokering classes are tougher than you think."

"Finished last night and passed with 96%."

❦

Discussions and serious planning consumed the next few days. Even though she hated to admit it, Em had her father's business sense. Carrie brought her office experience to the table. And Scott was setting them up with an unbelievable Internet system, website, everything. And Em had a few friends interested in working part time. If all went well, they might even go full time.

Everything was moving so fast; she didn't think she had time to breathe. She wanted to tell John about everything going on, but she wasn't sure she could make any sense. Or, that he'd understand.

Once things calmed down, when he got back and he could see what they had set up, and she'd explain everything to him.

For now, she just relished listening to him talk about what she was missing. Being on the truck, the freedom of it, the simplicity. A slow ache slid through her.

✁

"Oh, Em, I finally called Carl, John's broker," Carrie said as the black icon of John's truck moved on the monitor beside the picture window. He was just leaving *Big- D* and was on route to *Hotlanta*. She glanced at the weather monitor. Severe storms were moving east. She'd have to tell him.

"Earth to Mom, what did Carl say?"

"Oh. He's closing his office, and you won't believe it. He offered his client base to us. Should we?"

Emily exploded, charging around the office like a banshee. "Absolutely! Mom! That means instant trucks needing loads. It's perfect." She stopped in front of Carrie's desk. "What's he asking?"

"Let me say, we'll need a loan."

Em slapped the desk, scaring Carrie nearly out of her wits. "Then do it. We've got enough assets to swing it." She stopped. "Don't we?"

CHAPTER 52

JOHN CAME OUT of the shower area, looking for Carrie, and remembered she wasn't with him. These last ten days without her had been the worse. The miles were endless now.

Bottles of water filled Carrie's seat instead of her and, like before, he had to stop to make his own coffee or nuke his own meals.

He missed her handing him the papers, and filing them away. He also thanked her every time he entered his driving time on the computer.

In small ways, Carrie was with him. After all, she had warned him about the snowstorm coming through Arkansas. When it hit, he had to wait it out and loneliness hit him like a fist.

Not only that, waking up without his arm draped over her waist was pure hell. He'd gone to hugging her pillow scented with her perfume. If he didn't smell that, he couldn't sleep, and he paced his cab like a trapped animal. He couldn't get back on the road fast enough.

Offices asked about Carrie constantly. How some of these offices even knew she was brokering for him, he didn't know.

But she was excited about her new office that Em and Scott were setting up for her.

But he didn't see why she needed an office. She had managed perfectly well right there in the *rig* with him.

He wanted to call her constantly. But lately, she seemed distant, not her usual chattering self. He guessed she was just busy setting up that office.

John walked into the Subway restaurant outside *Hotlanta* and was picking out his sandwich when Brance strolled toward him. Something about that man always itched like a rash, and the smirk on the man's face only made it worse.

"Hey, Big John, guess we're kinda like business partners since Marshall Brokerage is setting up our loads now." Brance slapped a friendly hand down on his shoulder. "Can't thank you enough. Carrie's a good one."

What the hell? Marshall Brokerage? Before he could ask the man, Brance had disappeared outside.

John's appetite died instantly. Marshall Brokerage. Sure, it was Carrie's last name, but there could be plenty of other brokers out there with the same name. But if it was Carrie, why hadn't she said anything to him about it?

He grabbed the sandwich sack and made for his truck. By the time he climbed in, he could easily see she would need other drivers to make this work.

At least, she could have told him, asked his opinion, or let him help find reliable drivers. *Son-of-a-bitch.* Had he become just another driver to her? He threw the sack on her seat.

His guts were burning as he punched in her phone number hard enough to break the casing. "Carrie, what the hell? You're brokering for Brance now? Who else? Why didn't you tell me about this Marshall Brokerage? Why, Carrie?" It all just spewed out like vomit.

"Leave your name, phone number, and a brief message. We'll get back to you as soon as possible. In the meantime, *keep-the-sunny-side-up* and thank you for calling Marshal Brokerage." Her recording clicked off.

Brance was right. Carrie was a brokerage now. Why hadn't she told him? Unless she had other plans.

His phone lit up, playing her tinkling ring. He stopped turning circles behind the seats to answer.

 "What the hell, Carrie? Marshall Brokerage? What the hell is going on? You couldn't tell me? Why?"

"John. John. It's not what you think."

He took hold of the back of her seat to steady himself. "Then tell me what I think, Carrie."

"John, we needed a few more drivers."

"We? We who?"

"Emily. I told you she got her broker license. I can't believe she beat me by two points."

"No, you didn't tell me."

"Oh, I thought I had. But, John, it's gone crazy with all the calls we are getting. Did Carl tell you? We bought his brokerage. Which is likely why we are going crazy here. He must have told every *driver* out there."

Carl? Sold his brokerage? All his drivers? "No one told me anything, Carrie. That shit Brance had to."

"John, I didn't mean—"

"The least you could have done was let me advise you. Shit, Carrie, I know who drives and who doesn't. If you only had asked me first."

Silence filled his phone.

"Obviously, you don't need my help. So fine. Find another driver for the rest of your loads. I'll find my own loads from now on. So, as you said, *keep-the-sunny-side-up*."

ᗡ

It was Frank all over again *Obviously, you don't need my help. So fine. Find another driver for the rest of your loads. I'll deliver what I have and then find my own loads from now on. So, as you said, keep-the-sunny-side-up.* "Carrie stared at the silent phone as her insides incinerated.

Tears ran down her cheeks as she informed the silent phone. "So, find your own damn loads, John. And good luck. You'll need it." She dropped her phone on the desk like a rotten tomato and swiped at her cheeks.

"Mom, what's wrong?"

She looked across her desk at Emily, the one who had talked to Brance. She hadn't. What's more, why should she need John's approval or advice about the business? She had planned to tell John everything when he came home, but everything had happened so fast.

CHAPTER 53

J OHN STARED AT the bottom of the coffee mug, at the last of the cold dregs of the liquid curdling in his stomach. But when the waitress offered more coffee, he let her pour. This had been the longest three weeks of his life.

Carrie was brokering for every damn driver out there, or so it seemed, and never so much as bothered to ask him how he felt about any of it.

And she didn't need him now.

Never in a million years would he have believed that Carrie would have used him like this. Shit. All this time he believed she just wanted to help him. Janis certainly would never have done this to him.

How much of this was Frankie? John's guts twisted with that possibility. Yet, that didn't fit. Not after what that little shit had done to her. But then, maybe things had changed there, too

"You know mothers and sons," Janis had said more times than he could count. But she had been teasing because of their sons.

And, since he told Carrie that he'd get his own loads, everything seemed to go wrong. First, a blown trailer tire.

Getting that fixed had made him late with a half-load delivery, and that backloaded everything from there. And a *chicken-coop* in New York fined him. A *diesel-bear* had ticketed him for not balancing his load on the axles. Somehow, a tie-down had broken and the load had shifted.

Then, after going back to his old logbook that he'd used all these years, the *bear* scoured it for anything he could find wrong. And, he had found enough.

Now he had fines to pay. The real pisser was if he'd kept using Carrie's new app, the asshole would have found nothing. Now fog had closed I-70 at the bridge by Boonville, Missouri, leaving him stuck outside Columbia at the Midway Truck Stop.

All this time without Carrie, he couldn't find one decent load. He had had to eat crow and ask Phil to help. He made the call.

"What the hell, John? Why don't you just ask that new *seat-cover* of yours to fix this? After all, she's taking all my drivers and ruining me, you little prick."

Part of him wanted to kiss Carrie for that and, well, if things were different, he just might have. He didn't want to think of kissing her or anything else they'd done together. That was just a kick in the crotch.

However, Phil had managed to find him a half load of toilet paper for a general store outside Wentzville. Now he was deadheading back to *Bright-Lights*, trying to make up the lost time to the Walmart Distribution Center in Harrisonville, hopefully for a full load of anything.

He couldn't afford to continue working *the road* this way. He couldn't.

Steamroller Spike sat on the barstool beside John, motioning for the waitress to set a fresh mug of coffee in front of him. "Mind if I have a sit?" Spike asked.

John nodded to his weathered friend who had started driving about the same time he had. "Help yourself. Good to see you, Spike. How's your 20?"

Spike sipped coffee. "Heard on the *squawk-box* that you had a cute *seat-cover* working for you." Spike leaned on the counter and turned toward him. "Mind if I ask, what happened to her?"

He shrugged. "Went home."

Spike cradled his steaming coffee and watched the waitress. "Didn't like *the road*?"

Carrie loved being out there. Or, so he'd believed once. After firing her, she probably never would go out with him again. Maybe with other drivers, but not him.

The idea of seeing her with someone else cut through him like a butcher knife. In retaliation, he shoved away his coffee mug.

Spike slurped coffee. "Big John, I know it's none of my business why she ain't with you."

John shrugged.

"What I'm hearing is she ain't your broker now. Why or whatever the cause is, is none of my business. But Big John, this isn't like you. So, whether you want to keep her ridin' with you or not, best get your head out of your ass and do what needs to be done." Spike shrugged. "And *get-on-down-the-road*, my friend."

Spike laid a five-dollar bill on the table and set his hand on John's shoulder. "*Keep-the-sunny-up*, Big John. See you on the *flip-flop*." The waitress claimed the coffee mug and money.

Feeling totally alone again, thoughts burned. Maybe he should just *get-on-down-the-road*, like Spike said. Just add everything up to a good stretch of highway with Carrie. Very good time. Now it was over, and he best realize he was back where he had started…with Phil. Or not. He'd just retire with his kids.

John slid a twenty under his coffee mug and started to climb off the stool, when someone yelled from the front. "Big John, better get out here quick. It's your *box*."

⁌

"Son. Of. A. Bitch!"

John stared at the six-foot gash along the side of his trailer. Obviously, some idiot tried to back in and cut too sharp, gutted his trailer, and then took off.

He looked around as if expecting to see the bastard, but the shithead was long gone. A few drivers, who had seen it happen, said something about a red cab. And how many trucks were red?

Sympathetic hands dropped on his shoulder as drivers left to go back to their *rigs*. "Hang in there, Big John. You'll get through this," someone said. "Just a bad spell, is all."

One good thing, since he was *deadheading*, he didn't have to eat the cost of a load too. He had only one option now… get it fixed. Of course, if he had a good broker, she would call and reset the Walmart pickup date for him. Since he had Phil, he'd have to make his own call. Shit.

Tears burned behind his eyes as he climbed into the cab, reached across Carrie's seat, and dug into the glove compartment for the insurance papers and phone number. Piece by piece spilled into Carrie's seat until he clasped a small bottle of something—a bottle of her red fingernail polish. The memory of her doing her fingernails before they got to Ft. Lauderdale surged through him like a tidal wave.

He threw the bottle back into the glove box and rifled through the paperwork in a folded leather binder that Carrie had neatly organized. Claiming his agent's card, he fell back in the seat. "…do what needs to be done."

He clutched his phone like a lifeline and made the necessary calls. First, to the insurance agent and then the service center in *Bright-Lights* to arrange to get the sidewall fixed.

Maybe he should just sell the damn *box* and pick up ones already with loads. The idea of talking it out with Carrie pleaded in his brain, the way he had up in Maine.

None of that mattered. The trailer still had to be fixed, and he needed his coveralls to crawl under the trailer. He stepped on the tomato stain on the cab carpet as he went to the storage bins. It had been left after that last night together in the truck, another memory he'd have to forget.

As he pulled out the coveralls, Carrie's black negligee, scented with her fragrance, fell with it. His knees gave way, slumping him down on the foot of the mattress where she had stretched out like a kitten.

It was hopeless. The cab was filled with Carrie and there was no getting away from her. No way. Not unless he sold the *rig*, which was not an option.

The trouble really was he didn't want to lose those memories. He wanted more of them.

"So, whether you want to keep her ridin' with you or not, best get your head out of your ass and do what needs to be done."

❧

Carrie stared at the black dot on the monitor that appeared to be stuck at the Midway Truck Stop. The highway patrol was reporting that all traffic would be halted because the river bottoms were flooding from the March rain and fog was about to completely close off all traffic on I-70.

John, you've got to move now.

Instead of calling him, as she wanted to do a million times a day, Carrie just stared at her cell phone. She'd heard through the *squawk-box*, what he had been going through lately. Bad loads. Late loads. Tickets. Truck trouble. Obviously, he still didn't want her help. Every load hurt when she had to give it to another driver and not to John.

Voices in the great room cheered as the crew took a break to watch the finish of a NASCAR race. Apparently, Carl Edwards was winning. Emily appeared in the office doorway. "Can I get you anything, Mom?"

Tearing her gaze from the picture window, Carrie looked across at what was once the dining room. Now it was filled with monitors on the walls, a file cabinet, her and Emily's desks and an office credenza filled with office equipment and supplies. "Water."

Emily went back into the kitchen where dishes rattled, and more cheers erupted. Carrie's gaze returned to the budding redbud trees alongside the driveway. Every morning, as she sipped coffee from her blue coffee mug blazing the Marshall Brokerage logo, she saw John's car leave again.

The brokerage was now running extremely well in little over a month. Like with the ad agency, she ran the office and left Em to manage the meager staff, who found the loads, pickups, and deliveries. She couldn't do that part anymore because all she could think of was John not getting that load.

So, she stuck to the books. The brokerage was now paying for itself, as well as the household bills that were entered as office expenses.

Even though brokering was a 24/7 job at times, it was too close for too much comfort. Where was he? Check the trucking monitor. What was it like on his road? Check the weather monitor. Did he need anything…water, coffee, someone to talk to? Bring up the closest truck stop to where the black dot was. Was he *deadheading*? She didn't know, but she had plenty of loads if he wanted them.

Emily appeared with a bottle of water. Her gaze shifted to the screen that showed where all the trucks were at any time of the day or night.

"He's stuck in Columbia, isn't he?"

"Apparently."

The NASCAR race must have ended because of the screams of victory or grumbles of defeat and then everyone retreated to the basement to work. Once again, blessed silence reigned in the house.

"Mom, why don't you just call him, for God's sake?"

"You know why. I have enough to deal with here, Em. You know that. John knows my cell phone number as well as you do. If he wants our help, he can call any time." She opened the Excel balance sheet and started working on the expense report.

"Yeah. Whatever." Em walked over to her desk. "Oh, by the way, I'm going out with the girls tonight. Want to join us?"

"No. But thanks anyway."

"Just remember that I asked." Someone in the basement area messaged Em. "Gotta go down and look into this," she said and headed to the basement.

John still wasn't moving. Carrie didn't know why. Other than knowing where he was, she never knew what he was doing because he wasn't hauling her load. She closed her eyes and could smell his Old Spice and jerked her attention back to the spreadsheet.

Silence slowly filled the office for the next few hours until her cell phone honked. She grabbed it and stared at the caller ID displaying "John Graham."

Her finger lingered over the blazing answer button as the phone continued to honk, sending her heart to her throat. She couldn't breathe.

The message system picked up, "Thanks for calling Marshall Broker…" She answered. "John…?"

"Oh, Carrie. Uh. Thought I'd call. I'm caught here in Columbia. Fog."

Just hearing his voice soothed the pit of her stomach. She saw that he was nearing Blue Springs. So, she'd play along. "Should clear up for you soon enough."

"Yeah. Thanks." The sound of the engine rumbled through the phone, leaving a longing to be in her seat beside him, drawing tears in her eyes.

"Uh, I'm having the *box* fixed, and well, since I have to come through *Bright- Lights*, I thought maybe you'd, well, you know, want barbeque or something."

This wasn't his first pass along *The-Seventy* since he… and never called. Why now? "What happened…to the trailer?" she asked, but the *squawk-box* had already told her all about the gash.

"Some son-of-a-bitch left a six-foot gash in the side of my box. Insurance is paying, but no loads until it's fixed."

"Oh shit, John, that's horrible. Do you know who?" By the traffic on the *squawk-box*, eyes were watching for the guy.

"Some red rig." There was a silence over the phone, a breath that lasted a lifetime. "And, uh, I was wondering if you'd like to go out for some barbeque. I know a great place."

CHAPTER 54

J UST AFTER SUNSET, John drove the rental car into Carrie's driveway. Light from the dining room window lit up her profile where she sat at her desk.

When Carrie saw his car's headlights, she stood up and disappeared. Soon, the garage doors lifted, and she appeared just as she had the day he left. His heart slammed in his chest as he turned off the car and got out.

A stiff smile played across her lips as she walked toward him. "It's good to see you, John."

"You, too." How easy it would be to wrap his arms around her and feel her melt into him, erasing every stupid thing he'd ever done. Instead, she took his arm and led him through the garage into the house.

A fresh scent seeped from the dryer as it tossed clothes. The washer started into its spin mode. The delicious fragrance of chicken roasting in a Crock-Pot destroyed his desire for barbeque.

She left him for the kitchen, so he sat on a barstool. "Can I get you something to drink?" Carrie asked.

"Have any water?" He scanned the great room, rearranged for a better view of the television, which wasn't like her. Her bedroom door was closed. Was that a message to him?

"Place looks great," he said, tearing his gaze from where most of his fantasies had once lived.

Carrie claimed two bottles of water from the fridge. "Thanks. Em and I have been busy with everything." She left one on the kitchen bar and broke the seal on the other one.

"How're things going?" he asked.

"Paying the bills."

"So, this is Emily and you now?"

"Sort of. After we bought out Carl, everything took off. Growing every day. A few are even working on the brokerage classes."

Wow. That was…. good. "How's Em doing?"

"She loves brokering. She can't wait to graduate this May so she can work this full time." She smiled tauntingly. "Want to see what she and Scott set up? It truly is state of the art." She waved her bottle toward the dining room.

"Sure."

⤖

John couldn't believe the changes in the house. Shelves of maps, truck books, and manuals filled two bookcases on both sides of what he figured was Emily's desk by the doorway. Across from hers was Carrie's desk. He figured that because of the model of his truck and the souvenir from Mt. Rushmore behind her on a credenza.

Monitors draped both sides of the main window. One had a scrolling list of loads like the stock market ticker. Weather radar on another screen showed a downpour over *Gateway*. Another large screen displayed a map of the major interstate highways with different colored dots running all about the country. He walked over to it and saw a pink truck on I-55. He pointed at it. "Liz?"

"That's Liz." Pride gleamed in Carrie's eyes.

He pointed to a green dot moving along I-95 and looked at her.

"Bill and Browser. And the blue one is Brance on I-5."

In the heart of the map was a black dot stuck right over her house. "You've known where I've been?"

She nodded. "All along. I had to know you were okay."

Every stupid word he had ever said to her hit him like a bat. He staggered back a step and dove his hand through his hair. "Carrie, I'm sorry. I've been a fucking idiot."

Before he could go on, she reclaimed his arm and led him toward the basement stairs. "You won't believe what Scott's done down here. I still can't."

She wasn't letting him grovel. He felt as light as an empty trailer on a windy day as he followed her down the stairs into a totally different world.

He remembered a mattress and a single desk full of wiring. Now, three monitors displaying the same as the two upstairs. Four desks with computers.

"Carrie, this is amazing!"

"I think so." She walked over to one of the computers and hit a few buttons. He remembered how she attacked his laptop that first night in his cab.

The monitor showing the interstates changed as if zooming in. "If we have to, we can zero in for a closer look at the local roads for any road construction going on." The screen changed to his truck parked in the service lot.

"I'll be damned." They hadn't pulled the trailer inside yet.

Her gaze softened. "You were our test model."

He stared out the darkening basement doors. All this time, she knew what he was going through. That fact only made him feel worse after dumping her as he had. He sliced a hand through his hair. "I've been the dumbest ass God ever created, Carrie. I'm so sorry. Really."

She brushed her hand down his chest with a familiarity he needed to feel and walked toward the stairs. "Hungry?"

"Yeah." However, for more than that, he wanted to wrap her in his arms. Kiss her if she'd let him. He wanted her back.

She started up the stairs. "I have to change. You can come up and wait in my room."

Hope joined him as he followed her back up the stairs and expected her to turn toward her bedroom. But she crossed to the bedroom behind the kitchen, the one Carrianne had taken Frankie to. He followed her inside.

"You can sit here. I won't be long." Carrie motioned to an overstuffed chair in the corner by the bedroom door.

One glance about the smaller room, made Carrie continue. "I couldn't stay in that other room. It was too big, so Em and I switched rooms. This one is smaller and much more comfortable. At least, I think so." She plucked a green top out of the closet and headed toward the small bathroom.

It did seem to suit her better. A queen-sized bed, covered with blue and white pillows, separated him from the doors out to a private deck, not that different from the cottage in Key West.

⋞

Gripping the vanity sink, Carrie forced herself to breathe. Seeing John. Seeing him get out of that car. Smelling his Old Spice as he drew close. Watching his reactions at what she and Em had accomplished ripped open the wound that had refused to heal. It rattled every bone in her body until she could barely climb the stairs.

There was no need for John to apologize either. She should have told him everything. There was enough blame to pass around. Carl's warning had stopped her. It got busy and she had forgotten. She didn't think past her nose. But knowing he was out there, reminded her of his touch, of Key West, of lasagna in his cab, of…

Each memory rippled through Carrie like warm honey. Fantasies of her appearing naked in the doorway to see his reaction taunted her.

She jerked back from the sink, ripped off the white sweatshirt, and pulled on her new teal top. John was here because he needed a broker and to get his trailer fixed. Not for her.

That sense of reality calmed her as she brushed her hair and checked her makeup. Like before, this was business. She stared at her reflection in the mirror. Surely, he didn't expect to spend the night. There was no way she could let that happen.

Bolstered and steadfast, she nodded to the girl in the mirror and then walked out of the bathroom. "Sorry it took so long. I was a—"

John wasn't sitting in the chair. Panic cut through her until she noticed the open deck doors. When she walked onto the small deck, he turned from the railing.

"I didn't know this was out here. It's nice." His smile melted her insides.

Carrie walked to the rail and clung to it to keep from walking into his arms. "There are times I wish I hadn't bought this house. It's too big."

John leaned against the wood railing. "Seriously? You've only been in it barely three months."

"Yeah. Even with Em and Scott living here, the house is still too big. I'm thinking of either selling or renting." She laughed.

"Especially since the neighbors found out we are running a business and reported us to the homeowners' association." She shrugged. "Scott's found a perfect commercial space to move the office into. I offered the house to them, but both said it's too big even for them. I want something smaller."

John stared out into the darkness. "How much smaller?"

She rubbed her arms to ward off the chilly night air. "I don't know. An apartment maybe."

"I don't know how to say this, Carrie, but God, I've missed you every mile since I left here." John claimed her hand and held it to his chest.

"Not just because I'm an ass to have ever let you go as my broker either. I mean, I miss everything, hearing about the towns, having someone to talk to." He smirked. "Having someone to get me coffee. Or to rub my shoulders. Or kick my ass when needed."

The humor faded from his eyes, shifting to serious. He took her other hand and tucked it under his. "So, Carrie Ann Marshall of Marshall Brokering, would you be interested in something as small as the cab of my *18-wheeler*?"

Was he serious? Joy bubbled like New Year's champagne into every empty hole in her soul. She pulled back. "Are you serious, John? I mean, really serious."

"Yes, Carrie, I am."

"But the brokerage. Emily. I don't know."

"You can work from my *rig*. I mean, as you did before. Like last time. Would it work? Em could take it from here."

He clasped both of her shoulders with a desperate certainty. A dangerous sparkle danced in his blue gaze. "So, go on the road with me again, Carrie. Please."

Every part of her jumped at the chance. Except for her brain. Emily and Scott? Could they handle all this without her? She already knew the answer. Yes. And yes, she could easily work from John's *rig*.

But could she go down that road again and be dumped like road trash? "I don't know, John. I need to think about this. Talk to Emily."

He clasped her face and kissed her forehead. "I've also realized something, Carrie, something I never believed I would be able to say again. I love you. I do, Carrie. We both know life's too short to be lonely, and I know I have been lately. I don't want to drive another mile without you."

Carrie watched as John pulled something from his pants pocket and opened his hand to a ring with an emerald surrounded with diamonds. "Will you marry me, Carrie Ann Marshall?"

She studied the ring, his face, the ring. Struggled to swallow, to even breathe. Even her heart had stopped beating. "John, are…are you sure… of this?"

"Marry me, Carrie. I need you."

He was asking her to spend the rest of her life with him. And there was not a better man out there. She knew this to be a fact. No woman in her right mind would refuse John.

But did she love him? Did she really want to spend her life on the road with Big John? Her heart started thundering.

In fact, every nerve in her body thrilled with joy. "Yes. I will marry you."

She let him slide the ring on her finger. He leaned in to kiss her, but she stopped him. "And so, you know, I have loved you, John Eli Graham, for quite some time."

"That makes it perfect."

Epilogue

CARRIE CLIMBED DOWN onto the desert gravel of the Salt Flats with practiced ease. Memories of attempting to get into the cab on that icy day a thousand years ago danced in her mind. So much had changed. So much.

She joined John waiting by the front wheel. His emerald ring flashed on her hand in the morning sun as she reached for his palm.

"Not much different than before," he muttered.

She threaded her hand through his arm and looked at the vista surrounding them. Only the spirit of her car remained. Yet she could see it.

"It's totally different." She turned to John. "Because of you."

He looked at her with the world dancing in his eyes. "You still want to do this?"

"Only if you do."

The corner of his mouth lifted with humor. "Absolutely, I do."

"No. You aren't supposed to say that until after the vows."

They walked down the highway shoulder onto the flats basking beneath a pristine sky with no cloud blocking the view of the heavens above. They clasped both hands. John lifted her left one and kissed it.

She loved this man now more than life. "Before God, John Eli Graham, I promise to love you until the end of time."

"I hope God hears this, because I want Him to know Carrie Ann Marshall, I will always love and cherish you down to my last mile."

An eagle soared high in the sky as if to answer.

John clasped her face with both hands and kissed her soul, which she easily relinquished to him. Then they drew apart and sat on what was left of the crunchy asphalt-covered gravel coating the highway shoulder.

She leaned against her new husband, who wrapped his arm around her shoulder. They both sighed. "All I have left to say is thank you, John, for stopping that day and changing my life forever."

He looked down at her with a grin. "What?"

She grinned. "You heard me. Thank you."

"And all I can say is thank you for driving over that *gator*."

He got to his feet and then pulled her up against him. A cloud of Old Spice swept around her as he kissed her. Tongues played until she knew they had better get into the *rig* and off the road before she started ripping off his clothes.

"John, I don't think I can climb in," she teased.

He laughed. "No problem, my love. I'll catch you like before."

"I'm counting on it."

The End of this Road

And keep the sunny side up and the greasy side down, ya' hear.

CARRIE AND JOHN'S story came to me from the image of Carrie trying to climb into John's I and him catching her butt in his hands. It is harder than you think. And it was fun seeing that scene come to life.

However, no matter how much I wanted to write this story, I still had no knowledge of the trucking world, other than of my father, who drove a dump truck, saying truckers were the 'princes of the road.'

Then Spike, my husband's nephew, changed all that. He loved the world of *18-wheelers* and hauling goods around this country.

For a few days one summer, he stayed with my Joe and me. As usual, I shared my story. And, lo and behold, Spike made the story come to life, first, my changing the setting to the Salt Flats, explaining to me that you could easily survive for at least three days in a snowstorm, and that such storms happened often out there during the winter.

He took me to see a Peterbilt cab that became John's cab, drove me around in the truck he drove, and shared stories such as the man with no pants. With his help and his wife Barb, who Spike claimed knew more about trucking than he did, this story was born.

Spike and Barb shared their amazing world that I had taken for granted. They were right…everything I have in my house came by truck. Yours, too.

I also learned of the hardships truckers and their loved ones must deal with as holidays came and, like all *drivers* out there, went by without them being home, because Spike and all the other were simply on the road delivering something somewhere. Christmas. Thanksgiving. The Fourth. Birthdays. Anniversaries. It didn't matter. His family never knew exactly when he could come home to celebrate with them.

Life on *the Road* ain't easy, folks.

Not only did I learn about the world of trucking, I also learned a lot about brokering loads, a world as complicated as anything on Wall Street.

The most enjoyable part was learning a bit of trucker-talk. The highway patrol will forever be some kind of *'bear'* to me now. *Rigs, Fuel, Gators. Bright-lights.* It's fun. I hope you enjoyed that too.

I knew Carrie and John would need a trip across the country. So I asked friends what were their favorite places: Spike – The Big-Dig, Boston, Massachusetts; Peg – Bangor, Maine; Teresa – Flint Hills, Kansas; Becky – Loveland Pass, Colorado; Ernie –Yosemite National Park, California; Oregon; Candice – Puget Sound, Washington; Barb – Mt. Rushmore, South Dakota; Cora – Tahquamenon Falls, Michigan; Donna – Cedar Springs, Michigan; Jennifer – Gatlinburg, Tennessee; Anna – Myrtle Beach, South Carolina; Zoe – Jacksonville, Florida; Joe – Key West Florida; and James – New Orleans, Louisiana. That set their trip. And I thank Wikipedia for the historical information about these places. And a special thanks go out to Wild Bill for all the details about taking a bike run to Key West.

As for 'TAT' or Truckers Against Trafficking.org, is an actual group who are the eyes and ears on the look-out for victims of human trafficking, a global horror in the world, and since *drivers* are everywhere about this magnificent country of ours, they keep watch and do what they can. They are saving lives every day. May God bless and keep them all safe. If you want to help support this nonprofit group check out http://www.truckersagainsttrafficking.org or call 612-688-4828.

Writing this story was a blast until something horrible developed in my life. Not only did Spike discovered he had liver cancer, but my husband did soon after. I lost them both to this disease. So, John and Carrie's story is dedicated to both. I miss you.

Thank you, dear readers, for the time out of your lives to read this story. And now, as you travel this amazing country, may you *'keep the sunny side up and the oily side down'*.